Also by A.N. Steinberg from Headline Review

Manroot
An Eye For An Ear
The Cuckoo's Gift

First Hands

A.N. Steinberg

review

First published in 1997
by HEADLINE BOOK PUBLISHING

First published in paperback in 1998
by HEADLINE BOOK PUBLISHING

A REVIEW paperback

10 9 8 7 6 5 4 3 2 1

ISBN 0 7472 5658 6

Printed and bound in Great Britain by
Mackays of Chatham PLC, Chatham, Kent

HEADLINE BOOK PUBLISHING
A division of Hodder Headline PLC
338 Euston Road
London NW1 3BH

TO MY SON MARC
for lending his expertise that allowed
me a peek into the world of fashion.

And
with gratitude to
Betty Richards.

CHAPTER ONE

My steps are hesitant as slowly I walk into this alien room. Somewhere near the middle of the room I pause and feel caught by an unseen force. I'm cold – that deep-down, frozen-to-the-bone cold – yet I know it's not only the temperature that makes me shiver. Rooted to the spot, I pull my coat tighter around myself, while above me in the high ceiling, one bank of fluorescent lights wink on and off, lending the cavernous space a sense of movement. Clothes breathe and seem to leap off the racks, then settle restlessly back to their original positions.

I sniff the air and find the smell of lemon room-freshener does not quite cover it, that subtle mixture of scents – old velvet, fragile chiffon, warm silk, and crisp polished cotton – for the undertone is that of living creatures. Fox, mink, seal, and the heavy musk of leopard fight for a place among my senses.

Framed against the barred window, a mannequin seems to shiver, her leopard cloak caught in an unseen draft, wisps of her blonde wig under the matching hat moving like small waves.

Then there is stillness, and the mannequin is almost like another woman, alive, breathing with me in this quiet room.

I'm tired, so I blame imagination for these tricks of the light; still I stand frozen among the garments that seem to be waiting, remembering cherry trees where silk worms gorged themselves, or cotton plants that warmed in the sun, or, with a shudder of fear, I think of dappled jungles where silent cats trod on moist green leaves. I shiver more violently now, for I can see clearly in my mind's eye icy polar caps where carefree seal pups swam.

I blink and breathe rapidly, for over the sounds of traffic, I hear it distinctly – the buzz, the sounds mixed, crossed over, meshed into the cloth and fur, a sigh of love, a cry of disappointment, the low rumble of laughter, a shriek of terror . . . all these sounds trapped for ever in their yesterdays.

The noise grows louder, talking in a language without words, their past connection with living skin. It rises to a frightening cacophony of sound.

Gripping the door keys, I reach for the light switch to plunge the room back into darkness, so that they may sleep again, these carriers of memories.

Outside, I do not notice him huddled in my doorway, fetus-like under the cardboard cover, but I feel the physical connection of my foot touching his.

'Spare some change?' His voice floats up in the cold air.

Ignoring him, I search the ring of keys for the one which opens the door to the flat above.

'Bitch.' He spits the word out into the night as he readjusts his cardboard cover. 'Bitch,' he continues to mutter halfheartedly, and the sound of his slurred voice follows me up the narrow staircase.

Sighing deeply with relief, I find the light, only to discover that I am standing in the middle of the same riddle. *Her shop, her flat.*

The living room, too, contains echoes of other times, all jumbled together. The worn three-piece suite – a maroon couch with matching chairs – has wide arms and plush seats that scream 1950s, but hugging the furniture, a beautiful white Italian marble table jars the senses as the Art-deco nude reclines seductively upon it, holding up a lampshade of pale green isinglass which lights the room and softens the stained walls.

I make my way along the narrow hallway touching light switches; some lights choose to light and some do not.

Opening the first door, I find the room empty save for a large mahogany desk, its surface covered with papers untidily stacked, and one solitary chair, its back intricately carved and the fabric seat a delicate needlepoint scene of a deer standing among tall trees in a sheltering forest.

Leaving this door ajar, I make my way to the next room, where the heavy scent of incense overwhelms me. Tentatively, I squint into the gloom.

I see a massive shrouded bed. It reminds me of a galleon ghost ship on a strong sea. I cannot decide if it is really beautiful or only vulgar. The top of the massive headboard is festooned with veils of scarlet; the wood gleams where an intricate swan is carved, its wings outstretched, and at its feet a woman lies . . . Of course, it's a representation of the Greek myth, Leda and her lover, the god

Zeus, who came to her in the guise of a swan. I find the carving terrifying!

The bedposts are like entwined arms, holding up the canopy, where filmy red curtains descend around the silk-velvet blood-red spread; the color-scheme is inappropriate, but still reminiscent of tropical nights hiding from lethal mosquitoes.

On impulse, I slide open the mirrored closet door, only to find the shop below re-created here.

A 1950s waist-hugging suit leans protectively against a 1920s black satin bias-cut evening gown.

Sliding the hangers, moving coats, capes, dresses of various styles and periods, it seems impossible to believe that they all belonged to her. For they have no stamp of a definite style, no hint of a certain taste, yet I remember clearly that she had been vivid in her opinions and preferences.

Unconsciously I look for one remnant of her that is familiar, carefully examining each garment for even one large satin label announcing that it is an original piece of couture by Myra Dunhom.

Recognition would be instant, for Cynthia and I have kept a label in the sideboard for the last fifteen years, in our house back in Denver.

If only there were just one label here among the clothes . . . it would make the lie less brutal, more forgivable.

Reaching the end of the rack, I do finally spot a garment I recognize, and the same rage and hate flood through me that I felt for this woman, my mother, who had dishonored my father and deserted us all. The word 'Mother' is alien; she's Myra to me.

Myra had kept it all this time, the kimono – I cannot help but wonder why. As I touch the oriental robe I find the silk has grown paper-thin, the black background faded from many hand-washings. Yet the pattern of white chrysanthemums is still as vivid as it was then!

Feeling an overwhelming desire to bring the cloth up to my cheek, I draw it near and with the petals of the fabric flower against my cheek, crazily I ask, 'Did you love us, any of us – ever?'

I always knew that she didn't love Daddy, at least not after the accident, for the clearest picture in my mind is not one of her lovely face – no, it is one where Myra's lips were drawn thin and cruel as a razor and her eyes sharp as flint were looking down at my father's white, useless legs. I hadn't known then what the emotion was, but I know now that that look, that face, conveyed hate and pure revulsion.

Suddenly I feel too tired for this task of searching for the pieces of the life that belonged to a stranger. I cannot cry for this mother whom I never really knew; if ever I do, it will simply be because a human being has died.

Sadly I leave the bedroom and make my way to the kitchen, again not sure of what I am searching for or what I hope to learn. The sound of scratching at the window startles me, and I look up to see the large shadow of a black cat. He begins to meow piteously, rubbing his thin body hopefully against the bars.

Struggling with the worn lock, I finally succeed in opening the window and a gush of frozen air rushes in with the animal as he lands on the worn tiles. The cupboards are full of tins of cat food, and after hunting unsuccessfully for a bowl, I finally settle on a shiny new pie tin, for the cat is impatiently thrusting against my hand – his way of telling me to hurry.

Mounding his dinner on the plate, the smell speaks of faraway oceans. Hungrily the cat gulps the food and, satisfied at last, begins grooming his wet fur.

Among the cardboard cups from hamburger stands and Chinese take-aways, I eventually discover a green and orange bowl with bold black borders. Turning it over, I see it's an original Clarice Cliff. It doesn't matter, for it's mine now; I can choose to offer it to the cat.

Putting the bowl of fresh cold water on the floor, I call, 'Here, Kitty, Kitty,' but he has retreated somewhere into the flat and does not respond. So, running cold water over the tin, I erase the strong fish smell from the room.

One more piece of the puzzle has been found. She had loved a cat; if not loved, then at least cared for and looked after one – more than she had done for Cindy and me.

I catch myself, for I had almost slipped and called my sister by that hateful nickname Myra always used – *Cin*. Thinking of Cindy, I find a connection like radio waves in the air, and somewhere in the hall the phone begins ringing.

After only three short rings, a strange voice breathes out into the night: 'Hello, you've reached the Myra Dunhom residence. I'm not here right now, but I promise I'll return your call as soon as possible. Please leave your message after the tone.' The seductive voice making promises it can no longer keep.

I find gooseflesh rising up on my arms. It's eerie, this technology. How much of a dead person it can save – voices, pictures that move . . . and then my morbid thoughts scatter as I hear my sister Cynthia's hesitant voice. 'Tree-ne . . . Tre-Tre . . . Tree-ne . . . are you there? It scares – frightens me – hearing her voice. Call – call us. Jeff tri-tried earlier.'

I'm frozen, unable to pick up the phone. Whatever could I say? How could I explain what I have found here, knowing I must follow in Myra's footsteps and lie, color the truth, soften it for her. For I have always protected Cindy from anything ugly, always. Ever since . . .

I touch the now-silent phone, promising myself that I will call her in the morning. It's late in Denver – three hours later than here, I rationalize.

I lift the notepad, expecting to see old messages, strange names and phone numbers on it, but instead, in an angry scrawl, one sentence is repeated over and over: *I must find it. I must find it. I must . . .*

The night has grown still. Aware of the loud monotonous sound of the satisfied cat's purring, I glance into the bedroom to see its large black body stretched languidly out in the middle of the mammoth bed.

The room is bathed in shadows and the red filmy chiffon that hangs limply from the canopy encloses the creature which lolls so comfortably there. An invisible breeze moves the curtains.

Inexplicably, I shudder, and the word 'decadent' comes to mind. One thing is for certain: I cannot pull down that scarlet cover and join the animal in this disquieting bed.

With regret, I realize I've left my bags downstairs in the shop, along with the portfolio of papers from the lawyer. Too late – I'll get them in the morning. For it has been a very long, tiring day. The four-hour flight from Denver in the winter storm was one of ongoing turbulence, and the mad rush to find a taxi in the crowded, snow-covered streets of Manhattan was another nightmare.

Back out in the hall, I search for the bathroom and finally locate the door, in an almost-hidden alcove. Unlike the other tired rooms, the bathroom is extremely luxurious, with black tiles, a black tub, and just a touch of lime green, reminiscent of the Art-Deco period. She must have loved that era. On the ledge, I can see the evidence of her vanity – numerous jars, bottles of perfume, night creams . . . all the things a woman buys to try to cheat the calendar.

But she was only fifty! Had she changed so much over the years? I cannot help but wonder, for I knew, even as a child, that my mother was beautiful; everyone said so.

I cannot bear to touch the used soap, the soap that touched *her* skin, so instead I rinse my face in clear warm water, and with only water I brush my fingers along my teeth and rinse my mouth thoroughly.

Staring at my own weary face in the mirror, I remember how everyone always said I looked like her, and maybe I do. Not beautiful – no, I do not lie to myself. I appraise my large gray eyes that are set in a slender face beneath a tangle of wheat-colored hair. My cheekbones are high and I have a wide generous mouth. The coloring is correct – it is like hers – but something is missing in my face, some intangible thing that separates beautiful from merely pleasant.

No, I do not kid myself. Myra was beautiful, and if you look close, you can see that Cindy is beautiful too, in a different way. She's exotic, with her dark skin, eyes of the clearest blue, and hair that strange color of dark auburn. Yet she disguises it carefully, hiding herself in loose unflattering dresses or baggy sweatsuits, with a dull hair style and those wonderful blue eyes concealed behind a pair of large black spectacles, which no amount of coaxing can convince her to trade in for contact lenses. And her rare smile she hides behind a nervous cupped hand. I have tried, but I am too sad, too guilty, to force her to do otherwise.

I often wonder if you must pay for beauty in another way. In Cindy's case it's true she pays a terrible price, but in the end, it's my fault – Myra always told me so. *My fault*. An accident? No excuse, no excuse whatsoever! A tender age? Again, no excuse.

I stiffen suddenly when I realize I can see it again in the mirror, and I peer intently, straining in the light. Yes, it's there, not entirely erased. Written with the end of a bar of soap – *'I must find it'*.

The radiators in the old building begin to rattle and clang, and finally settle down to a faint gurgling.

I must sleep, I must get some rest. Turning out the living-room light I see, from the solitary window, beautiful shifting patterns playing across the floor and tracing designs on my stockinged feet.

It's easy to explain, for in this poorly heated ancient building, a thick coating of frost has built up on the inside of the window.

A chill strikes me, even though I am still wearing my winter coat. That's where it all began – with Jack Frost. As small children Cindy and I had chanted his name, singing to him in that attic window in that long-ago winter in Denver. I try to block out the guessing games, but in high clear voices I can still hear us playing, pointing to the images in the ice.

'Look, Trini, it's a dog!'

'Yes, Cindy, I see it. Look there,' and even now I almost find myself pointing, 'that's a flower, a daisy like the ones in the yard in summer.'

Yes, yes, we had called to each other of our marvelous discoveries of pictures in the ice, our voices tumbling over each other in the excitement of the game. 'Look, Cindy, look!' No, no, I stop the game. Oh, if only I had stopped it then, and hadn't seen the tempting shape that lured her to it like Eve to the forbidden apple!

I awake in a room which feels colder than it did last night. The thermostat is set on 62; I swivel the dial until the pointer is resting on 75, and in answer, almost immediately I hear the rumble of ancient pipes.

Stretching, for I'm stiff from sleeping on the couch, I walk about the flat vainly wishing for a large mug of hot coffee. But I know that before I go out, I must call home and talk to either Jeff or Cynthia. It's impossible to tell the time, for although the flat is full of clocks, none of them seem to be working.

For the first time I notice above me, covered almost entirely with snow, a skylight, and with an indifferent eye, devoid of emotion, I evaluate the flat. It's roomy by New York standards, and using my imagination, I transform it with light and space. Gone, I have sent away the clutter, and realizing the value of this property which I have been left, I feel the heat of excitement.

The attorney had included the last valuation of the commercial building and flat; it had come to a little over one million dollars.

Why the elaborate charade? Why couldn't Myra bring herself to tell the truth! And now I have the task of somehow telling Cynthia. It cannot help to stall, so I lift the receiver and dial and find myself greeted with my sister's painful stutter. 'Hell-hello.'

'Cindy, it's me.'

'Oh, I'm so glad you called.' Cindy's voice now smoothes itself out, the stutter put away, for it only emerges with strangers and persons she doesn't know very well.

'I would have rung last night, but it was late. I do apologize.'

'That's okay. But Jeff was worried, and so was I.'

'I know, but it was very late – the plane was, too. And it was very difficult getting around town. The taxis were all full. It's cold here, lots of snow still on the ground.'

'Oh, just like here.' Cindy waits expectantly.

There is an awkward silence and finally Cindy fills it. 'Trini, is something wrong?'

'No, it's just that things here are not exactly what we expected. She changed the salon since she wrote last.'

'Oh! How is it, real nice? I'm terrible with maps, but I've studied it over and over. Is it near Fifth Avenue and Central Park?'

'No, not really. It's in Greenwich Village. Trendy, the West Village is real trendy, always has been. The shops here have everything imaginable.'

'Wait, Trini, let me get the map. I can find Charles Street while we're talking.'

'No, don't. That won't help. It's on the other side of Manhattan – not near the park.'

'Oh, I've tried to imagine it, her salon, so many times,' Cindy says wistfully.

I take a deep breath and launch into my deception.

'There's a letter here for us,' 'I begin. 'She never got a chance to mail it.'

'Oh!'

'It seems she was tired of dealing with all those famous women. You know, they can be very tiresome, rich women like that.'

'Did she close the salon?' The disappointment in Cindy's voice is almost a visible sound.

'Sort of. She just got sick and tired of it, and she opened a shop instead.'

'Oh. Well, a shop full of her designs must really be something.' And as Cindy spoke, no doubt she thought of the satin label Myra had sent us years ago.

This was even harder than I had imagined. 'She must have sold them, her designs.' I cough, then go on: 'Her shop sells vintage clothes.'

'You mean old clothes?'

'Well, yes, they *are* old, but they're vintage. Lots of movie stars and famous people collect and wear garments like this. She probably had a lot of her old customers, too. You know Ma. Dad always said she was like a restless bee going from flower to flower. New ideas, new projects, that was what excited her. He always said so.'

'Yeah, I guess, but I would have liked to have seen the salon. I thought about it a lot.'

'I know. Me, too.' And I cast around for a tidbit that will erase the disappointment from my sister's voice. Of course! The next bit of information is important to both of us.

'Cindy, the building that the shop's in and the flat above it, it's free and clear – and it's worth a lot of money. She left it to us.' That wasn't exactly true; she had left it to me with a stern reminder to take care of my sister since, after all, it was my responsibility, my fault, my burden.

'Oh.' Cindy's voice brightens. 'I guess the salon was a real success then.'

'Yeah, it must have been. I wish you had come with me,' I finish, knowing I hadn't wanted her there at all, especially after finding out there was no salon and never had been. 'I don't know how long I'm staying. I guess I should put the property up for sale, and the things in the shop.'

'Could you save me some thing of hers, something that seems like her?'

'Of course I will. I've got to talk to Jeff about all this. I'll call him later and explain all the loose ends.'

'Don't worry,' and Cindy's voice softens. 'I made Jeff's breakfast this morning,' she says proudly.

I look down at my thick gold wedding band and feel sick. I have so much and my sister has so little. 'Thanks. That's really nice.' And our secret is held unspoken between us.

Trash and treasures, I think as I walk the flat again, searching, looking, appraising.

I wash my face, run a comb through my tangled hair; open the window so the cat can go out on the roof terrace, and notice for the first time the locks that would allow the bars to open, giving access to the roof.

It is a very desirable flat, I decide – large, roomy, with a roof terrace.

Making sure I have the keys, I go down the stairs to the busy street. The tramp has left it for me, his insult, right in the middle of the doormat – a pile of human excrement.

Seeing a newspaper in the trash, I retrieve it and with my face wrinkled up in a mask of distaste, I follow suit of those who clean up after their dogs and reach down with the paper and deposit the waste into the nearby trash can.

Letting myself into the shop, I go first to the bathroom and scrub my hands thoroughly with the kitchen cleanser I find there.

In the daylight, with the lights on, the shop appears far less ominous. It is apparent that there are some very beautiful pieces of clothing here, but hunger overcomes my urge to linger. So, leaving the lights on, I secure the lock and walk briskly down to 7th Avenue, where a smart café beckons.

I order a simple continental breakfast and cappuccino.

The brisk but friendly waitress, after placing the croissant and fruit before me, searches my face. 'You're her daughter, aren't you – Myra's?'

'Yes, I am,' and I offer a smile up into her curious face.

'Shame about Myra. You have my condolences. She was a nice lady. I can't imagine who would have wanted to hurt her.'

Puzzled, I just nod.

'Cremated, wasn't she? It was private or I would have gone. I would have sent some flowers, too, but the announcement in the paper said not to. I did send a check though, a small one, to the orphanage in Denver that was named in the paper.'

'Thanks,' I say softly, but I look down at my plate, wishing the woman would stop talking. The orphanage in Denver – what a joke! What black humor one could find in that. Even the lawyer's letter informing us of our mother's death came after she had been cremated.

I find it hard, even in death, not to hate the woman, although I have managed all these years to maintain a steady indifference.

I finish my breakfast and walk out again into the small, tight, busy streets of the Village, unsure of what to do next. I have to talk to Jeff, explain what it's like here, and together we'll decide how to go about settling things.

Meaning only to retrieve my suitcase, I let myself into the store, but before I can leave, a woman is knocking frantically on the door.

'Closed,' I mouth through the thick glass.

'I need something. I promise I won't be long.'

'Closed,' I repeat.

'Oh please – I'll just be a minute.'

Reluctantly, I switch the lock and hold the door ajar.

'Thanks. I need that Fifties' dress, the blue one with the draped side. I'm auditioning for a commercial and I thought I'd blow them away by being totally genuine from head to toe. I've got a friend who can do my hair right, too,' the girl gushes on as she threads her way among the racks, searching for the dress. 'I tried it on before; it's perfect.' She stoops down, looking for a certain pair of ankle-strapped shoes. 'Got 'em.' She holds the shoes up like a triumphant flag.

She puts everything down on the counter while I clumsily search for a sales book or something. 'I don't exactly know how to do this,' I apologize.

'That's okay. You're her daughter, right? Are you the one who plays the piano or the ice-skater?'

Surprised, I mumble, 'Piano.' I've never played in my life; I skated some, but nothing to brag about.

Evidence and more evidence of the lie that had been Myra.

'Visa,' and the girl holds out her credit card. Seeing my confusion, she says, 'I'll do it, if it's okay with you.'

I nod my consent and the customer comes around the counter, finds the correct machine and sales slip, and runs it off.

'See, you pull the numbers down with the amount – ninety dollars. Shoes, forty dollars; dress, fifty dollars.' And she pulls the slip through. 'I sign it and keep my copy and that's all there is to it.'

I nod.

'It's easy, you'll see,' the girl assures me. 'You're supposed to check the book, though, for stolen cards and stuff like that. Mine's okay, though.'

'I'm sure it is.'

'I don't need a bag – I live just down the street. Thanks, you saved my life, or at least my livelihood.'

Following her to the door, I find myself saying, 'Good luck. I hope you get the commercial.'

'Thanks.'

But before I can shut the door, a small dark woman shoulders her way into the shop. Holding out her worn hand, she says, 'I'm Clarista.'

Puzzled, I take the offered hand. 'Trini Woodruff, Myra's daughter.'

'I clean here Monday and Thursday, but I haven't touched the place for a couple of weeks now.' She looks around dismayed. 'Dust, it's everywhere. It's gonna take a lot of elbow grease next time.' She stops and then mumbles awkwardly, 'Sorry about Myra.'

'Thanks.' And thinking it wouldn't hurt to have the place cleaned, I say, 'Any time you'd like to do it would be fine.'

'Well, this is just as good a time as any,' and Clarista bustles towards the broom closet. She pauses and then asks, 'When you opening?'

'I'm not sure I am. I'm only here from Denver settling my mother's things.'

'Damn shame you're not opening; Myra had a good business here. All those damn designers poking around looking for the same thing, but they paid, they bought stuff, always hoping,' and she turns away, rustling in the closet for the feather duster.

Looking? Looking for what, I wonder. Like the note upstairs. But the woman seems intent on her work now and I have no idea how to ask her what she meant.

I take my luggage and tell Clarista, 'I'm going upstairs; I need to bathe and freshen up. How does this work? Should I come back to let you out?'

Clarista straightens up, puts her hands on her hips, and surveys the damage. 'Take me three or four hours at least. I usually only do two. But if you're not back, I'll close the door after me and make sure it's locked. I'm reliable – I worked for Myra going on ten years.'

'That's fine.' I pause. 'About payment . . .'

'Oh, I'll come back Thursday if it's okay with you. We can settle then. I'm fair, I won't charge you extra.' Her voice is a strange mixture of Spanish and English learned in the streets of Spanish Harlem.

'That sounds good,' and I lift the heavy suitcase and the folders of legal papers.

Upstairs, I run the water in the tub and search for a fresh bar of soap. There isn't one; I have to settle for bath salts, and I remind myself that I must find a store and buy a few essentials.

I lie back in the warm water and feel my cramped muscles begin to relax.

Images, thoughts, questions, flood my mind and I decide not to permit it, so with an effort I close them off and tune into the comfort and relaxation of my tired body.

It is only when the water has cooled, and might slop over if I top it up any more, that I pull out the plug, dry myself and put on my comfortable old terry robe. The flat is warm now and feeling wasteful, I lower the thermostat to 70.

On impulse, I go to the bedroom and tear down the sheer red curtains surrounding the bed and rumple the bedspread into a ball. The pristine white sheets are acceptable, so I crawl between them, still in my robe, and instantly fall asleep.

I wake up to the sound of Myra's voice echoing through the apartment. I must erase that tape; it is unsettling hearing a dead woman's voice. I would have thought there would be something familiar in her speech, a remembered cadence or inflection, but sadly, it's the voice of a stranger.

I play back the messages. A woman named Felicity has asked to be called back; Jeff has called again; and the last message is from a Lieutenant Burke, an officer from the 1st District.

Whatever can the police want? My hands are shaking as I write down the phone numbers.

The sound of the cat crying at the window delays me. I open the window, feed the animal, and then return to the answering machine, where I erase the tape and record a simple new message in its place.

I dial the house; Jeff's hearty 'Hello!' feels like a lifeline and makes me realize how disoriented and confused I am.

'Hi,' I breathe into the phone.

'You're a hard one to catch up with,' he says, his voice warm and not at all accusatory.

'I know, I don't know how to begin, Jeff, it's all so much different than what I had expected.'

'Cindy mentioned as much. No salon – finito – in its place some kinda store.'

'True – that's it.' I take a deep breath, trying to form the words that would explain. 'I never told you much about my mother. I couldn't really, I didn't know much about her myself!'

'Uh huh.'

'I was trying to soften the truth for Cindy. It seems there never *was* a salon. Myra never designed anything, but there is a shop. Seems she ran a shop all those years, selling second-hand, vintage clothes.'

'Oh?' he prompts, wanting me to go on.

'There's a flat above the shop. The store itself is full of jewelry and clothes, and the flat has some antiques, maybe valuable, maybe not. The real estate is paid for free and clear.'

'If you're putting it on the market, do you need Cindy's signature?'

'Well . . .' Again I hesitate. 'I didn't tell her, I knew how much it would hurt her. Myra left everything to me. She left Cindy a dollar.'

'What?'

'A dollar. She left her a dollar.'

'Gee, that's harsh. What did the poor kid ever do to her to deserve that?'

'Nothing, Jeff. For God's sake, she left when Cindy was only four. I barely remember her myself – I was only nine.' Silence . . . and then I feel I must continue. 'Of course, in the will there was a mention of my responsibility to take care of Cindy. Very clearly she spelled it out, that it was my fault.'

I can tell he has cupped his hand over the phone – his voice is now a harsh whisper. 'My God, Trini, you've always treated her like a retard! There's nothing wrong with her, nothing at all that taking responsibility for herself wouldn't cure. You can't spend your entire life feeling guilty.'

'I don't want to fight, Jeff. Please, it's difficult enough.'

'I know, I'm sorry. When are you coming home?'

'I'm not sure.'

'Should I call the ad agency for you?'

'No, I'll do it myself.'

There is a real strain between us, but it isn't anything new – it has been like this for months. It has absolutely nothing to do with the legacy. I look down at my wedding band and feel an overwhelming urge to take it off.

'Cindy just came in. You wanna speak to her?'

'Yeah, but first, how is she? I mean really.'

'Great, better than great. It's what I said before. On her own, she's fine.'

His words make me feel guilty. 'I just want to protect her, Jeff. You know that.'

'No, I don't, I really don't know that.' And again I can tell his hand is cupped over the phone. 'You treat her like the child we don't have.'

It's that painful subject again. I have stalled him for years on starting a family, and even to myself I can't explain why.

'Cindy, Cindy, it's Trini,' and I can imagine him holding out the phone to my sister.

Breathless from the recent exertion of clearing the snow from the front walk, Cindy says a soft hello, with no trace of the stutter. 'How's it going?'

'Slow. I've been in the shop and met a friend or two of Myra's.'

'Gee, was it someone famous?'

Resisting the urge to continue the elaborate fabrication, I answer truthfully. 'No, actually it was a customer and a lady that works for her and some people in the neighborhood.'

'Oh, I bet she was well liked. She was like you, Trini, I just know it.'

'Yeah, maybe so, but how about you, how are you doing?'

'Fine, I'm doing just fine. I didn't tell you, but I got it in the mail this morning, my degree – Bachelor of Science.'

'That's great. I'm so proud of you.' And I remember those years of Cindy sitting for hours in front of the TV at the Home University. I should have forced her to go out in the real world and attend a real university, but after her painful years at high school, I just couldn't. 'Anything else?'

'Oh, I've taken care of everything. I've ironed all of Jeff's shirts, light on the starch like you told me, and I've cleaned the house from top to bottom, and I made Jeff that pot roast he likes so much. Everything's fine. I'm doing everything just like you would if you were here.' She pauses and her voice grows trembly. 'Except I moved things around in the living room a bit. I hope you don't mind, Trini. Is that okay?'

'Of course I don't mind, but you take it easy; the house and Jeff will survive without your playing Superwoman.'

'I like doing things for Jeff.'

'I know you do,' and I feel that familiar pang of dread. How would it end – what I had started?

I hang up and call the next number on the pad. When I ask for Felicity, a pleasant voice tells me Felicity isn't in right now.

'This is Trini from "Repeat Performance" returning her call.'

'Oh, Myra's place. She was gonna come around in the morning and see if you were there. Someone told her you were open today.'

'Not exactly open, but I was in the shop and I will be there in the morning sorting things out.'

'I'll tell her.'

I hang up and looking down at the last number, decide not to call Lieutenant Burke right then. I imagine it's some sort of hassle about licenses or some legal thing about the shop.

I dress in a pair of comfortable jeans, a flannel shirt, and my warm, lined denim jacket. Gathering up the bedspread and the bundle of red curtains, I carry them down to the street and deposit them in the nearest trash can before entering the shop again.

This time, the scent of lemon is refreshing and I can see that the wooden counters gleam with Clarista's efforts. The thick gray carpet is now spotless and the racks have been straightened. On the counter a note from the cleaner says she'll polish the jewelry on Thursday.

I hadn't really looked in the cases before. I flick on the lights in the jewelry counters and see matched bracelet, necklace, and earring sets beautiful and showy like pieces from the old movies; stones in pink, purple, green, blue, and clear sets sparkling like precious diamonds. Small, hand-printed signs identify the pieces as collectible costume jewelry, and designer names run through my head as I read: *1940s Trifari, 1950 Coro, 1930 Haskell, 1920 Chanel, 1940 Schiaparelli.* I gaze at them in awe, not having realized before that some of the famous clothes designers from the past made jewelry as well.

My interest quickens. There is so much here at 'Repeat Performance' – the clothes, the jewelry, the flat. But I don't need to look for Myra in these things, for we lost her a long time ago.

I sit at the counter intending to make out a shopping list, but among the papers there I see an envelope addressed to me in Myra's distinctive scrawl. The stark message – it begins 'Trini' – not 'Dear Trini' – tells me to sign the enclosed cards and take them to the bank.

There are two cards to be filled out, one for a savings account and one for the business account.

I open the savings book. My name is on it, waiting only for my signature.

I can't believe it – there's more than a hundred thousand dollars in the account! Strange that over the years she had sent us virtually nothing. Maybe once or twice a year a package would arrive with a toy that no longer suited, or a gift of clothing – a sweater or blouse that was far too small.

The infrequent correspondence from Myra invariably made reference to a famous client or an article that was due to appear about the salon; she always promised to send these along later, but they never materalized. The satin label arrived with a brief note saying that these were sewn into every article of clothing Myra designed . . .

I'm beginning to feel dizzy for there is so much to take in. I sit back in the chair, realizing that when I sell the property, I will have a great deal of money. We aren't strapped for cash, by any means. With Jeff's position at the university where he makes a good salary and my position at the advertising agency, we have enough. It is only Cindy who earns nothing. I haven't forced her out into the world to do anything. She probably could have, for she is very bright, but for now she is a professional student, all of her education coming through the box – the TV university.

I hadn't told Jeff that the property is valuable; I hadn't mentioned it to Cindy either. I couldn't understand why, for I'm not greedy; I want nothing for myself that doesn't include Jeff and Cindy. Or maybe I do, but I'm just not sure what it is.

I dim the lights and set out to look for someplace to eat a quick dinner. It's early and the restaurants aren't crowded. I read the menus outside a couple of restaurants and decide on the Italian. The small intimate restaurant smells wonderful, the herby, red-wine aroma blending with the pleasant scent of the candles that sit atop each table on checkered red and white cloths. How quaint, I think – the prototype of Italian restaurants the world over. The owner obviously believed if it ain't broke, don't fix it.

When the young waiter looks my way, his face blanches momentarily, but recovering he says politely, 'Sorry, I thought you were someone else.'

I must resemble Myra a lot more than I had thought. 'My mother probably came in here,' I say. 'She was Myra Dunhom.'

'Of course,' he answers. 'Welcome to New York.'

'Thank you.'

'She was so proud of you both, her daughters. She bragged about her great athletes. I never learned to ski myself,' he admits.

'Oh! In Colorado we had lots of opportunity to do so,' I lie, and for a minute the pain of my father's broken promise returns. I have to get used to it, these elaborate lies Myra has told.

I glance down at the menu. 'I'll have a martini,' for suddenly I feel the need of alcohol.

'I'll give you a few minutes to study the menu, but here are our specials,' and he begins listing them with a memory that would make an elephant jealous.

After the simple meal of linguine, garlic bread and a tossed side salad, I feel the effect of the house wine coursing through my veins. I'm in a euphoric mood, and when I walk outside, I see it is already that early winter dark. Couples walk hand in hand and on Bleeker Street, two teenagers playfully hurl snowballs at each other.

Ahead of me, a couple under a streetlamp stop and embrace and kiss like they are totally unaware of anyone or anything in the whole world except for the urgency of their desire for each other.

Suddenly it makes me think of Cal. I haven't thought of him for a very long time. That's how I had felt about him . . . then, I stop myself. No good remembering, and in a moment of complete honesty I admit, if only to myself, that I have never felt that way about Jeff. I love him, but not like that – that all-consuming way, body on fire, I can't wait to touch you, can't wait for you to touch me . . . I think of the light and how I had loved looking at Cal and how much I enjoyed his eyes devouring me. No, it's not like that with Jeff; it never has been. With a feeling of shame and degradation, I think of the light – really meaning I think of the dark.

Further down the sidewalk I pass a young girl walking a parcel of dogs who strain at the leash as she reaches down, newspaper in hand, to clean up after one of her charges.

'Hi,' the stranger says. 'Great, ain't it?'

I'm not sure if she means the snow or early evening, but I meet the girl's friendliness with my own.

'It sure is.'

On Bleeker Street, I stop to glance in the shop windows. The evening is cold and crisp, but not unpleasant, just invigorating.

I walk on, passing men, women, couples, and meeting their greetings with my own. 'Hi . . . Hello . . . Nice night.' The Village is a friendly place; whoever said New Yorkers were not!

This small piece of the huge metropolis is an island unto itself, and when I arrive back at the flat, I see him bedded down in my doorway, swaddled in the velvet covers.

He peers out at me, understanding now that I'm not just a tourist passing through. I am one of them now, a part of the Village. He doesn't hassle locals, so he puts his head back under the covers, grateful for this find. It is cosy, he is okay, his belly is full and the wine in his veins keeps him warm. He can sleep and dream about his childhood back in New Mexico.

I walk up the stairs to the flat that seems familiar to me already. I need a plan, I need to put things in order. Where to begin, I wonder. A realtor, that seems a logical start, but somehow I dismiss it, thinking I'll take a few days and look around. I enjoy my freedom, the lack of ties. Here in this strange city I am free!

I click on all the lights in the flat and let out the cat.

The clutter of the place annoys me – it could be so much nicer – and with a vengeance I begin taking down pictures, removing knick-knacks, and packing them inside a large box. There are various bits of bric-à-brac scattered everywhere. All these things could go downstairs to the shop. That's probably where they came from in the first place.

I work for several hours; and the living room already looks different. In its sparseness it seems much larger. There is nothing I can do about the mix-matched furniture tonight and I wonder if there is a corner of the shop where the threepiece suite might fit. The 1950s is not a favorite period of mine, at least not for the furniture; it's so kitsch.

I move to the bedroom. With all the red fabric gone it already looks much better. Still, I don't fancy the bed with its savage swan, although in some large house it could be a real showpiece and should command a good price. I don't know woods, but something about the rosy hue in the grain makes me think the bed might be cherry, or even rosewood.

I peek into the next room, but the cluttered desk is not appealing, so I make for the kitchen instead.

My first task is to throw away all the cups, straws and plates from the take-aways; the debris half fills a trash bag. I look in the cupboards. The pots and pans seem to be brand new; it's apparent that Myra never cooked.

The cupboards contain no china; I'll have to get some.

I stop myself. No, I won't, for I will only be here for a few move days. I realize suddenly what I am doing – nesting – that female instinct to make a place my own. 'Stop it,' I say aloud, and my thoughts trail back to Cindy's words earlier: 'I moved things around in the living room. I hope you don't mind.'

I check the kitchen window to see if the cat is about or trying to get back in, but in the silver-blue moonlight shining on the snow I see only its footprints where it has made its way back and forth.

The wind makes dark shadows move across the porch, and I shield my eyes trying to see what is out there. I notice four trees, native to Colorado, in huge pots. These are the same trees that line our ample yard in Denver.

I feel surprised, for I would have thought that Myra wanted to get away from Denver, with no reminders of her life, or the lives she had left back there.

I look around the kitchen. It's tidy now and I take the full bag of trash and put it on the landing ready to be taken down in the morning.

The flat's chilly, so I raise the thermostat and go into the room with the desk and the solitary chair. I should really sort the papers and start making a dent in clearing things up.

I leaf through stacks of paid bills for the shop and look around for file folders or something to put them in. In frustration, I find nothing appropriate, so I stack the paid bills and put my shoe on top. I can't tell whether the bills in the other stack are paid or not; I'll have to check with the lawyer.

Shocked, I find three marriage licenses all clipped together and, in a different drawer, two divorce papers and one death certificate. Her husbands, all of her former husbands . . . I read the names on the papers over and over. Myra had married three more times. I feel a sense of outrage and betrayal for my father, who had never stopped loving her. Secrets, how adept people are at keeping secrets! It seemed she had never given up the name Dunhom. I drop the certificates into the metal strongbox with a feeling of revulsion, but I am glad that my father never knew – how it would have hurt him! – and for once I feel a small sense of kinship with Myra. It was a kindness, this secret of hers.

Next I pick up a folded piece of paper, a copy of a cashier's check in the amount of ten thousand dollars. It is dated one month earlier. Curious. I can't help but wonder what Myra bought for this large sum, but the line where the company or person's name should go was blank. Whoever cashed it evidently filled it in later.

In the bottom drawer of the desk I find a small gold box; opening the lid I see them – a stack of elegant satin labels, just like the one she sent us: *Myra Dunhom, Couture.* The stack has not been disturbed, except for maybe one or two.

I know where one label is: in the sideboard in the house back in Denver.

Sadly, I replace the lid and open a neat folder, to be confronted by sketch upon sketch of dress designs. I rifle through the pages and wonder at the hours of work that have gone into this portfolio.

'No,' I find myself thinking as I examine a sketch. 'It won't drape right like that.' As an artist who has many hours of sketching nudes in my background, I have a real understanding of the human body and I can see the obvious flaws in Myra's work.

'A raglan sleeve would work on this,' and I catch myself talking aloud.

I can hear the cat whining in the kitchen, so I put down the folder, let him in, and excitedly go back to look through the folder again. Myra's designs seem best on the evening clothes, but while she had been an expert seamstress, she lacked that crucial knowledge of anatomy.

'No, it needs tucks here, and this one needs darts at the back just above the waist.' The cat, now resting on the stack of papers, looks up again and again to see who I am talking to.

I feel an overwhelming desire to get out a pen and correct the designs; they're good, or could be.

Sad for Myra to have had the desire but not the ability; her expertise in reading patterns did not seem to transfer over to knowing how to create her own designs.

I hold the pen, longing to get started, but the mere act of holding it reminds me of all the work waiting for me at home.

The Anderson account, for instance. They won't accept anyone else's artwork but my own. They are old fashioned to a fault; they would never approve of any computer-generated designs. I have done their print-media work for the last six years and know exactly what they want – the Norman Rockwell look – but it doesn't stretch my talent and I am bored to death with it.

When is that deadline? I can't remember, but it's weeks off – at least, I hope so!

Carefully, I lay the folder aside and pick through Myra's correspondence – invitations to parties, short notes from women, reminders of luncheon dates, auction calendars, flea-market flyers – and I find several sheets of stationery which begin *Dear Jack,* but the letter that was meant to go with the salutation was never written.

At the bottom of the last drawer, I find it; it could have been the same one that is in Denver. Going through into the bedroom, I sit down and caress the cover of the photo album before opening it at the first page. This contains an enlarged picture of my father, Big Jack, and in the background of the photograph I can see the other dancers and Myra, a vision of loveliness in an evening gown tiered with ruffles. The pages seem to be a record of their courtship, both of them in swimsuits leaning against an old convertible, another in tennis clothes, one with Big Jack in a white tuxedo, and their wedding photo. They looked so young, so happy then.

I see myself, a fat happy baby of six months of age on the classic bearskin rug; then another on my father's shoulders at two; and one photo of Big Jack as a huge dirty Santa Claus in his oil-stained work-clothes, the hard hat tilted crookedly on his head and in his hands two enormous sacks of presents for us.

My tears spill over and like sporadic rain fall on the faded photographs. I close the book and fling myself down on the bed, sobbing into the pillow. *Daddy, I miss you* – and the sadness of his life overwhelms me. Why him, why did it have to happen to him? And Myra, she deserted him, not only ran out on him, but left her two children behind for him to cope with as best he could. I continue to cry and the cat snuggles up to my side and purrs, and the rumbling of his body next to mine is a comfort.

CHAPTER TWO

I can't remember in detail the days of Big Jack's glory. Our spacious house on Downing Street near the park was part of it, and that marvelous house was paid for free and clear. I do remember clearly his Fridaynight homecomings, his arms laden with gifts – toys for me, his princess, and perfume and jewelry and silly expensive baubles for his adorable wife, Myra – all earned by his sweat climbing oil rigs in Wyoming. It was dangerous work. I only knew this by the photo album that he later kept on his knees, often searching the pictures, peering intently at the large muscular strong man he had been before the accident.

Those times I sensed his anguish and would lay my head against his knee, waiting patiently for the day he would leave the chair with wheels and toss me up into the air again, squealing with delight. Every so often I found myself hunting in his pockets for a tantalizing present he might have forgotten. Days, weeks, months went by and I began to believe those happy times were only dreams or bits of happy stories I remembered.

In our house, change was slow but insidious; the phone began ringing with callers who made my mother angry.

'Not the house, Myra. Sell anything, but please don't mortgage the house.' This was Big Jack's constant plea from the prison of his chair, and so Myra's jewelry box was raided again and again until it was completely empty and the forlorn ballerina on top had no reason to whirl round and round.

One day, Myra thought she had found an answer to our financial problems. In one of the large stocked closets, she discovered the 'Singer', an old treadle sewing machine left behind by the spinster from whom they had purchased the house.

It was a happy time for Myra, for hope flared once more. The rocking horse and overflowing toy boxes were removed from the attic room. Then workmen began rushing about moving, painting, until in utter frustration, Jack called out: 'What is it, Myra? What's all the fuss?'

And with patience, she sat down to try to explain her idea. 'The insurance money is almost gone, Jack. We've only the monthly check now and it's so little. I thought . . .' She stopped and twisted her bare fingers which felt naked without the enormous diamond engagement ring. 'I thought . . .' Again she hesitated. 'Do you remember that formal dance, the first one you asked me to?'

Through tear-filled eyes he nodded.

'And dress, do you remember that, too? It was blue with a cloud of ruffles.'

He nodded, speaking in a whisper. 'Everyone looked at you. You were so beautiful and I was so proud that you were with me.'

'But the dress, Jack, do you really remember the dress?'

He nodded, but all he really remembered was her face glowing with happiness; he remembered too how he had promised himself that if she were his, he would give her the world – lay it at her feet. He started from his reverie as Myra continued.

'*I* made it, that blue dress. I made it myself on Momma's sewing machine, and all the girls in the powder room wondered and whispered, trying to guess where I had bought it.'

He nodded again, still not understanding.

'I'm making the attic into a workroom,' she said brightly. 'Well, sort of a salon where I can design and sew clothes.' She paused and then went on: 'I'm good, Jack. I know I can succeed at this.'

His eyes flared with sudden anger. 'A studio, a salon!' That was Myra's way of coating the truth. She always dressed up something ugly. 'You mean you're going to take in sewing for strangers.' His voice was a harsh sound in the quiet room.

'No,' she said as she rose up angrily. 'It's not like that, not at all, Jack. I'm good. Before we were married, I designed all my own clothes. You make it sound so awful, but it won't be like that.' She turned round and glared at him. 'How can you criticize me, sitting in that Goddamned chair doing nothing!' And she left the room, banging the door loudly behind her.

I continued to cower under the chair in abject terror, watching my father squirm his upper torso, still bulging with muscles, his powerful arms clutching the sides of the chair willing himself to rise.

I witnessed his fruitless struggle and was frightened of the strange tears running down his cheeks. As much as I wanted to, I couldn't give up my hiding place to comfort him by laying my head upon his knee and telling him everything was gonna be okay.

I wanted desperately to give him back the comfort he always gave me when I had a broken toy or a skinned knee or even a terrible nightmare. I wanted to tell him everything was gonna be okay, but somehow I knew it wouldn't be.

That autumn, the sewing machine hummed its endless songs and the sound of strangers' footfalls on the stairs was a common sound. Jack began to grow smaller; he shrank back further into his wheelchair, and like body parts which couldn't bear to be in disharmony, his broad chest and firm arms dwindled to match his shriveled legs.

I couldn't bear to watch him, so I took refuge in the attic, hiding among the lengths of satin and drawing endless circles on the floor with the dressmaker's chalk. Completely unnoticed by my mother, I gathered mislaid pins, bits of thread, ends of bias tape, and buttons, the extra ones, stolen from the cutting table. In my child's mind, I thought that somehow out of small pieces, I could magically make something whole.

Like my mother, I loved the cloth, the feel of the soft velvet, the shimmery satin, the magic of it all; it was one thing that became another. The unhappiness in the house smoothed out when I could feel the cloth; in it was something that would make things right.

Missing my mother's past easy caresses and my father's warmth, I found something important in the tactile sensation of the cloth. Touching, always touching, stroking, it must have been then that I lost the feel of loved ones and thought I found dreams in silk. It was a comfort, my only comfort, in that tragic house.

The humming of the machine and the movement back and forth of the treadle was steady. From my vantage point on the floor hidden under the dresses, I could see my mother's slim ankles and her feet, in inappropriate satin dancing shoes, coaxing the machine onward on a journey that never ended.

With a satisfying thumb, I sucked, clutching, smoothing the satin wedding gown – a fine replacement for the worn teddy bear forgotten downstairs on my bed.

My fingerprints caught me out, and Myra screamed with rage, her face as red as the autumn leaves. 'Out!' she screamed. 'Out,

Trini, and don't you ever come up here again. It's not a playroom any more, it's my work – and damn hard work it is, too!'

But I did return and hide in the cupboard among the bolts of cloth, or crept among the dressmaker's dummies, silently searching for bits and pieces, hoping to regain what I thought was my mother's lost love.

It was because of my ability to hide and crawl so silently that I saw them, both of them – unaware that I sat huddled among the finished dresses, careful not to touch the bridesmaids' gowns of lilac and yellow, which made me think of Easter and happy times, of when Big Jack hid the eggs and baskets on the big lawn out back.

But this man with my mother was different, not like my father at all. This man stood shirtless, his arms outstretched, as Myra measured him, the tape pulled firmly around his tanned narrow chest. It made me breathless with fear watching them, for slowly, like a serpent, Myra's ringless finger smoothed his skin. But why, why was she touching his cheek, her hand running over his trim dark mustache, and then seeking upward to touch his smooth dark hair, only to leave him standing in front of the mirror to disappear behind the dressing screen, pausing at the radio to click it on, flooding the room with music and the sound of a sorrowful tenor sax, its trembling notes imitating her slow progress. Shoes forgotten, Myra walked lightly, almost tiptoeing, and the oriental gown she was now wearing moved gracefully with her like a summer cloud, black then white chrysanthemums shuddering in a summer breeze, the folds of her gown teasing as the ripeness of her flesh peeked through.

They blended, the man's hands lost in the fullness hidden in her gown, until I could look no more, so I closed my eyes tightly, imagining the Easter-egg hunt, and began counting silently how many Easter eggs I had found, but the sound of mating breath soared through the room, reminiscent of the Singer treadle going back and forth, back and forth.

Forgetting that it was forbidden, I reached up to finger the gowns in lavender and buttercup yellow, searching the cloth and trying to erase what was on the floor before me.

'Jack, you've got to keep Trini amused downstairs. I can't have her up there in the salon. She dirties the clothes. Can't you read to her or something?'

It was an unnecessary plea, for I, seeing *His* polished shoes and freshly pressed trousers on the stairs, with hate roaring through me ran outside into the yard, for it was hard to breathe knowing! And one time, hiding in the bushes, I found a forgotten egg from a long-ago Easter-egg hunt, the red of its shell bleached pink, and only a tiny pinprick showing where the egg had been invaded, the ants carefully filing in and out until it was just an empty shell.

I crushed it with my fist, satisfied that it lay in tiny pieces, but then I cried because like everything around me, I couldn't put it back together again.

Like one thing transferred to another, *He* didn't come any more, and only in my dreams did I see the polished black shoes going up, always going up, ascending the stairway. Instead, I saw my mother changing. No longer was her hair curled; the lipstick stood forgotten on the bathroom shelf and the high heels lay under the dust-ruffle of her bed, while she wore terry-cloth house shoes; the stylish clothes had gone, replaced by a clean loose smock.

Jack could never raise his eyes to the level of her face, but stared as if, like a magician, he could make what was growing under his wife's smock disappear.

'Her name's Cynthia. She's your sister, and you have to help, Trini. I've got to work. My clients need me – I have to work.' And she shook me roughly. 'Do you understand?

I didn't, but I nodded yes.

And when I looked into the basket, I felt a mixture of hate and love. Something wasn't right, I knew that – but I didn't know what. I only knew that Daddy would not look at my new sister, and that it felt good knowing he loved me best. He obviously didn't love my new sister at all.

At times, I could forget my jealousy and sometimes when I learned to give the baby a bottle, I felt protective and strong. And above me, in the attic, the hum of the machine was the center of our universe.

The man never came back. Only ladies came now, giggling and planning a wedding or a special dress for a tea dance. And while Myra's hands were busy with the cloth and other women's hopes and dreams, her hands became so full that she let go and I inherited the child. I was the first to see Cynthia crawl, take her first step, and utter the word 'Momma' in error while touching my face.

The dual nature of it tore at me. That child stumbling on uneasy feet could make Jack frown, biting his lip, losing himself in the pictures in the album, crying out for yesterday, and it was those times that I hated her, that beautiful child following me like a shadow.

It was a house of silence, minimum words spoken softly and the sound of the radio playing in the attic competing always with the monotonous hum of the sewing machine upstairs.

It was the first snowfall of the season; the radio predicted a white-out. Somehow the snow made Daddy happy, and he dozed in his chair, remembering clearly how it felt to ski, flying down the hills, expertly dodging trees. He had always promised me next year, always next year: 'We'll go to Steamboat Springs, honey, and I'll teach you how to ski.'

But it never happened, and now he could only ski day dreaming in his chair.

I never forgot the broken promise, although a tiny part of me forgave him.

With a heavy storm like this one, I needed to see the mountain, to imagine that it was Steamboat Springs; I still remembered snippets of life, what it had been like before the wheel chair, before Cindy.

Momma was at the dining-room table sketching dresses, Daddy was watching television, and Cindy was bedded down fast asleep. I felt the restlessness of wanting to run in the pristine snow, wanting to throw snowballs . . . and just wanting to see it – that secret place – the mountains.

Stealthily I crept up the two flights of stairs and entered what Momma called the studio. I didn't intend to touch any of the dresses that hung there waiting to come alive, to be admired and treasured clinging to warm skin.

No, I only wanted to see the tip of the distant mountain.

The attic room was silver with the glow of distant streetlamps, and the window was covered with frost designs intricate and unique; I imagined that magical creature Jack Frost creeping in with his magic brush to paint those beautiful pictures just for me.

Reluctantly, I chipped at a spot of ice with my fingernails, clearing the glass, but spoiling the pattern. I could see the snow coming down like a moving curtain, in waves, but now and then I glimpsed it, the highest peak of the snow-covered Rockies. 'There,' I pointed to a spot. 'There – he was gonna take me there,' and bitterly disappointed, I began to cry about everything – the chair, Momma and the sewing machine, the man with the shiny shoes, and even about Cindy. Maybe it was her fault; her coming could have changed everything. But I knew that wasn't right; it changed way before Cindy. Why couldn't Daddy just get out of that chair? 'He could if he wanted to,' I said aloud.

'Trini . . .' I heard the whisper. 'Trini . . .' Startled, I looked about the room, imagining ghosts where the shadows seemed to move. On shaking legs I rose, intending to run downstairs, when I saw the silhouette in the open doorway.

'Cindy, what are you doing here? You're supposed to be asleep!'

My voice released her and my four-year-old sister ran to me, knocking over a dressmaker's dummy, which clattered loudly to the floor.

'Ssh,' I urged and we both held our breath, but downstairs Myra only looked up and imagined it was a clap of thunder, common in a winter storm.

'What are you doing up here?' Cindy asked.

'I'm looking at the mountain. Daddy's gonna take me there someday.'

'When?'

'Oh,' I stalled, 'someday soon, maybe tomorrow.'

'Can I see?'

'Here . . .' And I held her up to the spot of cleared glass. 'Over there – see them? That's the Rockies.'

'It looks far away.'

'It is, but he's gonna take me there, he promised.'

'His chair don't do that,' Cindy stated importantly.

'I don't mean in the chair, stupid. We're gonna take the Jeep and drive, then we're gonna put on skis and fly down the mountain.'

Cynthia covered her mouth and giggled. 'No, you're not. He's a bigger baby than I am. Momma's gotta carry him to bed; he can't even walk.'

'Yes, he can!' I exclaimed indignantly. 'Yes, he can.'

'I never seen him. Does he get up at night when we're all asleep?'

'Yes, that's exactly what he does. He doesn't like you, so he's never gonna take you there or teach you to ski neither.'

Cynthia began to sob. 'I know he doesn't like me. Why doesn't he like me? I drew him a picture once, but he tore it up. Oh Trini, nobody likes me. Momma doesn't, Daddy doesn't, but I thought you did.'

Feeling guilty, I said, 'Of course I like you. I love you, but we can't talk about Daddy walking; it's a secret.'

'Okay, but you don't like me either,' and Cynthia resumed crying.

'Sure I like you, and I know somebody else that likes you, too.'

'Who?' Cynthia asked.

'Jack Frost. Look, he painted all these pictures for us.' And I pointed to the eerie designs on the panes of the window where frost had gathered thickly.

'Let's play the game,' Cindy begged. 'I'm first. I see a puppy,' she indicated the top of the window, 'right there.'

'Oh yes, it is a puppy. Let's see . . . there, that's the North Star,' I announced proudly. 'Daddy taught me all about stars.'

'There! There!' Cindy squealed, pointing. 'It's a teddy bear.'

'Yes, it looks just like yours. Let me see. Oh Cindy, look at that, it's a big delicious ice-cream cone, with two dips; first dip is strawberry, bottom one chocolate.'

And with that mouth-watering description, my sister moved forward and stuck out her tongue and licked the likeness of an imaginary ice-cream cone.

She stood frozen to the spot, caught, with horrible sounds issuing from her terrified child's throat. I was rigid with terror. What was happening? Cindy's arms flailed helplessly at the air and the sound of urine splatted on the wood floor. But the inhuman sounds still came out of Cindy's throat as she stood in front of the frozen window, held fast by her tongue.

'Accident . . . Accident.' That terrible word raced through my mind and I found myself running away, tumbling down the steps, to hear my mother call, 'Trini, quiet! I'm trying to work.'

I hid under the bed. It was an accident, just like what they said about Daddy, but accidents are terrible; they cause all kinds of repercussions.

Still hiding, I heard the grandfather clock in the hall bong several times, yet Cindy didn't appear.

Then Momma came into the room and screamed when she saw our empty beds. Then my father was circling wildly in his chair around and around endlessly in the entrance hall and Myra was running through the house screaming in every empty room, until at the top of the house we heard her voice, hysterical with disbelief. 'Oh my God, oh my God, who did this to you?'

Then there was the banging of pots and the sound of water and Myra coming down the steps carrying the unconscious child.

My father looked out through the curtains and said helplessly, 'You can't go anywhere, the car's completely snowed in.' But he wheeled himself to the table and dialed 911.

'That devil, that little devil Trini, hurting her sister like this!' And Myra paced and listened for the welcome sound of the ambulance screeching through the blizzard, unaware of drops of blood on her blouse from her daughter's bleeding tongue.

It was only after they left that I came out of hiding. 'I didn't mean to hurt her, honest. It was an accident, Daddy, honest. We were pretending that Jack Frost had painted an ice-cream cone on the window.'

'I know, I know,' he soothed. His voice dropped and gently he said, 'You shouldn't have left her, Trini. It was your responsibility to come and tell.'

'I'm sorry, I was so scared,' I sobbed.

'There's lots of times in life when you feel scared, but remember, if it's your responsibility, you've got to do something even though you're scared.'

'I promise,' I gasped. 'I promise I will from now on.'

Later, I heard my mother talking quietly. 'It will affect her speech; a great deal of damage was caused by the delay.'

'I'm sorry, Myra, but Trini's just a child herself. She didn't know, she didn't realize.'

'She should have. It's on her head, whatever happens.'

And when Cindy came home from the hospital, she was silent, afraid to talk. When she did, it was apparent she had a lisp and a stutter that might or might not go away.

Now Daddy softened to the child that was not his. He invited her to sit upon his lap, telling her endless stories of oil rigs and adventures in the oil fields of Oklahoma and Wyoming.

'You're bad, Trini,' Cindy managed to blurt out. 'I was scared; it was so dark and I hurt so much.'

'I'm sorry, so sorry, baby sister. I'll never leave you again, ever, no matter what.'

But Momma found a new refrain. 'She's your sister; it's all your fault. She's never gonna talk right and it's all your fault.'

Her prediction seemed correct and, like any affliction, it seemed to grate on Myra. Instead of arousing her sympathy, that damaged voice annoyed her and she took to calling her Cin.

'Sin's a bad thing, Momma. Don't call her that. Cindy doesn't like it,' I pleaded.

'I'm not calling her Sin. It's only a nickname, short for Cindy.'

'But it sounds like you're calling her a Sin, a real bad one like they talk about in Sunday School.'

'What do you know, you're the one that's committed a sin. It's your fault and don't you ever forget it,' my mother spat at me.

And the accident seemed to give Myra an excuse to pull further away from her younger daughter, who trailed her helplessly like a lost duckling.

'Trini, come get her, she's wrinkling my dress . . . Trini, come wash her face, it's so dirty it's disgusting . . . Trini, come put her to bed, I hate her whining . . .' The requests to hand her child over to me, her elder daughter, went on endlessly until it was clear she rejected her younger daughter totally.

And then it was springtime and Myra seemed to remember the curlers and the lipstick and, staring at herself in the mirror, she began to dream of other cities, other men, other lives that could belong to her.

When she left, her message to Jack was brief.

Jack,
I'm sorry, I've gotta go, I'm dying here. Maybe I'll write.

Myra

It wasn't until I was eleven that Myra wrote us a brief note.

Dear Jack and girls,
I'm in New York, working in design. Everything going well. I'm sure you'll see my stuff in Vogue *very soon. Take care!*

Love, Myra.

'What's *Vogue*?' Cindy asked with her slow careful speech.

'It's a magazine with pictures of beautiful clothes, and beautiful ladies wearing them,' I explained.

Cindy ran to the dresser and pulled out a small, years-ago outgrown party dress. 'She made this for me. Momma made this for me special.'

'Yes, she did,' I agreed. 'She loved you; she'll be back someday, or maybe she'll send for us.'

'We can't go unless we can take Daddy.'

'Sure,' I agreed, hating the lie, for I was certain Myra would never send for us.

I was grateful that maybe Cindy didn't remember the total rejection, or maybe somewhere deep down she did!

The years flew past. We managed with the old housekeeper and only Cindy looked forward to the pale ocher envelope that came once in a while filled with formal words of success, great and small, in that faraway city.

Even with her gone, the three of us found a measure of happiness.

And now my father welcomed Cindy as a beloved daughter while knowing she wasn't his. He gave his love as he had always given everything; he was a generous man. And it was so much better when he found the thing that supported us.

He never had to give up the house. No, his love of fishing in the cold mountain streams saved us all. He tied fishing lures and invented several new kinds of spinners that worked on wide-mouth bass and trout, and eventually a large corporation bought his patents and financially we were comfortable. He could care for his daughters.

He took pleasure in his old buddies, who visited and played poker into the wee hours of the morning. And weekends, when the weather was good, they loaded his wheelchair into one of their vans and he spent the day in the mountains fishing in streams, which was his inspiration for making other lures.

Jack spent time in the large study that he had filled with books. Before, he was a rugged outdoorsman, and now he lived this life again in the pages of Hemingway, Norman Mailer and others.

He knew so much about so many different things that it was a pleasure for me to go to him, while in high school and college, and ask his advice. We only quarreled about one thing – Cindy.

'Don't protect her so much,' my father urged.

'But Momma said she's my responsibility; it was all my fault.'

'No, it was an accident. That happened when you were a small child.'

'I left her, so it was my fault.'

'You were a child, Trini, and it was an accident,' he repeated.

But I remember whispering to him, 'She does talk funny, and around some people she can't talk at all.'

'Making her hide isn't helping her.'

'I don't make her hide. It hurts her, Daddy, when kids make fun of her.'

'There are worse things in the world,' and he looked down at his useless legs.

'It is my fault; no one can tell me different,' I said.

At eighteen, I fell in love. He was a big blond handsome guy walking the paths of the University of Denver; sitting next to me in class confiding that he couldn't draw a straight line, but needed an art credit. Admiringly he flattered my work, not recognizing that it was really good.

The physical attraction overwhelmed me, and within a week I thought I was madly in love.

Cal was my first love. I gave my body to him, and felt I gained as much as he did from the physical relationship. I didn't really know him, what he dreamed of, how he felt – it was the discovery of sensation and touch, and often the smoothness of his skin reminded me of bolts of satin, and that made me feel safe.

Our romance lasted only one summer, and I realized it was not love, not complete, rounded human love; it was a relationship of only sensation, feeling. His was a magic touch that seemed to know my body and my needs. The physical chemistry between us was perfection, and I missed him when that autumn he was off to some Eastern university. He promised to write, but he never did.

Often when I thought of him, I could remember nothing about him other than his touch. I dated others, but never succumbed and never felt again that strong pull of physical attraction, of perfect sex.

* * *

It was a year after Daddy died when I got the position of art director at the agency, and then in walked Jeff. He was led into my office because no one else knew what to do with his requests.

'Hi, I'm with the University of Colorado, Boulder.' He glanced at the wall and saw my diploma. 'You, too.'

Instantly, I admired his open charm. 'No, I graduated from Denver.'

'Same difference.' He handed me a stack of scratched-up papers. 'No one seems to know what to do with them, not even me.'

'That's a good beginning,' I quipped.

He sank heavily into a chair. 'Let me explain. I'm a mechanical engineer, working mainly on equipment for oil fields. I have these ideas for a new way to design the bits, but I need clear drawings, not specifications; I can do that after I have clear drawings. I also have an idea to modify the pumps.' He laughed. 'I can say it, but I can't draw it.'

I studied his muddled notes and he watched me studying them.

'Some of it's language of the oil fields; I could interpret.'

'I understand. My father worked in them all his life.'

'Whereabouts?'

'Wyoming mostly. He wildcatted a few in Oklahoma.'

'Well, you're a girl after my own heart.' He smiled. 'How about dinner and we can talk about it?'

'I can't, truly I can't,' I said with a sincerity that made him pursue it.

'Another date?'

'Not exactly.' I looked into his crestfallen face and decided to soften his disappointment. 'Not a date. My sister and I live together and she makes dinner.'

He smiled wickedly. 'I don't eat much and I bring wine and flowers.'

'Okay, okay, you convinced me. Eight o'clock.' I scribbled the address on my business card.

He studied it. 'Which apartment?'

'It's a house.'

'Oh.' He turned before leaving. 'Red or white?'

I shrugged and he offered generously, 'I'll bring both.'

At 7:30, Cindy was still asking, 'Does the table look all right?'

'It's fine, honey, it's fine. This is no big deal.'

Cindy rushed back to the kitchen to stir the pots and toss the salad, but what she really wanted to do was hide.

Jeff was there promptly at eight and looked younger and handsome in a pair of corduroys and an Icelandic sweater that made his face seem tanner under the thatch of warm brown hair.

He was entranced with the study, where the walls were cluttered with photographs of oil rigs and the oil-streaked faces of the men who worked them.

'I wish I could have known him,' he said, pointing to Big Jack in the photographs.

I nodded. 'He was an interesting man who loved his work.' I paused. 'His work before the accident. It crippled him, but he was never bitter about the rigs,' I lied.

He nodded, unsure of what to say, for my face was drawn and closed and it was clear I didn't want to elaborate.

The small tinkle of a dinner bell summoned us, and he smiled at the formality of it all, for there were just the three of us in the enormous house.

It was a nice homey dinner – roast pork, baked apples, corn on the cob, a salad, and fresh-backed sourdough bread. Dessert was warm apple pie with a scoop of vanilla ice cream melting tantalizingly on top. 'You're a marvelous cook,' he told Cindy. 'Reminds me of home, or what used to be home.'

We took our coffees to the den, where Cynthia had lit a fire, and Jeff felt like he had truly come home. Furnished rooms, and finally the sterile apartment in Boulder, had been his life for years now since his parents had gone, one after the other, and he had sold the small farm in Oklahoma.

He was used to his solitary bachelor's life. There had been a girl or two he thought of marrying, but it never felt right so he remained single. But here in this house he felt a strong nostalgia for something lost and now refound.

We dated, and for me it was a friendship I fell into that was comfortable and easy. Jeff was a very warm person who loved life and people, and his pleasant nature made it impossible to send him away. I loved him, but not in that same Fourth of July firecracker way. Over and over he pleaded with me to marry him until finally I did! And on our wedding night I knew I had made a dreadful mistake.

In the warm candleglow of the bedroom at the inn, I stiffened in his arms and with a great effort pretended I felt pleasure. But he knew, for I saw the raw hurt in his eyes.

He never asked and we never spoke of it, and mercifully I found a solution. One evening in our bedroom I reached across and turned out the light. In the velvet darkness, I imagined it was Cal's sun-bronzed hair that brushed my face and that the arms holding me were the same which had held me that long-ago summer, and the vivid fantasy made my body come alive. I responded to Jeff with a fervor that he had never experienced with me before and together we were good.

Later, he smoothed wisps of fair hair from my sweaty forehead and whispered, 'You should have told me that having the light on bothered you,' and from then on he turned out the light before I did.

It shamed and puzzled me, this fantasy, for as I thought back, I couldn't remember one thing about Cal – not one word or one meaningful conversation. I could only remember our lovemaking. I felt dishonest, for I loved Jeff as a person, as a man, but not as a lover, and it made me wonder how many people in the world lived their whole life like this in a relationship that wasn't honest.

It was much later when I realized that Cindy loved him, too. It was when I went to her room one day to borrow a pair of stockings that I found it, the hidden photograph of Jeff carefully secreted among the hosiery, the edges of the photograph limp with the many times it had been touched.

After that I watched my sister closely and I couldn't miss the way she looked at him, shyly, across the dinner table, and even in candlelight, I, who knew my sister so well, could see the slight upturn of color in her cheeks, the telltale blush of desire.

I felt an incredible sadness for Cindy, who did not venture out in the world, who had never dated, never experienced the back and forth dance of a courtship – and guilt overwhelmed me again. Myra was right. The arid desert of Cindy's life was entirely my fault, and I searched my mind for a way to make it up to her, all that she had missed.

CHAPTER THREE

The cat licking my face startles me awake. I had been dreaming of a strange city in Mexico, with Trini Lopez playing calypso music. Daddy used to laugh when he said Myra named me Trini because she loved the Trini Lopez band, Mexican salsa, and all things south of the border.

I wonder if she named Cindy so that she could mentally call her Cin. Suddenly it makes me think of Myra's note – *'I'm dying here'* – and I realize that just lately I have felt that same way in Denver. It's guilt – it lies on my shoulders like a lead weight. I feel the guilt of denying Jeff the child he so desperately wants, and every day I face the desert of my sister's life. I, who caused it, have no idea how to change it.

In broad daylight, it now seems incredible, the thing I did to her. Crazy and obscene. Why, oh why, had I ever thought of such a thing?

I realize for the first time that it feels good to be here in Manhattan away from Jeff and Cindy.

I welcome the ringing of the phone and answer it. A gruff Lieutenant Burke is asking if he may come over and speak with me.

'Do you mean now?' I ask.

'Yes, if that's convenient. I've been trying to reach someone for days and so much time has elapsed!'

I agree to see him and freshen my make-up, run a comb through my hair.

I answer his buzz and within minutes hear heavy footsteps treading upon the stairs. I open the door and he stands on the mat, wiping his feet and brushing fresh snow off his overcoat. He is about fifty, his suit is rumpled, and his overcoat barely buttons over an ample beer belly.

'Want him removed?' he asks.

'Who?'

'The bum sleeping in your doorway.'

'Where would they take him?'

'Shelter downtown. Course, they do come right back.'

'No. He's not really bothering anybody.'

As if suddenly remembering his manners, he offers a large hand. 'Lieutenant. Burke. I'm in charge of the case.'

I return his firm handshake. 'Trini Woodruff, Mrs Dunhom's daughter,' and I wonder at the word 'case'. What case? 'May I take your coat?'

He shakes his head to refuse and I indicate the one easy chair. 'Won't you please sit down?'

He sinks into the chair and looks around the room, then takes out a peppermint, offers me one, removes the wrapper, and pops the candy into his mouth. It is a minute or two before he speaks.

'Have you had the locks changed?'

Surprised, I respond, 'No, should I have?'

'It's a good precaution, of course, but it seems like Mrs Dunhom knew the person. She must have let him in, or maybe he had a key.'

'I'm sorry, I don't understand.'

He rubs his chin thoughtfully and without any adornment, blurts it out. 'It seems she knew her murderer.'

'Murderer.' I say the ugly word and experience a quick jolt of anger and denial. I demand, 'What are you talking about?'

'You don't know the circumstances of your mother's death?'

'No – the lawyer said she died as a result of a fall. He didn't give me any details.'

He nods. 'That's right, she did fall. She was pushed off the roof.'

'The roof? Which roof?'

'The one in back. In Queens we call it a roof; here in Manhattan it's a roof terrace.'

My hands begin to shake and a wave of dizziness washes over me.

The Lieutenant sees the look of shock on my face, finds his way to the kitchen, locates the only clean cup, and brings me a drink of water.

'I'm sorry, miss, I had no idea that you didn't know.' He sits back down and we are both silent. He goes slowly now. 'That's why I needed to speak to you. I thought maybe you knew of someone who might want to harm your mother – an enemy, an old boyfriend, someone with a grudge – a business acquaintance, maybe?'

I shake my head vigorously. 'I haven't seen Myra in twenty years.'

'Myra?'

'We weren't close. She left my father when my sister and I were children. We rarely corresponded; she wrote a postcard or a short note only once or twice a year.'

The Lieutenant nods, wondering what sort of woman would leave her children and voluntarily not see them for years – the sort of woman who got herself murdered.

'I'm sorry to have troubled you,' he apologizes and starts to rise from his chair.

'No, please sit down. I need to ask you some questions. I need some answers.'

He sits back, licks his lips nervously, and hopes he can answer my questions with tact.

'Do you have any suspects?'

He shakes his head no.

'Do you have any clues?'

'Yes, a few, but they haven't turned up anything concrete yet.'

'What sort of clues? I should be told whatever it is that you know.'

He clears his throat before speaking and nervously unwraps a mint. 'We know it was a man; his footprints were etched into the ice on the roof alongside hers. Good thing there was ice – we still got the cast even though the snow covered over the prints.' He clasps his hands and looks up at the ceiling. 'Her footprints were going backwards; his were not. We found the shoes that made the prints in her bedroom closet. Course, there were lots of her footprints on the roof going backwards and forwards; can't make out exactly what happened out there.' He doesn't mention that one of her slippers was caught on the ledge.

'You mean after he—' I put my hand across my mouth and barely mumble, 'then he put his shoes in the closet?' I feel sick.

'Yes.'

Again we both fall into an awkward silence.

Nervously, the Lieutenant starts to crack his knuckles, but stops himself. Delivering bad news to the next of kin always makes him jumpy. Again he clears his throat. 'We've looked through her things.

I insist that my men take care, but while you're clearing up, if you see anything that looks odd, please give me a call.' He rises and hands me his card. 'I'd change the locks right away, miss, and keep the chain on till you do.'

I nod in agreement and walk him to the door, slide the bolt on and regretfully listen to his footsteps fading away down the stairs.

The cat comes and stands in the hall; his fur bristles and he gives a low growl. 'What is it?' I ask, but realize he is probably responding to the smell of my newborn fear.

The apartment feels alien and frightening now and I rattle the door to make sure it is securely locked. The safety chain looks terribly fragile, and with a great effort I begin pushing the large sofa against the door.

I go into the kitchen to reassure myself that the bars on the window are securely locked. There is only a small narrow window in the bathroom, and the other windows are all barred.

I see the cat look up, and a minute too late I follow his glance. There was a subtle movement, but I assure myself it was only snow blowing across the panes of the skylight window.

I walk back to the kitchen, turn out the lights, and gaze over the snow-covered roof. It looks deceptively peaceful with moonlight shining silver on the snow. I feel a pang of incredible sorrow. She died out there. My mother died out there in the frozen night, and it is a horror I can't even imagine. Did she cry? I wonder. Did she scream? Did she plead with this man whom she must have known? In this city full of so many people, did no one hear or see her caught in this moment of danger?

The morning is abuzz with activity. The locksmith comes early and a breathless voice on the answerphone informs me that it is Felicity and she simply has to see me today – she'll stop by the shop in the early afternoon.

In the bright sunlit morning, my fears dissolve, but the knowledge that Myra was murdered sits in my stomach like an uneasy rock. I take the portfolio of sketches and go downstairs to the shop.

In the doorway, my resident vagrant shakes his covers, smiles at me, and mumbles a, 'Good morning.'

I am surprised to see that he isn't an old man; under the swaddling rags he has a slim dark face covered with a sprinkling of whiskers. He is ethnic in appearance, but which nationality escapes me.

'Good morning,' I answer cheerfully, and wonder if I should reach into my purse and give him some spare change. But he doesn't ask, and I feel it could be a precedent that I wouldn't want to start.

I reach for the keys and struggle with the lock, which appears frozen. I tug at the door and with my effort the portfolio slides to the ground.

'Whoops!' I hear someone holler, and turn to see a slim girl dressed entirely in black who seems to be dancing as she sidesteps gracefully, catching my wayward papers that threaten to blow away.

The vagrant, too, joins her and manages to catch a page or two.

'That's my man, Tonto,' the girl says as she retrieves the pages from him.

'Thanks,' I say.

'I'll hold 'em till we get inside,' the girl offers. 'By the way, I'm Felix.' She laughs. 'Felicity, but to my friends I'm Felix. I got the morning off so I'm early.'

We go inside. I turn on the bank of lights and the rows of garments seem to welcome me like an old friend. I thread my way to the counter with Felix trailing me.

Before laying each sketch on the counter, Felix studies them. 'I'm afraid our friend got a few fingerprints on them,' and she brushes the paper, but the dark smudges remain. 'Tonto means well, but I guess you could have gotten along without his help. He sure got 'em dirty.'

'Tonto,' I repeat. 'What a strange name.'

The girl laughs. 'Oh, that's not his real name. No one knows what that is so we just call him Tonto, him being an Indian. You know, Tonto and the Lone Ranger. I guess it is pretty insulting. I think he told somebody once that he was from Gallup, New Mexico, or Arizona or somewhere out West.'

'Why on earth would he come to New York City?'

'There's a lot of 'em here. You know they hire Indians to work on the skyscrapers. They make good money, too, before the booze gets 'em. I guess they can't help it. Alcoholism is a disease.'

I am puzzled by this information. 'Why Indians to work on skyscrapers?'

'It's their inner ear, makes them desirable as workers. They have fabulous inner ears; they don't get dizzy a hundred stories up. Good genes, bad genes, fabulous inner ear, and then there's that bad gene that makes their whole race terribly susceptible to alcoholism. Can't blame them for that – it *is* a disease,' she said again.

'It's strange that most people don't think of it that way. They just think of it as no will-power et cetera,' I say.

I turn on the lights in the jewelry cases and the girl follows me, still talking.

'Sometimes when there's a new building going up, I take my lunch, of course I mean in the summer, and sit and watch the workers. It's like a marvelous ballet. Those men up there are so graceful moving along the struts barefoot like they own the sky, and some not even wearing a safety harness. It must feel wonderful!'

'How interesting. I never knew that.'

'Yeah, I've seen Tonto down on Wall Street plenty of times watching his building. I've heard they put eagle feathers in the mortar, right near the top when they're almost finished; it's their connection to the building – like an artist's signature. Nobody can see it, but they know it's there.'

I nod as I subtly examine the young girl before me. She is slim and waif-like, her red hair a mass of unruly waves that frame her angular, pale face that is dominated by large blue eyes. When she smiles, she seems very attractive, whereas with her face at rest, she's merely a slender girl with the right body and a contemporary look.

'I'll make the coffee,' Felix offers, 'and don't worry, I know where everything is.' And she walks to the back of the building from where I can hear the clatter of dishes. She sticks her head out of the pantry. 'By the way, are you Trini or Cindy?'

'Trini.'

'Glad to meet you and I'm sorry it's under such sad circumstances. My deepest sympathies. She was one hell of a lady, your mother.'

I mumble something in answer to what I assume was a compliment.

I smooth the sketches, annoyed at the black fingerprints at the edges of two of the pages. I search the drawer of the counter and finding a pencil with an eraser, rub the prints until they are only faint gray blurs on the page.

Satisfied, I examine the sketch. It is of an evening coat. I study it again carefully – it doesn't work. After a minute I find the error in the design; the sleeves aren't right. My hand trembles above the page until finally, with one swift motion, I begin to draw. I soften the silhouette, and the curved motion of the raglan sleeve makes the design flow. Better, it is so much better.

Again I search the lines of the garment. Too much fullness for the altered sleeve. I straighten the lines and it all meshes; it is perfect.

I start as I hear Felix's voice behind me. 'It's magic – reminiscent of pure Christian Dior.'

'Oh,' I laugh, 'I was just playing around.' But still I feel pleased.

'Those Myra's sketches?'

'Yes, I just altered it a little.'

'She asked me to look at her sketches once, but I wasn't really any help to her. I saw they weren't right, but I couldn't tell her that, and I couldn't tell her how to fix them either.'

Felix slides the coffee along the counter. 'It's cappuccino. Myra bought the machine a while back.'

'Smells great. Thanks.'

Still examining the sketch, Felix asks, 'Do you design?'

'Not really. I'm a commercial artist. I work for an ad agency in Denver.'

'With your corrections, it's obvious you should design. You've got it, the eye. God, I hope I do; it's what I want most in the world. Oh, I almost forgot what I wanted to talk to you about. I need my paper signed; I really need the credit. I'm at Parsons School of Design, second year. I was doing an internship with Myra. When she died, they were going to pull the credit . . .' She looks at me and smiles that wonderful smile. 'Now you're here. This really bails me out.'

'But I'm not planning on staying. I'm just here trying to straighten out Myra's affairs.' I look around the overflowing shop. 'I don't even know where to begin.'

'That's okay. If you leave before spring break, they'll never know. Oh please, I really need the credit.'

'Okay.' And I reach for the paper Felix offers and sign without reading it. 'Now what is it you're supposed to do on this internship?'

'Anything. I'm sort of like an indentured servant.' Felix laughs. 'With Myra, I did everything. I did the windows, sales, straightened the racks, but mostly we talked about design. She loved the stories about Europe. I went to a few cat-walk shows in Milan and Paris, my first year. I had to sleep with the Professor, but it was worth it.'

Felix sips her coffee and looks dreamy-eyed, remembering. 'God, it was exciting, the gossip, the designers kissing the model when they were finally satisfied that a particular creation worked. And honest to God, they cried at their own shows. Those Italians, they've got it all – the cloth, it's like it was made in heaven – and the talent. God, they know how to cut, fit . . .' She stops and then screams with a brainstorm that has just occurred to her. 'We could do it!' She picks up the sketch. 'I'd get an A; of course, it's your design. I know a model, she'd be perfect and she's down on her luck so we wouldn't have to pay her much.'

'Whoa, Felicity. I'm not a designer – I'm an artist. I don't know anything about sewing. My mother, I mean Myra, did. She was wonderful. Why, in Denver . . .' I stop myself. It isn't fair. Myra wouldn't have liked people to know she had been a housewife taking in sewing in the attic of the old house in Denver.

'No, you don't have to know how to really sew, just the design. The design is the creative part; you can hire people to make the patterns and cut and sew. Even I can do it. I'm studying that right now, pattern-making.'

I chuckle. It's fun to be around someone so young who still believes anything is possible. At thirty, responsibility weighs heavily on my shoulders. I sip my coffee slowly and one by one I study Myra's designs, with Felicity glancing over my shoulder.

'Can you fix them?' the girl asks.

Before I can deny it, I find myself saying, 'I think so. Yeah, I can.'

Our conversation goes no further as the bell clangs and Felix walks over to help a customer.

Somewhere in the bowels of the building a phone rings persistently and Felix rushes over. 'It's the one in the office. I forgot to explain how it works. The extension from upstairs can be switched over so when you come down it turns off your answerphone so all your calls come in here to the shop.'

I lift the receiver and say, 'Hello.'

Cindy is seated on the chaise in Trini's bedroom. She is wearing her own flannel nightgown, the one that her sister always threatened to throw out, but over it she wears Trini's peach satin robe with its scent of Chanel perfume still lingering faintly.

'It rang so long I thought you'd gone out, Trini, but I couldn't imagine why the answerphone wasn't on.'

'Oh, I'm downstairs in the shop; there's an extension here from the apartment. I can have my calls switched.'

'Oh, that's convenient. What are you doing in the shop?'

'I'm not doing much, just looking through some of Momma's sketches of designs,' I say. The word 'Momma' sticks in my throat, but when referring to Myra I force myself to say it for Cindy's sake.

'Oh, I bet they're great! I hear voices. Is someone else there?'

'Yeah, some customers and Felicity. She's the college girl that was doing an internship at the shop.'

'You have customers?'

'Yeah, they're at the counter. Seems like they're buying something.'

'Do you have to go?'

'No, Felicity, or Felix as she likes to be called, is taking care of it.'

'So you'll be staying in New York a while?' And Cindy soars with happiness at her sister's answer.

'I'm afraid so.'

'Well, I'll let you go. I'm fine and Jeff's fine. Don't worry about us, I'll take care of everything.'

When they hang up, Cindy takes it out of the package that arrived that morning and, sitting at her sister's dressing table, puts it on, the wig. The color is perfect, and the styling is, too. She stares at herself in the mirror. At a quick glance, one might have mistaken them for each other. She listens for sounds in the large old house and the creaks and groans of the furnace pumping away make her feel afraid. If Jeff came home unexpectedly, what would he think? He would think her crazy sitting there in a blonde wig pretending to be his wife.

She knows everything has been done. The stuffed green peppers for dinner are cooked and only need to be reheated; all of the laundry is finished; and instead of sending Jeff's shirts to the laundry, as he requested, she did them herself. She even hung them outside in the cold winter sunshine, for she remembered Jeff had mentioned once that he loved the smell of clothing dried outdoors.

Everything is done. The house is clean, dinner is made, and she has a surprise for him. She hopes with all her heart that he likes it. Recently Jeff complimented her on the rearrangement of the furniture in the living room; he said the room seemed much cozier. This morning she placed the elegant chess set on the low table between the chairs – the surprise.

She knows Jeff was a chess champion in college. When she saw the marble chess set in the window of an antique shop on Colfax Avenue, she couldn't resist, so she took her hoard of money and bought it, thinking of the long winter evenings that they might spend together. She would tell Trini and Jeff that she found it in one of the closets in the attic.

With a burst of anger at her sister, she speaks aloud in their bedroom. 'You wouldn't have done that for him. You wouldn't have read all those books and watched that training video over and over, the one that bragged that "You, too, can be a chess expert in twenty-four hours". I love him best!' she shouts to the empty house. She lies down on their bed, on his side, and inhales the pleasant aroma of him that still lingers in the sheets, and like a prayer, mumbles over and over in the silent house, 'Queen to rook – to knight – check. Queen to rook – to knight – *checkmate*.'

CHAPTER FOUR

At six I switch off the light, shut the door of the shop, and turn the Open sign to Closed.

'It was hectic, but fun,' I admit to Felix.

'Yeah, Myra has some good customers. She kept the stock replenished so it was always fresh, and she'd run the flea markets every weekend – the annex over on Sixth, the one in Soho, the one uptown – she worked hard. When desperate, she'd run the boroughs of Queens, Brooklyn, Staten Island, and go outside the city. Course, she had regulars that would bring stuff in.' Felix pauses. 'I could show you.'

'I'm not staying,' I say, then correct myself. 'I can't stay. I have a job, a husband, a sister, all back in Colorado.'

Felix nods, but something inside makes her think that maybe Trini *will* be staying. It is the sketches, something about the sketches and the woman's innate ability. When Felix got feelings about things like this, most of the time they were right. 'Do you know about the banking?'

I look down at the stack of Visa and Mastercard slips. 'Yeah, Myra left some notes on that.' I'm not sure what to offer the girl for her hard day's work which produced so much money. 'She didn't leave any info on the pay scale, though.'

'Oh, she didn't pay me. I'm on the internship; you know, the paper you signed. I do three days a week for the credit.'

'But you do so much! All those sales you made!'

'That's all part of it, the work experience. I get a generous allowance from my parents. I don't need money; my stepfather, he's loaded.'

'Well, thanks. I'll see you – when?'

'Thursday, I'm in again Thursday.' Felix looks around the darkened shop. 'Well, I'm off to get my pizza. You gonna go upstairs and cook?'

'No, God no. Myra had pots that she never used, but there aren't any dishes.'

'You can order in. Here . . .' She opens the counter drawer and hands me the Diners Book. 'Anything you want – Chinese, Mexican, barbecue, pizza – they all deliver. Oh, I almost forgot. I'll show you how to switch the phone back up to the apartment.'

I desperately want to ask Felix about Myra, whether she knew any of her men friends, and whether she had talked to the police, but it is so late and we are both tired. It can wait.

Outside, Tonto is already huddled into his red covers, but he is still awake; his dark eyes stare up into the night sky and he does not blink as the snowflakes gently rain into his face. Feeling generous with the stack of bills and credit slips in my purse, I take a ten-dollar bill and put it into his ever-present tin cup at the edge of his covers.

'Thank you, lovely lady,' he mumbles, and then suddenly, through his alcoholic fog, he remembers he didn't do what he'd been asked to do by the other lady that looked like this one!

The letters she had asked him to mail are still here somewhere; he's certain they're still in a carrier bag in his stolen grocery cart, and he is sure it's parked in the gangway. It's her fault that he forgot; she was too generous and the money that night bought two-fifths of 'Rosie O'Grady'. By the time he drank the wine and found his way back into the gangway to escape the biting wind, he forgot all about mail-boxes; he was seeing things like that big white eagle on the roof. But it didn't soar up into the sky like the ones he had seen as a child in New Mexico. No, sadly, this eagle fell to the ground like a rock.

If Tonto had been sober that night, he could have seen clearly that it wasn't an eagle on the roof at all, but a woman in white, her lingerie trimmed in extravagant feathers that seemed once again to have a life of their own as they swayed in the cold wind. The rapid fall of snowflakes dampened them, only to rise again and again in the frigid air. The feathers, like a tethered kite, yearned to be free of the thread that held them fast.

It was not the sound of a bird chattering that Tonto heard, but the combination of taxi tires on Seventh Avenue and voices whispering. Like wine in her veins, the false courage coursed through, a combination of Scotch and tranquilizers.

She wasn't afraid as she walked unsteadily backwards toward the edge. She could clearly see the footprints of the size 10½ men's Gucci loafers that were a companion to her size 6 high-heeled slippers.

The journey was slow, and slower still. She would not plead, and drunkenly promised herself she would not even cry. She tried to think only of what was positive in this terrible situation and her ego, which was and always had been voracious, found it, the crumb to feed upon.

They would write about her murder and about the sadness of a wasted talent; surely her death would warrant a full-page spread in the *Village Voice,* an article on page six of the *Times,* and maybe her passing would be the cover story of *Women's Wear Daily.*

It was one o'clock in the Village, and the shades on all the many windows were firmly pulled down; no insomniac stared out into the snow-filled night. Only Tonto watched and dozed and listened to the sound of voices, but he wasn't sure if they were human voices or the chattering of birds.

Closer and closer to the edge she backed up, only to pause for a moment as her ankle twisted. She felt one tear escape her eye and roll down her frozen cheek, but told herself again, 'I will not cry, for I will be beautiful, so beautiful, like a snow angel greeting the morning, spread out gracefully on the pristine blanket of snow.' It was only when she felt the sensation of flight and speed and frozen air rushing around her that she betrayed herself and screamed into the night, *'No-ooo!'* her protest echoing off the brick walls.

She had always lied to herself and others – she painted the world in different colors – and she even lied to herself at the moment of her death. Her body did not drift down slowly like a feather to a blanket of soft welcoming snow; no, it crashed down swiftly to be broken on the paving stones and quickly covered by the falling snow. It was only discovered three days later when a woman who spent her days looking out of her fifth-floor window wondered at all the rodent tracks in the snow and called the police.

Myra Dunhom's murder was reported on the back pages of the New York papers, listed among the many homicides on 15 January.

[illegible] would not ever [illegible] in this [illegible]

[illegible] story [illegible] and the [illegible] developed [illegible]

[illegible] in different [illegible]

[illegible] quickly [illegible] after [illegible] looking out of her [illegible] window [illegible]

[illegible] New York [illegible]

CHAPTER FIVE

After checking all the windows and inspecting the new lock, I still feel the need to pull the heavy couch in front of the door. I feel tired, but it is the good kind, the result of a long, hard-working day. I like Felix. Her bubbling personalty is refreshing, and I find the subject of her talk – designers and couture – interesting.

I take a long warm bath, close my eyes and soak until the water cools. I hope Jeff won't call tonight, for it's almost five days now and absolutely nothing has been settled. How can I explain that I've been working in the shop, have called no realtors, and have been dealing with the police? I know I could tell Jeff, but not Cindy, the dreadful fact that Myra was murdered. Every time this thought comes back into my mind, I feel the fear, the nervousness that makes me almost faint.

I hear the phone ringing and after four rings, my own voice echoes softly through the apartment urging the caller to leave a message after the beep. No one comes on the line, but I can hear the sound of heavy breathing and then the finality of a click as the caller hangs up.

I get out of the tub, rub my gooseflesh skin briskly, and put on my gown and terrycloth robe. For a moment I yearn for the peach satin robe – it is my favorite – but I didn't pack it.

I glance up at the bathroom window. The steamy room still hasn't dispelled the frost on the glass. These old buildings that have settled seem to have ill-fitting windows and doors, where cold drafts seep in.

As the steam clears, I see it, just as it had been then, in the center of the window, the perfect image of a tantalizing ice-cream cone. It is always the guilt. If for a time I can forget, something always comes back to chastise me. Then I remember how often I have tried to expiate it, my sin. 'Mama, Cindy can have my best toy. Mama, she can have my music box. Mama, Cindy can have my strawberry shortcake.'

But it never worked out. My mother only frowned. 'Some things you can't pay back, Trini; it's your fault and she's your responsibility. You must take care of her always.'

All my life I have tried; anything I have, I would give Cindy if only I could erase that one day. But it is only now that I am away that the tie to my sister feels so tight, a stranglehold for all time.

With a sense of shame, I remember what else I gave her. No one would understand what made me do it, and now that shameful secret ties us together for ever. There is no way to take it back, and I cannot see what to do about it in the future. Maybe this is why I feel so relieved to be away from that large old house that hoards all our sordid secrets.

Surprisingly, I fall asleep quickly, but the dreams are there waiting for me. So real, the feel of cloth against my face, bolts and bolts of Duchess Satin caressing me as I hide among the fabric. In my sleep my thumb and forefinger move as they did then, finding comfort in the feel of the cloth.

The rhythm of the old Singer treadle machine was comforting in its symphony of sound; like *Bolero*, it repeated over and over, seeming to grow louder. I remember the foreign language of my mother, words I had no understanding of then, words spoken to strangers. 'Brocade, you must have brocade, the fabric of kings.' Once I even heard my mother say to a customer, 'The kind of cloth Rumpelstiltskin would have woven.' Odd, talking to strangers of fairy tales that even she knew.

My mother's voice, on and on, now speaking of ruffles. 'Just a soft ruffle there, like sea foam around the neck, or perhaps pleats; we could drape and pleat, but oh, my dear, the drape can be so disobedient.'

In the dream, I recalled the extravagant language my mother had used and the women customers, expecting to be superior to the seamstress, left intimidated by the strange-talking woman.

Giant hands appeared in my dream, sewing, always sewing beads, one by one, attached to silk, gathering like clouds, stretching toward the design that was meant to be. Beads dropping to the hardwood floor, rolling away, disobedient like the drape of cloth that refused to be tamed.

Warm and safe among the lengths of tulle and the tickle of

organza in my cave of cloth, I relive it all in my dreams until the dream shatters as I see the twin mirrors of *His* black shoes. 'You,' I scream at my hated mother, 'you are the most guilty one of all – not me!' And trembling with anger, I am propelled awake to find myself sitting in the middle of the huge bed; and for a moment the giant swan above me seems to shudder its wings.

I rise from the bed, trembling from the disturbing dream as I wonder, was it the contact of the sheets, or the pillow where my mother's head had lain, in the same valley – was it this that was bringing her back so vividly? Or perhaps the walls, the rooms which had known her, the clothes hanging in the closet where memories of her dreams and disappointments are still sheltered . . . My contact now seems closer than the sparse nine years I had with my mother.

I wrap the robe around me and feel comforted by the gurgle of the radiators. I go out to the kitchen and watch the sun rise over the tall towers of Manhattan and its beams glittering on the snow, and my presence in the window brings them to me, a flock of chattering sparrows that hop closer and closer to my window, clowning and begging in their spirited dance. I search the cupboard and find a half-pack of crackers, and struggling with the window, I scatter crumbs to the small brown clowns. It is obvious that as well as harboring an alley cat, Myra had fed the birds.

CHAPTER SIX

I awaken and feel the luxury of being without ties; there are no places I have to be, no appointments that I must keep. It is wonderful, this complete sense of freedom. With an effort, I cleanse my mind of worry. I will not dwell on Myra's murder. I leave it in the hands of those who search, and I tell myself that in time they will find answers.

My thoughts do touch upon the subject of money. It is something that in the past I never dwelt upon, but now Cindy and I will have so much. Money is, after all, a tool; it allows one to be the architect of one's own life. It buys that exotic commodity – freedom.

As I shower, I go over in my mind what I would like to accomplish today. I decide to shop for some dishes and groceries, for I am tired of eating out, and maybe I'll call a couple of realtors to see if they would be interested in listing the property. I feel energetic and would like to really achieve something today, for it is over two weeks now that I've been in New York. I can't imagine why I've slipped so easily into the routine of opening the shop, but it does interest me and with Felicity's help and direction, I've learned a great deal. To my surprise, the place is a real money-maker and when the shop is closed, I allow myself the luxury of sightseeing.

Here in the city the January thaw is pleasant and I've done a lot of interesting things. I've seen the many museums, spent a day in Central Park, where the street actors were a great deal of fun, and on top of the observation deck of the World Trade Center, I found myself thinking of the Indian. How odd that in the past, that man climbed among the clouds and owned the sky, and now his only niche is two feet of New York pavement inches from the gutter.

Surprised at myself, I realize I have fallen into this other life in New York much as I suppose Myra did. But I don't belong here, even though it feels like I do; I have ties, obligations to my family back in Denver. Jeff barely calls any more; he seems disgruntled by my obscure answers about when I will be finished and will return to Colorado. The agency, too, seem irritated at my absence; they have assigned my accounts to a junior artist and I was told the client was dissatisfied and that I lost them the Anderson account.

But these things don't seem to matter, for finally it has dawned on me that the property and bank accounts *belong to me* – although of course I will share them equally with Cindy. It's a great deal of money. Enough for me to change my life and have the luxury of doing whatever I like – if I only know what that was.

With this new knowledge comes a revelation: I haven't really been satisfied with my life. In five years of marriage, I've never been away from Jeff and, in the last twenty-five years, I've never been apart from Cindy.

In Denver, my life had become routine and predictable. Every morning I left Cindy at the door of our large house and every night I returned to find her waiting in exactly the same place. Many times I tried to imagine what my sister's days were like, polishing the oak banisters, vacuuming the oriental rugs, dusting off Daddy's pictures in the study, sitting in the kitchen planning menus, but not for a loving husband or a raft of noisy children.

Jeff had been understanding about Cindy living with us; he knew before our marriage that it would be that way and he never complained. The house has twelve rooms and it is more than large enough. But still we both felt her silent presence, someone else in the house, carefully making sure she was not in the way. Maybe it was this that stopped us from growing closer, but Jeff never seemed to resent her and more than once he tried to convince me to get Cindy help. He suggested a speech therapist, or even a psychologist. As he pointed out, it wasn't normal for a young girl to hide herself away from the world. I agreed, but didn't know how to make my sister get the help; for years and years I had helped her hide.

Finally realizing how barren, how sterile, Cindy's world was, I did it, that unbelievable thing. Even now, it's hard to face the fact that it really happened, and I know it was my fault entirely, my twisted brain that dreamed it up. I can't even imagine where such an idea came from, but still I harbor the uncomfortable feeling that this bizarre seed of an idea had been planted long ago.

Thinking of them both makes me pick up the phone. I want to tell Jeff that there is progress. Realtors will be coming soon and I am moving forward – only yesterday I mailed Cindy a check for half of the shop's takings for the last two weeks. This sort of sharing salves my conscience.

'Hi,' Jeff answers, his voice breathless with hurry.

'Hi, it's me. I wanted to catch up with you before you left for work.'

'Oh. Anything important?'

'I've got realtors coming this afternoon.'

'That's good,' he answers, but his voice seems preoccupied.

'I'd like to talk with Cindy after you leave for work. It's good news; the shop is very successful. I've sent her a check for over a thousand dollars.'

'Great. That's good. Only yesterday she expressed a desire to buy some new clothes. I'm sure you won't mind – she's had to borrow a few of your things.'

'Of course not. I'm just pleased that she's showing an interest in clothes.'

'She wanted to look nice for the office.'

'The office?'

'Yeah, she's been helping out at the college. She's working in the Student Aid department.'

'Cindy has a job?'

'Yeah.' He lowers his voice so as not to be overheard. 'I had to be a bit sneaky about it. At first she outright refused, but I put on a real act about how that department was so screwed up. I asked her to do it for just a day or so as a personal favor to me as I owe Mrs Denton, head of that department, a helping hand . . .' He pauses. 'It's been a week now and she's doing great. She seems real happy.'

'That's fabulous,' I say. 'Could I speak to her?'

'For just a minute. We don't want to be late. We drive in together.' And I hear Jeff holler, 'Cindy, it's Trini, but we've only got a minute or two.'

Cindy comes on the phone with a breathless, 'Hi.'

'I'll just keep you a minute. Jeff said you don't want to be late.'

To herself, Cindy repeats over and over, 'Don't come back. Please don't come back.' Then, realizing she hasn't heard what her sister was saying, she says, 'Sorry, Trini, I didn't hear you.'

'I said I mailed you a check – proceeds from the shop. It's doing good.'

'You mean it's my money – I can spend it?'

'Sure, of course it's your money. Momma said we should share half and half; that's how she wanted it.'

'If I get time, I could call you tonight.'

'Okay,' I agree and hang up with mixed feelings coursing through me. Jeff has accomplished what I never could; he has gotten Cindy out into the world, but I feel afraid, too. Would someone hurt my sister again? Would a situation arise when Cindy would start stuttering so badly that it would end in hysterical crying? It happened so many times before in high school.

I have to put it out of my mind, for my productive day is already planned. I call the first realtor and get an answering machine. I call three more and leave a message.

I dress casually in jeans and a sweater, for the weather is deceptively spring-like. Tonto is already gone from my doorway and I can see that his covers are damp with the melting snow. I walk to the diner where I always have breakfast. The waitress and the owner greet me pleasantly and I feel like I am a part of the Village.

'Know where I can get some dishes?' I ask the waitress.

Katy smiles and teases, 'I shouldn't tell you, for then we'll lose a good customer.'

'Not really. I'm a lousy cook; I'm just tired of waking up at one a.m. without a bite of food in the house.'

'Just kidding. Course, there's all those shops on Bleeker, but they're fancy and expensive. If you're just looking for functional dishes, I'd go over on Fourteenth Street; there's a Woolworth's there.'

'Thanks.'

I pass the shop and put a note under the Closed sign that says the store will reopen Thursday at eleven. It feels good; as the owner I don't have to open up if I don't feel like it. I have gotten a lot of confidence about running it and I do well even on days that Felix isn't there.

The unseasonably warm weather is so pleasant I decide to walk to 14th Street and up Bleeker Street I go, leisurely pausing to window shop. When I get to 6th, the Avenue of the Americas, I browse among the many book-vendors who dot the pavement. With no reason to hurry and no time-clock controlling me, I stop and search through the titles. A pristine copy of *Chic Savages* by John Fairchild of *Women's Wear Daily* attracts my attention. It isn't a new book –

it was published in 1989 – but it promises gossip and a peek into the fascinating world of the famous designers. I decide to get it for Felix. I've come to like her very much. I see other books that look interesting, but not wanting to carry anything more, I don't buy them.

When I reach 14th Street, I am greeted with a cacophony of sound. On one corner a man has set up a small table, and is playing the shell game. I join the crowd to watch. The man's rapid spiel challenges anyone to beat the game. Quick as a flash, he grabs a man's two twenties and shoves them into his overflowing pocket as rapidly he moves the three walnut shells back and forth over what appears to be a small coin.

He stops – the moment of drama – the crowd waits expectantly. The gambler, puzzled, scratches his head in deep thought; the woman at his elbow advises him, shaking her head no. Then he changes his opinion once or twice until finally he points to the end shell. It is lifted up to expose nothing. A moan of disappointment goes through the small tight crowd, and the approach of the policeman on the beat makes the man quickly whisk the shells away, fold the small table, and innocently begin a leisurely stroll down 14th Street.

I smile. How gullible people are, but it makes me wonder how he did it. Does this mean that there is no work for magicians pulling rabbits out of hats, for this man clearly possesses magic hands.

I make my way past the open stores, but pause often to examine the tables and racks outside; most containing souvenir merchandise. On impulse, I buy Cindy a white T-shirt with the slogan *I Love the Big Apple* and for Jeff I buy a funny hat, one that can hold a beer can securely. With a sudden twinge of nostalgia, I think of him at our summer barbecues with our friends gathered around, and after three or four beers, someone predictably would coax him to play the saxophone.

Here on the busy New York streets, if I closed my eyes for just a moment, I know I could see it clearly – early evening, Jeff happy with friendship, good food, and a few beers, standing in the gazebo in our back yard wailing away on that saxophone a melancholy blues song, with the magnificent panorama of the snow-covered Rocky Mountains like a stage behind him.

I stop and try to will myself not to think, for I feel the physical pain of loving him – a quirk, a quick jolt of breathlessness – for it is the first time I haven't lied to myself. I love him like one would love a cherished brother, but there is a whole chunk missing out of our relationship.

In the beginning, and even now, I felt no physical desire for him. I have deceived him over the years with my fantasy of Cal, but that, too, is fading and is becoming harder and harder to maintain. It has been months since Jeff and I were intimate. I start as a man interrupts my painful thoughts.

'Wanna buy a watch?' And he opens his coat to show row upon row of watches pinned to the lining.

'No,' I say firmly, and sidestep him as he still trails behind calling, 'Designer bags, great knock-offs, and cheap!'

I walk into the doorway of the Woolworth's dime store and make my way to the coffee shop counter, where I sit down and order a coffee and a piece of pecan pie. I stroke the Formica counter; it is like a touchstone that in this rapidly changing world some things remain the same. This could be the same Woolworth's in the Denver mall where Momma and I sat twenty-five years ago. It is odd – I'm beginning to refer to her as Momma. I always ordered the same thing – a hot dog and root beer. The waitress could be the same one, too – old, overweight, and cheerful as morning sunshine at least on the surface, showing no unhappiness with her lot.

It is a pleasant memory of Myra, the dime store, the lunch, and the small toy I was always allowed to pick in the 'Happy Days' before Daddy's accident – and way before Cindy.

The steaming hot coffee and the pie are placed before me. 'I'm sorry, I made a mistake. I'd like a root beer and a foot-long hot dog.'

'But you said . . .' the waitress starts to protest, but not in an irritated manner.

'It's okay, I'll pay for both, but I really want a foot-long hot dog and a root beer.'

Seeing the unexpected tears in the eyes of the woman sitting at the counter before her, the waitress offers, 'It's okay, honey. Someone will order the pie, and the coffee I'll pour down the drain; costs the management less than a nickel.' She winks at me. 'It's okay, really. One hot dog and root beer coming up.'

I buy a set of plain crockery; mugs, knives and forks, paper towels, and all the things I need to create a working kitchen. Loaded down with shopping bags, I hail a cab and stop off at Balducci's, the gourmet grocer on 6th Avenue, where I buy essentials like bread, milk, cereal and coffee, and then find I can't resist all the exotic foods they offer. I buy pâté, artichoke hearts, fresh-filled pasta, and laugh at myself, for I know I'll never eat it all, but so what. I am practically wealthy. I own a valuable building, have a going business, and there is a lot of money in the bank account that Myra left me.

It takes several trips from the taxi to move my packages to the doorway of the apartment. Tonto, who has crashed early, mumbles, 'Need some help?' as he struggles awkwardly to rise.

'No, I'm fine,' I assure him as I see him rocking unsteadily, and he finally stands, only to come crashing down in a heap on the brick sidewalk.

I lean down. 'Are you all right?'

'Go away!' he shouts angrily. 'Leave me alone – go away!' And he pulls the damp covers up around himself.

I make several trips up and down the steps with the packages, but Tonto's presence bothers me. After all, he is a human being; it's cruel to be left on the streets in this harsh winter. I wonder how street people manage to live through it. Of course today it's mild, but still he lives there in the rain, in the snow, with only the liquor in his veins to keep him warm.

I can't invite him in, it would be too crazy. I simply can't have a street person sharing my apartment. But it comes to me in a flash that I could offer him the landing; I could let him sleep right inside the door. It is some protection from the elements and there is a stairway and another secure door between us. At least he would be out of the cruel wind.

I have read that many of the street people are mentally ill, but that with money so tight, the hospitals turn them out to live as best they can.

Without debating or thinking it over, I select a down quilt from the linen closet, remove the extra key to the bottom door from my key ring, and go downstairs.

'Tonto,' I call firmly. 'Tonto, wake up.' I hear only a deep cough issue from beneath the covers. 'Tonto, come inside now.' His head peeks out and he blinks up at me. 'Come inside, there's a dry blanket.'

He issues forth from the damp covers like a reluctant tortoise, not understanding what I want.

'Come,' I urge, beckoning with my finger. 'Come inside.'

Unable to stand, he crawls into the doorway, dragging the crimson spread behind him.

'No, it's wet,' and I kick the cover outside with the tip of my shoe. In a heap, he lies inside the doorway; like a parachute I fling the down cover above him and it settles over him protectively.

From my jacket pocket I take a length of ribbon that holds the key. Once or twice I lean forward in an attempt to place it over his head, which is now at rest on the first wooden step. 'Tonto, look up – I need to give you the key.' Sleepily he raises his head, and trying desperately not to touch him, I ease the ribbon over his shaggy head.

'It's the door key. At night you come in, don't lose it; at night you come inside and in the morning you go.' I try to give my voice authority; it wouldn't do to have to step over him every morning.

He nods and clutches the key and his fingers run up and down the ribbon like it is a precious string of prayer beads. Then he lays his head down and I hear his deep sigh of contentment.

I lean towards him, feeling good about myself for offering him shelter. But it isn't right, so I ask, 'Since you'll be sleeping here, I should know your name.'

'Tonto,' he mumbles.

'No, I mean your real name.'

He raises his head and looks up at me bewildered, for it has been years since he was asked that question. Suddenly his eyes fill with tears and he knows clearly that the man who sleeps in gutters has no name but the one they bestowed on him. 'Tonto,' he repeats, and he lays his head back down to hide himself in the covers.

I hold my breath, for the smell of liquor and his unwashed body assails me. Only later do I open the top door and, when I hear the steady rhythm of his snores, I spray room freshener into the stairwell.

I re-close the door, put on the night latch, pull the couch in front of the door, and finally sit down, hoping that my generous offer will not turn into a dreadful mistake. But I know I couldn't deny shelter to a homeless cat or dog in this weather, let alone a human being.

In the kitchen I put away the groceries, feed the cat, and sit down at the table to munch slices of baked ham without bread. Again and again I dip my fingers into the jar, eating almost a third of the Spanish olives. It feels nice not having to go out every time I'm hungry.

The cat rubs against my leg and I say affectionately, 'You no-name cat, I'm gonna have to give you a name; not fair being called Cat.' When the tea kettle whistles, he jumps down and runs away to escape the high-pitched sound.

I pour myself a cup of herbal tea, put my feet up on the chair, and feel extremely comfortable and satisfied at the productive day.

CHAPTER SEVEN

On Monday, I put up the Closed sign, pull down the shade on the shop door, and promise myself I won't answer any knock, no matter who it is.

I look about the crowded room indecisively. What to do? How to go about it? Should I try to sell off the stock in total? But I have no knowledge of how to go about finding the right buyer.

A sale, that's the answer. With my experience at the advertising agency, I know I can write some effective ads.

I begin looking through the racks, checking prices. The couture section, while small, has some hefty price tags. The old Chanels, Balenciagas and Schiaparellis are priced in the thousands. I could offer a half-price sale on the entire stock. As I handle the dresses, I feel a sense of awe. Some of these garments are truly works of art. One by one, I examine the couture pieces, the tiny careful stitches, the linings, the details, and I notice they were as carefully made inside as out. In my mind's eye, I can actually see the original pattern – which is curious, for I can't sew a stitch. I think all my life I avoided learning to sew, for it was so much a part of my memory of Myra.

I go to the counter, find some blank paper, and begin working on the ads. Now that I have decided what to do, I feel a sense of urgency about getting it done.

I shall place ads in the *Sunday Times*, the *Village Voice*, and a couple of the daily papers. I address the envelopes, determined to mail them off tonight so the ads will appear as soon as possible.

I find myself wanting to linger. I touch a beautiful gray cashmere suit; it is a size nine and suddenly I want to try it on. It is an Adrian and it seems familiar. Maybe I have seen it in an old movie. It is a perfect fit. I turn and look at myself in the mirror and begin to really understand the fascination of clothes. These old, beautiful garments beguile.

One by one, I begin trying them on – formals, suits, dresses, pants suits. Clothes, after all, are the face you present to the world. You are this or you are that – you can be anything you want to be – and I wonder what they felt like, those artists, the designers who created these costumes we were given to walk the world stage in.

Suddenly I want to keep them, this pile of clothes I have gathered, and I feel mixed up and sad, for I have found a fascinating world that I will be leaving soon.

In the morning, when Felix and Clarista come, I tell them of my decision to put on a half-price sale. 'But I want you both to look around and pick out things you like, anything at all. I did, I took a whole stack upstairs. I don't know when I'll ever wear half of it.'

'You mean it?' Felix gushes.

'Of course I do, and Clarista you, too. Look around. There must be something you like.'

'Oh I do, I like it all, but me . . .' and she pats her ample stomach. 'It's not meant for ladies my size.'

I notice Felix glancing lovingly at the couture rack. 'Go on,' I urge. 'I said anything at all. I took a few pieces of couture myself.'

'There's one dress I've always been in love with – it's a Valentino.'

'Take it. I intend to put up the half-price signs today and I've got some newspaper ads that will be running in the next couple of days. Take it, Felix, before somebody buys it.'

'Oh thanks, Trini!' And I find her hugging me tightly, raining kisses on my cheek.

After taking the dress and carefully wrapping it, Felix goes to the office, returning with poster board. 'Two signs for the window and one for the door. What do you want to say?'

I sip my coffee. 'How about "Closing Down Sale, Fifty Per Cent Off Everything". No, that's too long. Just "Fifty Per Cent Off Entire Stock".'

Felix nods and begins making the signs, and shyly Clarista holds out a brightly colored caftan. 'Is this okay?'

'Of course,' I assure her.

'But it's silk . . . I wasn't sure.'

'It's fine, Clarista.'

'Thank you. I never owned anything silk before,' and like Felix, she carefully wraps her gift in pink tissue paper.

We all begin going about our own work and half an hour after the signs go up in the windows, people begin drifting in and the clink of the cash register is a familiar sound all afternoon.

CHAPTER EIGHT

It has been a busy Thursday and Felix has rung up several sales before he comes in. It is impossible not to notice him, for he is dressed fashionably, but with a touch of the eccentric. A Paisley scarf is flung over the shoulder of his camel-colored cashmere coat, a trim beard covers his face, and his dark eyes, which dart eagerly about the room, are shadowed by the large black lady's hat he wears so proudly.

Felix abruptly leaves the customer she has been helping and comes over to me. 'It's Josh Wainwright,' she hisses.

'Who?' I ask.

'Editor of *High Fashion Today*,' and just as abruptly she leaves my side and hurries over to him. 'Good morning, Mr Wainwright,' she says effusively.

'Good morning, my dear.' And as he speaks, his eyes never stop scanning the room.

The saleslady in Felix prevents her from simply leaving him alone to explore. 'We've some wonderful pieces on sale, fifty per cent off, as the shop is closing down.'

'Closing down?' he booms. 'Impossible, irresponsible, the end of an institution. Why? Where's Myra?'

Felix lowers her voice and tells him, and I can see them gazing in my direction. He threads his way through the racks and holds out his hand. 'Josh Wainwright, my dear. You have my deepest sympathies. I didn't know, I've been out of town, but I'm here today considering doing a piece on the shop for my magazine.'

'I'm afraid it won't be open much longer,' I answer, almost an apology for being an inconvenience to him.

'Too bad,' he sorrows, and with a theatrical gesture wipes a pristine handkerchief across his brow.

Ignoring me as if we hadn't spoken, he puts his briefcase and hat on the counter and briskly begins flicking through the racks.

'Schiaparelli – where have you put the Schiaparelli?' he calls to Felix impatiently and she indicates the correct racks. 'A major part of my collection over the years came from here,' he says aloud, speaking to no one in particular.

I hear a customer whispering, 'He's that fashion editor, you know – *Vogue* or *Elle* or one of those magazines.'

'Young lady, young lady,' he calls to Felix again and starts handing her a group of dresses while cautioning her, 'Not buying – considering.'

At the counter, I straighten the pile and feel glad that this morning Felix talked me into wearing a flattering 'Jean Muir' with a simple string of pearls. I feel like Manhattan rather than Denver.

I smile to myself as I think of Cindy. At least Myra did know some important people, even though it was through her shop rather than a design studio.

A woman brings a summer gown that's on sale and a pair of sandals to the counter. 'Going to Florida,' she says as she hands me her Visa card. Expertly, I run off the sale slip, bag her purchase, and thank her.

'Coffee anyone?' I offer.

'Yes, please,' Josh answers. 'Black and plenty of sugar.'

'Felix?' I question.

'No, thanks.'

I leave his cup on the counter and proceed to the window to cover the spaces where two handbags had been that were sold this morning. I select a beaded bag and a 1920s crocodile clutch bag. I fuss with the scarves and step outside to check my arrangement. It's okay, but not as artistic as Felix would have made it.

A customer leaves, apologizing, 'I'm sorry, I just can't decide today. I need to bring in my silk blouse; it's a strange color, not exactly green, not aqua either. I really would love one of the Fifties suits, but since they're on sale and there's no return, I need to bring in my blouse.'

'Sure, that's a good idea.'

'Are you open tomorrow?'

'Yeah, ten to five.'

The door opens and a blast of cold air rushes in; back at the desk, I see their heads bent over the sketchpad.

'As pure as Balenciaga,' Josh says.

'I told her that,' Felix answers with excitement. 'She thought I was only being kind. I told you that, didn't I, Trini?' and she looks up for my agreement.

'Yes, you did,' and I feel embarrassed that they are poring over my sketchbook.

'Are these really yours?' Josh asks, indicating the book.

'No,' I answer truthfully. 'They're Myra's.'

He flings the book down on the counter. 'Myra couldn't design shit!'

'I made some changes,' I say softly, 'but they were originally her designs.'

'As different as chalk and cheese. Get your coat and let me buy you a drink.'

'We're still open,' I protest.

'She can ring my things up. I smell a story here, a feature. The daughter who can do what the mother only dreamed about.' And I find myself hustled into my coat. 'We're only going across the street. Casey's has hot buttered rum. Have her close the shop if you're concerned about her being alone.'

'I'm okay,' Felix protests. 'Go on, I can handle it.'

And as I'm helped into my coat, I find him reciting the vintage and make of the clothes I'm wearing.

'Jean Muir 1970, swimming-suit fabric topped by baroque Miriam Haskell pearls.' He turns to Felix. 'Remember, child, that in fashion and taste, less is more.'

Felix nods and smiles at me, excited because this icon in the fashion world has found me of interest.

'I always *think* hot buttered rum, but gin and tonic seems safer,' and with this pronouncement, he orders for both of us. 'Talk, tell me about yourself,' he coaxes.

'There's not much to tell. I'm a commercial artist working at an ad agency in Denver. I do ads that could be done as well by a photographer. I'm married and live with my husband and sister in a big old house in Denver.'

'That's a very wholesome picture, but you left out two small children and a dog.'

'Oh, I don't have any of those.'

'So I should take no mind of Myra's stories of champion skaters, symphonic pianists, famous poets . . .'

I interrupt him. 'My sister and I hadn't seen Myra for over twenty years.'

'I thought as much,' he muses. 'She had a rich inner life, but I firmly believe she enjoyed her creations as much, if not more, than if they had been real.'

I feel comfortable with this strange man, so I ask, 'Did you know her, really know her?'

'No, no, my dear. In New York, we kiss the air near someone's cheek, we listen to their stories till they merge with someone else's. No, I didn't know her, not really. I came in the shop occasionally. I did a piece on it five or six years ago. Like us now, she and I shared a few drinks – in this same bar, as a matter of fact. We talked about the fashion world, gossiped about the designers but no, I didn't really know her.'

I amaze myself, for suddenly I blurt out, 'Do you think she was mentally ill?'

'Who isn't?' He laughs at my naive question.

'I mean the lies – she told so many lies,' I clarify. 'She made up all those stories about my sister Cindy and me and she hadn't seen or spoken to either of us for twenty years.'

'As I said, my dear, she had a rich inner life. If the world didn't suit her, she simply made up one that did.'

'Is that sane? Is that normal?'

'Who can say? I only know one thing very sad about her – she desperately wanted to be a famous designer.' I nod. 'And she got it in the end. She has you.' His eyes grow bright. 'It's what they talk about – immortality. A child – blood of your blood. You can accomplish what she couldn't.'

I blush. 'You're making me feel very foolish.'

'I don't mean to.' He reaches over and pats my hand. 'I never married, never wanted any children, can't stand the brats, but don't you see that this proves that crap they always talk about. Her DNA lives on in you.'

'Mr Wainwright, I live in Denver. I'm not a designer, I'm a third-rate artist and I can't sew a stitch, but thanks to Myra's generosity I won't have to do anything I don't like any more. When the shop and the flat are sold, I'll leave Manhattan and have a wonderful life because I'll never have to worry about money ever again.'

He sips his drink and thoughtfully corrects me. 'It's Josh – not Mr Wainwright.'

'All right, Josh.'

And without missing a beat, he begins telling me about his collection of vintage couture. We enjoy another drink, but I beg off a third by saying I have to get back and close up with Felix.

We walk silently through the falling snow and he grips my arm, steering me over the icy patches.

Inside, a little tipsy now, I hear him gently arguing with Felix, saying that Myra always gave him a fifteen-per cent discount, and like the born salesperson she is, Felix points out he is purchasing sales items that are already reduced by fifty per cent!

'Oh, I see,' and he tips his hat and leaves with the old-fashioned parting, 'Till we meet again.'

'He really liked you,' Felix says. 'I think he found you interesting.'

'I can't imagine why.'

'He was real impressed with the sketches.' Felix pauses. 'My God, can you believe it? He snitched one.'

'Snitched what?'

'The sketch. It was right here on top. He tore it off the pad. See, a bit of the paper's still there.' And Felix holds out the tablet to show me.

'It's not important, but I can't imagine why. It wasn't that good.'

'He must have thought so. Oops, I almost forgot. While you were out, Lieutenant Burke called. He wanted to know if you changed the locks.'

'Yes, I did.'

'Good. I never mentioned anything about . . . you know what. I figured you didn't want to talk about it.'

'That's right. I don't, Felix – or I guess I should say I can't.' I pause. 'But there is one thing I'd like to ask you. Did she have a boyfriend that you know of?' I feel breathless even talking about Myra.

'No, I didn't know of any man that she was involved with. She had friends, men in the fashion business, but no, I can't think of anyone that she was close to. I can't think of anyone who would want to hurt her, either. I told the police that.'

'Thanks,' I mumble and hope we have closed the subject, for it's true – I do feel uncomfortable discussing it. It makes me somewhat uneasy that I can put all this out of my mind as if it never happened. I go on, knowing my mother died, but seldom facing the fact that she was murdered. *And the murderer has not been caught.* Like Myra, I feel I must create a world that I can live with.

[illegible] now and [illegible]

[illegible]

[illegible] "What [illegible]

[illegible]

[illegible] a world that I can never walk.

CHAPTER NINE

Each time I allow the cat in or out of the window, I try not to look at the expanse of white snow, for I know I will only imagine the terror of what it was like being chased across a frozen roof. Murder, the word is so alien to me. It's in stories, in movies, a part of a make-believe world, but it doesn't happen to real people. And even when I face the unpleasant fact that it does, it's never to anyone you know, so it stays an unreality for me anyway.

I must still feel it's unreal, for I haven't even told Jeff. I know he would insist I leave New York immediately or that he will come up, and I wouldn't want that, for it would mean that Cindy would be left alone.

I do feel vulnerable, even with the barred windows and a couch pulled in front of the door, for the mysteries swirl around me, unsolvable.

It's not love of my lost mother that holds me here, but sheer outrage that whoever did this to her is out there free, unpunished. In addition, there is something about the city, the shop, the clothes, my sketches . . . that has created a quickening, an interest. In spite of my misgivings, I have no wish to leave here, for Denver seems like a dim memory that belongs to someone else.

To justify my staying, I need to help solve the crime. Somewhere in this house there must be clue to the murderer's identity. The Lieutenant mentioned that it had to be someone Myra knew – someone she'd invited in, or who had their own key.

I go through her papers again. Surely her ex-husbands had been questioned, and I look for photographs that would give faces to the names on the marriage licenses, but I find none, only the album with her life in Denver.

I pick up the photocopy of the cashier's check for ten thousand dollars. Lieutenant Burke said they had been through all of her papers, but I remind myself to call him in the morning. Something about this check niggles at me.

I put the papers untidily away and as is my nightly habit, I go round the flat assuring myself that the windows are still barred and the door firmly locked.

I lie in bed and try not to, but I find myself wondering: is he still here in this city, or has he disappeared somewhere far away and is now invisible, never to be found!

CHAPTER TEN

In another part of Manhattan, a phone rings persistently in the hallway of a cheap hotel. The caller insists to the old man who answers, 'I need to speak to Willie Butts, Room Four. It's urgent, man – I mean *urgent*.'

'It's late,' the man grumbles, but the caller hears the phone banging against the wall, so he holds the receiver away from his ear – although it's a full ten minutes before he hears a slurred, 'Hello.'

'It's me, man. You're in a lotta shit – I kid you not.'

'What's wrong? What do you mean?'

'I seen her.'

'Who?'

'The dame – the one you were supposed to hit.'

'You seen her?'

'I was delivering pizza up in the Village. I been calling you all day. It was her all right; she was coming out of the apartment, large as life. I stopped to make sure and she went right to the door and opened up that store of hers.'

Willie tries to think and come out of the fog he is in. It was weeks ago, the night of the first snow. He was tripping, but he was there that night and he knows what he saw, or at least he thinks he knows what he saw.

'Are you sure it's her?'

'I told you, she came out of that apartment, went like a bird dog right to that store. You took their money, man. I'm surprised you haven't heard from them yet.'

'Yeah, I'll look into it.'

Willie hangs up, goes back to lie down on the sagging bed, and stares up at the spider-web cracks in the ceiling, trying to figure it out. He knows he went there; it was snowing – he remembers that it was snowing hard. He looked the place over and when he went out back, that's when he tripped over the bum sleeping there. He crouched low in the gangway when he heard voices above him. He searches his mind. What was she saying? He knows. *I won't* – she was saying. *I won't.* That's it – the woman was saying: *I won't plead, I won't cry.*

Somebody was up there doing the job he was paid to do. He remembers it so clearly, that sound that went on for ever – *No-ooo!* He remembers laughing. He can't recall exactly why, but it seemed so funny to him, for she looked like a toppled snow angel struggling against the frozen air, free-falling, and then there was only silence and the sound of taxi tires on 7th Avenue and the bum lying snoring in the snow.

Now Carlos is telling him it wasn't real, that night. How could that be? Carlos is telling him she is alive, leaving an apartment, opening a store, closing a store, entering an apartment. Maybe he did dream that night. For he had been bullshitting; he never killed anyone. But he needed the cash, so he bragged, opened his big mouth, and took their money. And it was almost gone now. Oh Jesus, he'll have to do it, and all the while he thought he was home free . . .

He scrambles up, pulls open the dresser drawer and sorts through the pills, but he can't tell what is what. Randomly he selects two of them and looks for water, but finding the glass empty, throws back his head and swallows them dry. He'll sleep for a while and then go tonight to check it out – for sure he'll do it tonight. It gets dark early. If there is no way into the flat, he'll check out the store. Info said most of the time she worked there alone. He can do it, he has to, for if he doesn't, as Carlos intimidated, he'll be a dead man.

He falls into a drug-induced sleep, but it doesn't last – it never does. He is breathing hard and heavy when he awakes; it is those Goddamned dreams again – someone chasing him, always chasing him. He has dreamed that dream all his life.

The luminous hands of the clock tell him it is 2 a.m. He turns and tosses, but it is no good. He feels strung as tight as a drum; he has to get the tension out. Again he searches the drawer and finds the pill with the apple impressed in it. Appropriate, he chuckles to himself. 'Have an apple in the Big Apple.' He swallows the last Ecstasy dose and it is only a few minutes before he is Superman, Batman; he sure as shit knows he could even fly if he really wanted to. As he begins dressing, he feels himself growing stronger and more powerful. Damn, there is nothing he can't do! And for the first time, he realizes he can do *that*, too – he can even kill!

CHAPTER ELEVEN

I come upstairs sometime after five. It has been another hectic day. The sale has been working so well that at times the shop was mobbed.

It wasn't a day that Felix worked, so I had to press Clarista into service, and she was so complimented that she had been elevated to Sales Clerk. She learned quickly, and she had a genuine way with customers. If one asked her what she really thought about a dress that was being tried on, if she didn't think it looked good, she said so.

The sale is working better than I anticipated. The racks are looser and a great deal of merchandise has been sold, so each day, when the shop empties out a bit, I go back to the office to run the figures to see how much we are making. Only yesterday, by one-day post, I sent Cindy a check for fifty thousand dollars – half of the money in the savings account.

I still haven't brought myself to tell Jeff or Cindy the true amount that the property is worth. I try examining my real feelings about it and I admit, here in New York, I feel free, relieved of burdens. I hate myself for thinking of Cindy and Jeff as such, but maybe the reason I can't face giving up the property is because, down deep, I know I don't want to leave. If the building is sold, I will have no reason to stay.

It is something about the shop, the touch of the cloth – it awakens something within me. I remember as a child, in that attic, the one thing that made me feel safe was the shine of the satin, the softness of the velvet, the rustle of the cotton – it spoke to all of my senses. The heady smell of the new material that came from exotic lands was a world of touch, scent, sight. It spoke to me of its magic, and before *Him,* and the tread of *His* shiny shoes on the stairs, I thought my mother was a magician who molded and created things of beauty. It was awe and jealousy, pure and simple, that drove me to stroke the cloth, feel its texture, search the threads so they could tell me their secrets, so that I, too, could one day create magic like hers in the flick of an eye.

Buried deep in my subconscious, they surface now, those forgotten sensations. It's like a germinating seed that has finally burst open and finds itself stretching, seeking a lost sun.

I close the shop after another successful day. In addition to a salary, I give Clarista a small commission on her sales. It makes me feel good to see how proudly she holds her head now and how eagerly she agrees to work with me on the two days that Felix isn't in.

'Maybe you could give me a reference?' she asks timidly, her eyes lowered.

'Of course,' I agree.

'I mean a reference about sales. Maybe I could get out of cleaning. My kids would be real proud if I was in sales.'

'Well, sure, of course, I'd be happy to do that.'

'I know I need to learn more, like checking the Visa book and learning how to do Telecheck, technical stuff like that.'

'Felix or I will show you. I didn't know any of that either. It's easy,' I assure her.

She looks up at me and I swear I can see tears in her eyes. 'Thanks, Miz Trini, thanks for the chance.'

'Now you do have to stop that, though. Cleaning ladies say "Miz Trini", sales ladies say "Trini".'

'Yes, ma'am,' she answers.

Clarista leaves humming to herself and I turn out the lights, feeling pleased that I have made someone hopeful, and maybe a little bit happy.

I take Felix's advice and phone for a take-away. I order tacos, burritos with salsa, and it makes me think of Myra. Daddy said she truly loved everything south of the border.

I take off my shoes and sit down in the easy chair, and then I remember I hadn't switched the phone through, so maybe there are messages.

Almost like ESP, I hear the click and Cindy's voice spills out into the room. 'Trini, I couldn't believe it! I got the check today. I was so excited I couldn't go into work. I've been home all day trying to decide what to do. I thought I'd keep a little and buy some clothes. I guess Jeff told you I had to borrow some of yours. I couldn't go into the office with what I had. I'm sorry, I'll have them cleaned. I've been real careful with them. I thought I'd buy a few things for the house. If you don't like what I choose, you can put them away. And I asked Jeff if he'd help me with investment advice. You know he's good at stuff like that . . .' and I listen for the message to continue and hear only soft sobs, but after a moment she continues: 'Momma loved us, she must have. I miss her so much.'

I stare at the phone. Money has convinced Cindy of our mother's love. Maybe Myra didn't like the Cancer Society or the Home for Stray Dogs. I take comfort in the fact that our inheritance has, after all these years, confirmed for Cindy that she was beloved at a distance.

CHAPTER TWELVE

Clarista and I worked together all week, as Felix was off studying for exams. Clarista was thrilled with gaining the experience and the extra cash was very welcome as she has three kids.

Felix had convinced me to wear garments from the stock, and I initiated Clarista into the practice.

Every day I sought out an outfit by Courrèges or Biba, or one of the designers from the late 1960s to the early 1970s. I chose that era as it was a fun period, and Clarista also took great pleasure in selecting a generous-sized outfit from about the same era. We were like two children playing dress up, but Felix was right – it did lend a certain air to the shop. The fact that we, too, loved the old things seemed to give it all credence.

It is late Saturday with the door locked and the lights dimmed that it happens. Clarista looks out the window and says, 'He's been there all week watching the shop, I'm sure of it. I don't like it, not one bit. I know he was there Thursday and Wednesday for sure.'

'Who?' I ask as I come up to her and stand by her side, and the two of us peer at the figure of a man standing across the narrow street. She wasn't mistaken – he *was* looking towards our window. His coat collar is pulled up and the hat he is wearing does an excellent job of hiding his face.

After only a moment or two, he notices us, for he turns and hurries away. It is only five o'clock, but the winter dark has already descended on the Village streets.

'I'm Sangria,' Clarista says suddenly.

'What does that mean?'

'It's a religion; it lets me sense things. That man was evil.' I can see pure fear in her eyes. 'He meant you harm, Miz Trini.'

I laugh uneasily. 'No "Miz Trini", remember?'

She reaches over and touches my hand, patting it urgently. 'You gotta lock your doors. Do you have a gun?'

'No, of course not, Clarista. It's because of what happened to Myra that you're worried about me, but I'll be okay. The police said it wasn't a stranger who killed her. They feel she knew him.'

'Miz Myra was never in danger from that man. No, no evil was ever near her. I know that for I can see the aura and hers was black, down and dirty black, it was her depression you see. That man never hurt Myra, but I feel it now strong as anything, that he means you harm. He means you bad harm.'

'Clarista, please stop talking like that. He just looked like a street person. Maybe he was a robber, but the shop's closed now and we're safe. He's gone – see?'

We crane our necks and look both ways but the street is deserted now. Nothing out there but one ginger cat carefully crossing the snow-packed street.

'Just the same, Miz Trini, you bolt your doors and sleep with a hammer by your bed. Baseball bat's good protection, too, long as you don't have a gun.'

'Clarista, please, you are frightening me. Please stop,' I plead.

'Yes, ma'am, I'm sorry,' and we go back to change into our regular clothes.

When we return to the door, she wraps her coat tight about herself and seems to be struggling with some inner debate.

'I'll be fine,' I assure her. 'I do bolt the door and Tonto sleeps inside my stairway. I know it's silly, but I also pull a heavy sofa in front of the door and all the windows have bars. I'll be safe, I promise you.'

'Tonto? You mean that drunken Indian, you let him in your house?'

'No, he's not in the house, he's in the hallway at the bottom of the stairs. I have another solid oak door upstairs that I double bolt, and I told you, I put the sofa in front of it. I close and lock the bedroom door, too. I have a phone right next to my bed and I swear I'll sleep with a hammer on the night-stand. I'm sure Myra doesn't have a bat.'

'He could be one of those crazy people they let out of the nut-house,' Clarista persists, and I can see by her face that she's still concerned.

'No, he's not dangerous, he's just a sad, pathetic alcoholic. He's no danger to anyone but himself. By nightfall, he can barely stand up.'

Clarista nods and loosens her coat, searching under her sweater; finally she pulls out a pendant on a chain. 'You take this now, Miz Trini, it'll keep you safe. It did me on the subway and on the mean streets of Spanish Harlem.'

Her concern makes her lapse into calling me Miz Trini, but I don't bother correcting her this time.

'What about you? If it's a medal or something that kept you safe, you can't just go giving it away.'

'I'll write off for another one tonight. For an extra five dollars, they'll send me a new one in just two or three days.'

I see the medallion glitter in the dim light. 'Is it a St Christopher?' I ask, for I am thoroughly touched by her concern.

'Oh no, it's much more special than that. It's the sacred Virgin of Fatima.' She holds the medal out to me.

I look at it. 'It's very beautiful. Thank you.'

'Put it on,' she urges. 'You must wear it next to your skin. Don't take it off, not even in the bath.'

I pull the chain over my head – but still she isn't satisfied. 'You need to wear it next to your skin.'

Obediently, I tug at the neck of my dress and the medal, still warm from her skin, settles between my breasts.

'You'll be safe now,' Clarista promises. 'When you get a chance, look at it real close. It's got a small glass place that has the real earth inside it from Fatima. It's all the way from Portugal, where people saw the Virgin, saw Her with their own eyes. It saved Pope John Paul II's life, too – he even said so on TV. Millions of people heard him thank the Virgin of Fatima.' I nod. 'You'll be safe now,' she says again and squeezes my hand once more.

'Thank you, Clarista. I'm very touched that you would give me something that means so much to you.'

'I'll get another one real soon,' she promises. 'Can't feel safe without one.'

For a brief moment I watch her walk to the corner, for now I am anxiously looking for the strange man that she seemed so worried about. But she turns and she is out of sight.

So I put the key in the lock and walk up the stairs to the flat. I feel a little foolish wearing the medal, for I know they are advertized in the *Enquirer* and in the back of every pulp magazine. But who am I to make fun of belief? Believing in things often makes them possible, so what if positive thinking and a feeling of protection comes from the medallion of the Virgin of Fatima? What harm is there in it?

It was such a busy week that I sleep until noon on Sunday. I have the luxury of eating in, so I make myself fresh squeezed orange juice, toasted bagels, and scrambled eggs, and I even take the time to make a pot of filtered coffee.

It feels so luxurious to stay in my nightgown and robe, and I take the week's receipts into the room with the desk and do the bookwork and calculate the profit, after taxes, Clarista's salary, and expenses, and I write out Cindy's check that I'll put in the post in the morning. She has been so grateful to receive the weekly checks and she has been ecstatic over the large amount from the savings account. It makes me feel good to know she can finally feel independent, that she has her own funds, and for the first time in her life she can make choices. Myra, for all her faults, has left us well taken care of.

The phone begins ringing and after three rings I hear my own voice saying, 'I'm not here right now. Please leave a message after the beep.'

'Hi, it's Felicity. If you come home—'

Quickly I pick up the phone. 'Hi, Felix, what's up?'

'Something really exciting, but it's a surprise.'

'Oh.'

'I'll be there in the morning to work, but I called to see if you're busy after the shop closes.'

'No, not really. What's this about?' I ask.

'I can't tell you, I gotta show you. I promise it won't take too long.'

'Okay, okay, we might even have crackers and cheese. You know I went out last week and bought dishes.'

'Who ran the shop when you were out carousing?' she teased.

'No one. I closed. I'm the owner, remember? I can do that.'

'Well, la de da, important lady.'

I laugh. 'I really couldn't stand it any longer; no dishes, no coffee in the morning . . . it was getting to be too much.'

'One should be comfortable,' Felix replies, 'but I'd better hang up now before I blurt it out. I just can't wait to see what you think of it. By the way, how did Clarista work out?'

'She was great. It was really sweet. I made her dress up and after her initial embarrassment, she really got into it.'

I can hear Felix's peals of laughter. 'Honest to God, what'd she wear?'

'Well, mostly she liked those Sixties caftans, but once or twice she found a larger size black crepe – you know, the 1940s Joan Crawford-style with shoulder pads and all.'

'You're kidding!'

'No, I'm not. She looked terrific and I think the clothes gave her an air of confidence. She was great with the customers, too.'

'Oh, shut up, you're making me jealous.'

'I meant to,' I grin.

'Oh, you meanie. I better hang up now. I'll see you in the morning.'

'Okay.'

Sitting by the phone, I know that I really should call home. I don't want to, for Jeff sounded so disapproving the last time we spoke; no realtors had shown up and I had nothing positive to report. It is beginning to seem like I am avoiding talking to them both. Deep down, I know I am.

It is only 10 o'clock in Denver; they'll still be awake. I really should call, so reluctantly I dial and the phone rings and rings. Puzzled, I redial in case I had gotten a wrong number. But again the phone rings and rings in the empty house. I know that Cindy never goes out alone at night and the feeling that something is wrong nags at me.

I try again at eleven and at midnight, and finally go to bed telling myself not to worry. If something is wrong, surely they'll call me!

I toss and turn, and my feline companion, who decided to stay in tonight, rises and patiently resettles himself each time I roll over, and when I am finally still, the cat begins to purr contentedly.

I try to quiet my mind, but again and again my thoughts return to Downing Street and the unanswered phone. So after an hour, I get up, and the cat, who has had enough of my restlessness, streaks to the kitchen and begins meowing to be let out.

I dial the number and finally, after seven rings, breathlessly Cindy answers, 'Hello.'

'Hi, it's me. I was really getting worried. I called a few times and . . .' I stop myself from saying I couldn't imagine where on earth she'd be, out so late at night.

'We're just getting in. Jeff's parking the car in the garage.'

'Oh, where were you?'

'This thing at the college – it was a cocktail party for the new Professor, a John Freesum, or Freedom, or something like that.'

And while Cindy's voice is free of a stutter, her voice is different – fuzzy, blurred – and I can tell she's been drinking.

'Sounds fun – food, booze, nice people.'

'Yeah, Trini, all of the above, and it was hilarious. I lost one of my contacts in my drink. At first I was horribly embarrassed and I thought I'd burst out crying 'cos everyone was laughing, but Jeff explained they were laughing with me, not at me, so it was okay.'

'Gee, I'm so glad. Sounds like you had a good time.'

'Yes, I did. I was scared to go at first, but Jeff told me how awkward it would be for him with you out of town. He didn't want to go alone.'

'Thanks for keeping him company. You should go out a lot more,' I urge.

'I am. I went to a play with Steve Brady, the film student, and I went out to lunch with some girls from the office.'

'Great, that's just great.'

'Jeff'll be here in a minute. I gotta go to bed soon. I had two of those Long Island Teas before it dawned on me that it wasn't tea, didn't even taste like tea, but they were good.'

'I think they're made with bourbon.'

'Yes, I think so. Jeff's here,' and I hear him thank Cindy.

'Thanks. You were great. You did just fine. Everybody liked you.' I hear his kind words of assurance before he takes the phone.

'You're up pretty late. Must be three o'clock in New York. Anything wrong?'

'No, I called earlier and when no one answered, I got worried about Cindy.'

'Oh,' and I hear the coldness in his voice. 'I told you she's doing fine. Really, she's doing better than fine, so please, Trini, don't start with her. You know doubt can undermine her progress.'

'You make it sound like I want to hurt her.'

'No, I never said that. I just think you go about it wrong. Give her space, don't coddle her. That way never helped her.'

I feel that same anger whenever we talk about Cindy. 'Well, I didn't really call for anything special, I just wanted to know everything was okay, and I don't appreciate being yelled at for being concerned about you both.'

'Trini, I wasn't yelling.'

'It sounded like it to me,' and it was there between us, the discord that always arose when we discussed Cindy. 'I'm going to bed now, it's late,' I said softly.

There was a silence before he responded. 'Take care. Bye now.'

I went to bed feeling left out, which is how Cindy must have felt all these years.

This was a husband I was certain I didn't love in the right way, and a sister I professed to love, who sounded like she was making so much progress without me that my past love of her became suspect. It seemed I had caused her nothing but harm.

I couldn't really understand my feelings. Here in my new life, with my new interests, I hadn't missed Jeff or Cindy at all. Yet this conversation somehow made me feel hurt and wounded, and I knew I was further away from both of them in a dimension that had nothing to do with miles.

CHAPTER THIRTEEN

Morning dawns and I am back in my New York persona and business at the shop starts off with a bang. A showbiz group is having a 1950s party and they need to rent twenty costumes. I assist Felix as they scan the racks searching for sizes. Felix urges them to buy instead, as a sale is on, but they are set on renting.

Two young women fight over a poodle skirt until Felicity finds a floral skirt with a huge appliquéd cactus and shows one of the girls how great it would be with a stiff net petticoat underneath. The customer tries it on and is happy with the transformation – and fortunately, both girls are satisfied.

There's a mad flurry of trying on garments and two hours later, we ring up all the charges and the group of chattering actresses and would-be actresses leaves.

'Rental is really good. Myra loved rentals. They fetch a good rate, the customer pays for the cleaning and we get to keep the things!' Felix chirps.

'Sounds perfect,' I agree.

Clarista comes out of the office with a worried frown. 'Mary Jane, we need the cat again; we got mice.'

I can't imagine who she is talking to. I look around the room and there are only the three of us, Felicity, Clarista and myself.

'That's me,' Felix confesses, looking toward Clarista angrily. 'Mary Jane, Mary Jane,' she mocks herself. 'I've told you a hundred times, Clarista, I'm not Mary Jane any more. You can say Felicity, can't you? If not, surely you can say Felix.'

'Sure I can say, but your mother, she name you Mary Jane. Out of respect for your mama, I call you the name she gave you.'

Felicity rolls her eyes and follows Clarista back to the office, where she points to a shredded napkin that contains a few crumbs left over from a pizza slice. 'See, mice, mice been here. They leave tracks.'

Felicity nods and comes back to the counter. 'She's right. Myra used to leave the cat in the shop overnight, and in just a couple of nights he cleaned them out all right.'

'I think she's pouting because you're here today,' I say. 'I couldn't even get her to change her dress.'

'I'm sorry. We're both being big babies. I did feel a little jealous when you told me she did so well in sales,' Felix admits.

'I know. I guess she thinks you know so much more. I asked her to pitch in when we get busy, but no, she's intent on cleaning today. I guess I'll just ignore it.' It is very silly for two grown women to feel competitive with each other, I think.

'I'll remember to bring the cat down tomorrow. By the way, Felix, what's his name?'

'I don't know. Myra always called him "the cat". I guess he doesn't have a name, or maybe "the cat" is it.'

'Well, that's gonna change. How about it, what should we call him?'

'I don't know. After all, Trini, he's your cat.'

'Just this morning I was telling him that he needed a name. I think I'll call him Rogue; he is one, you know, all that fighting and caterwauling. I guess I should have him neutered.'

'It's up to you, but remember that you're gonna change his destiny when you name him. I read that somewhere. Judy Garland used to be called Frances Gumm – can you imagine that? She only got famous when they changed her name. When I design, I'm only going to use one name – Felicity. Sounds English or European, doesn't it?'

'Yes, it does,' I agree. 'It's very unique.'

'Hmm,' we hear Clarista mumble as she dusts the shelves faster and faster. 'No use messin' with the fates; best you leave things be. There's a man in Harlem messes with them chicken feet, black ribbons. No, best leave things be. Keep the name you were born with.'

We both smile and Felix begins showing me exactly how the rental file works and how to record the stock numbers with the dates they are due back. I call Clarista over so she can learn how it is done as well.

We send out for lunch and the three of us share the various dishes from the Chinese take-away.

While the morning was busy, the afternoon is slow. Only a few customers drift in and Felix wants to redo the window. 'I thought red and white – as Valentine's Day is coming up.'

'Good idea,' I agree, and together we search the racks for just the right dress to put on the mannequin. We work well together, and with one mind we agree on the red silk-velvet bias-cut gown. I remember to ask Clarista for her opinion.

'Shame it doesn't have a famous label; it'd be worth a whole lot more,' Felix muses. 'But at half-price, it's a terrific bargain.'

'We do have some great labels. Recently I looked through the racks and was terribly impressed when I noticed Dior, Yves St Laurent, and my God, who is Adrian? Myra had that gray suit of Adrian's priced at over a thousand. I tried it on and it looked good, so I kept it. He did designs for the movies, didn't he?'

'Yes, he created costumes for Garbo, Joan Crawford, Katharine Hepburn – all the greats. He died in the late Fifties, so his stuff is in the collector's category now,' Felix informs me.

'Well, I'm glad I kept it then.'

Deftly, Felix continues dressing the mannequin. 'Shoes, shoes,' she mutters as she holds up a pair in silver, then one in black.

I shake my head no. 'How about gold, and you could use gold gloves and gold jewelry,' Clarista suggests boldly.

'Brilliant,' Felix pronounces, and with a few red boas and a gold fan, she continues decorating the window. The final touch is a huge Valentine box and, sprinkled tastefully about, dainty antique Valentines frilled with lace complete the picture.

The three of us go outside to survey the window.

'What do you think, Trini? I'm not sensitive about criticism. Is it okay?'

'It's better than okay, it's great!' I say.

'Yeah, I like it, too,' Clarista offers.

We stand quietly for five minutes admiring the window. The three of us have arrived at an easy friendship. Felix has been invaluable to me with her knowledge of the shop and all the details of running it, and my arrival has set her to dreaming. She has ideas, she has plans, which were born the day she saw how successfully I altered the sketches. And once or twice, when she peeked into Myra's folder of designs, she saw that I had worked on some of the other sketches and that my alterations were right on. She thinks the designs are wonderful now.

Felix can hardly contain her excitement about tonight and the surprise she has in store for me. She's desperate for me to understand, to agree with her plan, she says. It's such a good one!

Just as we are closing the shop, Gemma appears. She is a tall dark girl and with clean hair, she could have been considered very pretty, but it hangs lankily in greasy strands about her slender face. Her eyes appear too large, and she is dressed entirely in black, which makes her look too somber for someone so young. When Felix introduces us, Gemma simply nods to me, and says, 'Nice to meet you,' in a voice so low I'm almost not sure if she really spoke or whether I imagined it.

Both girls follow me to the apartment door and when Felix notices the down cover folded neatly on the first step, she offers, 'Shall I carry this up?'

'No, it's for Tonto; the other spread he had got wet,' I explain.

'Want me to put it outside for him?'

'No, leave it there,' and I walk briskly up the stairs with the two younger girls behind me.

Felix circles the living room. 'Gee, it looks so much better in here. Myra always was such a pack rat. Who was it that said "less is more"? It was someone I can't think of, and recently.'

'It was Josh and I agree. Have a seat and I'll get us some refreshments. I have food in the house now – or should I say snacks.'

'Can I help?' Felix asks.

'No, I'll just bring things out and we can use the little table there. Do you want coffee – tea – Cokes – bottled water . . . ?'

Felix comes closer to me and whispers, 'Have you any wine or whiskey? Gemma could sure use a drink.'

I glance over to where Gemma has sunk into the couch and is staring ahead, zombie-like. 'Is she all right? She doesn't look very well.' I wonder how these two could be friends; there seems to be no common denominator here.

'She'll be okay. It because of her modeling work that she's bulimic. You can't get any work in that field unless you're slim, and I mean *really* slim. She probably won't eat much, but she likes her spirits.'

'I have some Chablis,' and I go off into the kitchen to gather up the food. For a moment it strikes me as funny, for I have a bum sleeping in my hallway and a girl who looks like a junkie in my living room. How much I have changed in only four weeks. Jeff and Cindy would think I've gone mad.

I put out a generous plate of ham and cheese, and another tray of pickles, olives and rye bread. I carry the tray out to the living room and the three of us sit on the floor and, without speaking, eat. I watch the strange girl and Felix was completely wrong, for Gemma wolfs down the food as if she hadn't eaten for a week.

We sit back contented and sip the wine; only Gemma gulps hers. Felix meets my eyes and conveys the message, so I reach over and refill Gemma's glass.

In the awkward silence I rise, and not looking at the CDs, select one and click on the player. Steve Reich's music fills the room; the minimal music seems to flit over and over itself, the chords repeating endlessly. Without asking, Felix politely gathers the plates and only leaves the nearly empty wine bottle and glasses.

She returns carrying the cat. 'Here he is. Shall we drink to him since he now has a name? To Rogue,' and she lifts her glass in mock salute. 'To Rogue,' we answer and drink, toasting the newly named cat.

She puts him down and looking at me says, 'According to Clarista and me, his life will change now. Maybe he'll get together with the gorgeous Persian over on Perry Street. Remember – Judy Garland instead of Frances Gumm.'

I smile, but I feel uneasy. What is this evening all about? As if reading my mind, Felix opens her large backpack and pulls out a clumsily wrapped package. 'Open it, go on,' she urges, and she looks as excited as a child on Christmas morning.

At first I politely pick at the Sellotape, but finally tear into the tissue paper and find myself looking at what appears to be a white linen blouse. Puzzled, I mumble an embarrassed, 'Thank you.' I can't imagine what the occasion is.

'Put it on, go on,' Felix urges, her excitement almost at fever pitch.

I undo the top buttons; it appears to be longer than a blouse. I put my arms through it and without speaking, Felix comes over and buttons the garment for me.

Again I mumble a confused, 'Thank you.'

'It's a smock – the sort of smock that the master wears. Dior or Balenciaga started the tradition and it's said that Givenchy, among others, still follows the custom today. In all the Paris ateliers – that's what the workrooms are called – they wear them, the "White Smocks". Please, oh please, Trini, don't say anything, not yet.' And I watch in amazement as Felix moves the coffee table and swift as lightning whips off Gemma's coat, unzips her dress, and with a helping hand urges her to get up on the coffee table wearing only her bra and pants. Gemma obediently waits, standing on the table, as if this was an ordinary everyday occurrence.

'She's your mannequin; a bit too thin maybe, but clothes always look wonderful on the tall and skinny.'

For a minute I wonder if Felix is drunk or high; this is total madness, this bizarre scene of the girl dressed in her bra and pants standing on my coffee table.

'Look, look, I have it for you,' and Felix's hands scramble frantically into her large bag to retrieve several pieces of cloth. 'It's your toile – we've had it made, the pattern of your opera coat. See, Trini, the pattern, we've had it cut in muslin just like the couture houses do. It was Josh's idea – he used a woman from France who taught at my school. A long time ago, when she was young, she was "first hands" in Milan.'

'Josh's idea?' I ask, totally puzzled.

'Yes, that day he was in the shop he gave me his card and asked me to call him. Remember I told you he snitched the top sketch – this one – the opera coat.'

'But why?'

'People like Josh want to be the first to spot a new talent. He called you a rising star. He arranged this whole thing. He'd be devastated if he was wrong; his ego couldn't take it.'

It is happening too fast. 'Felix, I'm touched, this is so nice, but as I've said before, I'm an artist. I don't know anything about designing clothes. I'd love to know how, but I don't.'

'Yes, you do,' she urges. 'Every designer must know human anatomy. As an artist, I'm sure you've studied it a lot. Now you only need to learn about the properties of fibers and fabrics. Please, Trini, I can tell, I've studied all about the greats. You have the eye, the talent – this coat of yours is wonderful. Josh knows: he noticed something special in you straight away.' And holding out the first piece of the fabric pattern, she puts it into my shaking hands.

Like directing a play, Felix barks orders. 'Gemma, you are the mannequin. You stand perfectly still; you do not give an opinion.'

Half-hypnotized by this craziness, I find myself standing by the table with Felix thrusting parts of the pattern toward me. One by one, she hands me the straight pins; and like a player who does not want to play, I find myself fascinated with the reality of my design. The front piece is pinned on, the back attached, and only the cowl collar stubbornly will not lie properly. But then, like a finished puzzle, my creation is there in muslin and my imagination soars. I can almost see it in cut velvet or perhaps duchess satin; the choice of fabric could let it flow with the contours of the body, or with a stiff interface, it could be sculpted to have a lot more form.

'What do you think?' Felix asks, her voice breathless.

'The armholes are too narrow and the hem . . .' I put my finger in my mouth and gnaw on a hangnail. 'It depends on the fabric; if soft, the body of the coat is right, but if a stiffer material is used, the bottom of the coat should be fuller.'

Both Felix and I circle the girl, who does her part perfectly; she stands as lifeless as a mannequin.

'Either way, the armholes are too narrow for the design,' I say, as if speaking to myself. Carefully, Felix lifts off the pinned fabric and lays the pattern out on the rug.

With eyes like a wounded doe, Gemma catches Felix's eye. 'All right, all right, I guess we don't need you any more,' and walking her to the door, Felix furtively hands her something from her pocket.

Reaching for my purse, I ask, 'How much did you pay her?'

'It wasn't much, honest. Josh gave me her fee.'

'Come on, I can't let you do this. It is a wonderful surprise, but you've done so much, you both have. You must tell me what's been spent—' I'm interrupted by a loud crash and a timid scream.

'My God, what's happened?' we say in unison and, childlike, I almost add, 'Make a wish.'

Felix flings the door open. 'Tonto's down there in your hallway. How'd he get in?' We watch Gemma untangle herself, straighten up and go out, loudly slamming the door.

'I gave him a key.'

Felix sinks down on the couch and runs her fingers through her unruly head of red waves. 'Wow, maybe where you come from, but no, not here. You give the street people a blanket, a bologna sandwich, a cup of coffee, or the occasional dollar, but you don't invite them in to share your house.'

I pour myself a glass of wine and sink into the armchair. 'It's not my house, it's only my hallway.'

Felix shakes her head in disbelief and pours herself the last of the wine. We both drink silently until finally she can no longer contain herself. 'What did you think?'

'About what?'

'Your toile, the pattern. I'm sure the design works. Josh was adamant that it was perfect.'

'It was fun. No, it was more than fun, it was thrilling to see a vision become real. On paper it's so easy, but to actually see it, muslin or not, it's really thrilling. I'll remember it all my life,' I say truthfully.

For a moment, Felix's shoulders slump with dejection. Then with the determination that is the core of her personality, she continues planning. 'There's a fabric store in the garment district which has great ends of rolls. It's cheap and the owner gives all of us students a break on the prices. Maybe tomorrow we could go down and you could pick out the right fabric.'

I lean back and stretch. 'It's been a long day. I am very tired, and I'm sure you must be, too. Oh Felix, you're a dear sweet child and I'm so flattered, but I told you, I know absolutely nothing about sewing, toile or pattern-making. I'm totally hopeless on that score.'

Felix sits up. 'You don't understand. A designer doesn't really have to know those things. Some do, some know part of it – why, Chanel at eighty used to cut armholes on a live model. The story goes that she even drew blood, but like a good mannequin, the model never flinched or moved. Damn, I bet Gemma would have freaked out. No, it's the vision of what can be beautiful on the human form – most designers only have that one important part – the vision. Someone like Balenciaga, who was a genius, a true genius, could do it all – the toile, the cut, and the finished sewing, but he was rare – he was a genius. Most designers only have the vision. That's all you need.'

It is late and I am too tired to argue with this enthusiastic young woman. 'We'll see. We'll talk about it later.'

'Tomorrow?' Felix asks hopefully.

'No, some time later,' I say firmly.

'Think about it, Trini – promise – and you must start planning the dress, the one to go with the opera coat. Josh has the woman on standby. She can make the toile quickly.'

I nod as I walk Felix to the door and watch as she goes down the stairs and gracefully steps over Tonto, who is snoring loudly and doesn't turn over or wake up even when she slams the door after her.

As usual, I slide the night latch on and pull the couch over.

Exhausted, I brush my teeth, undress and fall into bed. The cat begins whining and wearily I get up and follow him to the kitchen.

I lift him up to the window. 'Look, you silly cat, it's starting to snow. Rogue, are you sure?'

His persistent whine convinces me, so I struggle with the window, unlock the bars, look out into the silvery night, and release the cat, who streaks off like a dark shadow towards some unknown destination. I relock the bars and the window, and gratefully go back to my warm bed.

My dreams that night put me back inside the attic in Denver. I crouch under a bolt of grass-green silk shantung and hear the comforting sound of the Singer – its treadle a Steve Reich symphony. And my mother, young and lovely as I remember her, pauses to play with me that forgotten game – parachute.

She picks up the bolts of cloth one by one and unfurls them. First there's the satin in daffodil yellow. Softly, like rain, it billows over my head and I giggle as it drifts down to cover me like a blanket of love, and I feel its touch and hear the sound of her high playful laughter as she uncovers me in this hide and seek game, only to unfurl another bolt – this time of rainbow-colored silk – and I shiver in anticipation waiting for this one to come down and caress me. On and on, into the afternoon we play, until we are a laughing heap caught among the different fabrics, and the touch of the cloth and her perfumed arms holding me are the last moments I ever remember of her loving me.

The dream was disturbing and I wake to find I have sleepwalked into the hall. I am facing the locked closet, the one opposite the bathroom door.

CHAPTER FOURTEEN

The phone wakes me at eight.

'Hi, I didn't mean to call so early, but I have to go to work, and I needed to ask you about something.'

I yawn and stretch. 'That's okay, Jeff told me about how well you're doing on the job. That's great, Cindy.'

'It's been four weeks, but it's not permanent, I'm sure. I only took it 'cos Jeff asked me to; he said they were really stuck. I'm probably not,' Cindy pauses, 'probably not good enough.'

'Ssh, ssh, baby sister, I don't like for you to talk that way. You're probably *too* good. After all, you have a Bachelor of Science degree.'

'I know, but this is only clerical. It's helping young people with their student loans and stuff; it's not permanent, either.' Cindy's voice drifts off with the same helpless sound she usually has when talking to me.

I hear alarm bells ringing. Maybe it is my fault, maybe I don't talk to her in the right way, for Jeff has gotten her to take a giant step out into the real world. So quickly I change the subject. 'I don't want to make you late. What'd you call about?'

'The check. God, Trini, it's so large! I can't believe it's all my money.'

'It is, kiddo. Share and share alike; that's half the takings for two weeks from the shop, and the other big check was from the savings account. Go on, splurge, have fun. After all, money is to be spent.'

'Well, that's just it. I saw some things at the Boulder Fifth Street Mall – a lovely handmade Indian rug and a couple of other things that would look so good in the den . . .'

'You mean Daddy's room?'

'No, I mean the den. I've been calling the second living room the den.'

I interrupt. 'Look, honey, you don't need my permission to spend your own money.'

'I . . . I . . . I mean . . . I mean . . .' Cindy stops helplessly as the stutter prevents her from going on.

'Slow down, honey, it's okay. Take your time.' Patiently I urge her on in the same way I have many times before.

'It's for the den,' Cindy finally blurts out. 'I mean the second living room I call the den.'

'That's fine, I understand. It's for the den, that's fine. Sounds good.'

I can hear Cindy taking several deep breaths the way she has always done in the past while trying to calm the stutter.

'I'm here. Just take your time.'

After a moment, Cindy speaks more slowly. 'I meant, you always did the house. Is it okay?'

'Of course it is. Do whatever you like. Daddy left the house to both of us. Change whatever you want, it's your house, too.'

'Thanks. Oh Trini, thanks!'

'You don't have to thank me. As I said, it's your house, too. You know that, or you should.'

'Thanks, Trini. I gotta go now. I don't want to be late. Jeff said he'd call you tonight.'

'Good. I'll wait for his call.'

I hang up and I feel bad that Cindy is so uncertain. She seemed almost frightened to change anything in the house. It was always *our* house – I thought she understood that. How sad that she felt she needed my permission to change anything.

I hated to hear her stutter, for lately she seemed so changed, so much improved, and I try to envision Cindy's progress. It seems unbelievable to me that she has a job, that she has actually been working for four weeks! If only I had been there when she needed me, I could have helped her with clothes. But I guess that was okay, for she mentioned borrowing some of mine.

Her hair – God, I hope she realized how outdated it looked! Maybe she pinned it up or something. But she sounded okay about everything except changes in the house, so I guess no one teased her and was cruel. Stop, I say to myself, stop, it's me that's so negative about her. Jeff is right. Whatever he's done, it's been the right thing. So it's me, *me* who's been wrong all along.

I go to the kitchen, pleased that I have the convenience of making a cup of coffee and some toast. I glance toward the window, but Rogue isn't there scratching to get in. I take a tray and go into the living room. I push away all thoughts of my sister and Jeff. I will not play the game of who's right and who's wrong.

The muslin pattern lies there, exactly where Felix had placed it, but my wayward thoughts insist on returning to my sister. Have I done wrong, always protecting her, hiding her from the big bad world? Perhaps I have always sent her the wrong message; it could have been taken that way – it must have been! Down deep, I acknowledge that I, too, must have felt that Cindy was as worthless and undeserving of love as she herself believes, or I wouldn't have done what I did! Why didn't I believe that this beautiful sister of mine, with only such a small affliction, could make it in the world, find a man to love, instead of always living in my shadow, hiding away in that big sad house.

Finally I see it clearly. It was Cindy's lack of self-esteem and Myra's total rejection of her that scarred her far more deeply than the stutter, and I, with my misplaced kindness and the heavy burden of guilt, sent her the very same message – *you have no value.* It will change, I promise myself. When I go back I'll treat her differently. I'll learn from Jeff. I know that someday Cindy and I will have to talk about it, this thing that festers between us. I can't imagine how or even why I did it, but it must have been because I didn't believe in my own sister's worth.

Denver and the house on Downing Street at times seem unreal to me, as if they exist somewhere in another time, another place, and I wonder if it really happened, this perverted thing, or is it something I only imagined.

I must distance myself from things I cannot change, so I look down at the toile. 'Crazy kid, that Felix. And Josh, what a character,' I say out loud. 'Designer my foot,' but I find myself going down on the floor to touch the muslin. With my fingers, I measure the distance; maybe another inch larger or even an inch and a half on the armholes. The urge to find scissors and clip the armholes to the correct dimension is overwhelming, but I glance up at the only clock in the house that seems to be working, and I see that I only have an hour before the shop is due to open. Time enough for a leisurely bath and later, after work, maybe for fun I'll experiment on the pattern. In my mind I try out different fabrics. I can see the coat in elegant black velvet or champagne-colored satin . . . I imagine it over and over – I'm hooked.

I lie lazily in a warm bubble bath and notice that for the first time, the window isn't full of frost. It must be warming up. Earlier, in the kitchen, I saw that the snow has stopped; it must have quit sometime during the night.

I dress and put my hair up in a chic bun. Going through Myra's costume-jewelry box, I find a large pair of black Bakelite earrings and a nest of bracelets that match. With a tan knit sweater dress and the bold jewelry, I look fashionable; I look like a New Yorker. With this outfit, I have no need to change downstairs.

Felix isn't scheduled to be in today – she has more exams – but Clarista will be working sales, and even on the days that I have worked alone, there have been no problems; whatever came up, I handled it. I must remember to switch the phone through as of now. Disappointingly, not one of the realtors has returned my call. Business must be too good. Hard to imagine in the dead of winter.

I grab my coat, purse, and the keys. I almost forget the cat – not fair to leave Rogue out all day. I open the window and call, 'Rogue! Here, Kitty, Kitty.' I start to unlock the bars when I notice them, perfectly clear, large, man-sized footprints in the smooth blanket of snow, footprints that lead right up to my window.

I look down below the sill and see something black. It's the cat, his head twisted almost all the way around; someone apparently has broken the poor creature's neck. I gasp with shock and slam the window down so hard it cracks one of the panes of glass. Shaking, I go to the phone to call the police. Where did I put Lieutenant Burke's card? I can't find it, so I call Information and then dial the number of the police station. A brusque voice answers, 'First Precinct.'

'Lieutenant Burke, please,' I ask, my voice cracking with nervousness.

'He isn't in. Can someone else help you?'

'I'm not sure.'

'Who's calling, miss, and in reference to what?'

I give the officer the particulars and I'm told patiently, 'I'm sorry, miss, but policework doesn't include investigating the death of a cat.'

'You don't understand, it's on my roof. The cat was killed on the roof.'

'You might want to call the Humane Society. They might be able to help.'

'No!' I shout, anger now joining my fear. 'I need Lieutenant Burke – he knows all about this matter. He asked me to call if anything happened.'

'Then call him on his private number, miss.'

'I can't find his card. Please connect me.'

'I can't really do that,' the officer objects, and it finally dawns on me that I'm making absolutely no sense at all.

I start over. 'This is Trini Woodruff on Charles Street. My mother, Myra Dunhom, was murdered here several weeks ago and today someone killed my cat.'

'I remember that case. I'll beep Lieutenant Burke now, but in any event someone will be dispatched to you right away.'

In less than ten minutes, the buzzer rings and on the answerphone I hear an officer's voice. 'It's the police.' I buzz him in and open the top door to see two uniformed policemen coming briskly up the steps. I notice that Tonto is gone and has neatly folded his covers.

I lead the officers to the kitchen, where they open the window, but they do not touch the metal bars. Both lean out and observe the footprints and the dead animal and I hear one of the men saying to the other, 'We better wait for Forensic,' and with that they close the window. I hear their whispers, 'Woman . . . roof . . .'

I offer coffee, which they refuse, and both men stay in the kitchen until the buzzer rings again and I admit Lieutenant Burke, who briskly asks me to wait in the living room. Within minutes, more officers arrive.

I can hear men going back and forth in the hall and can tell by the draft that the window is now open and they are probably out on the roof terrace. I sit down on the floor and nervously pick at the pins on the muslin pattern, trying desperately not to think of a stranger in the dead of night walking on my roof terrace, a stranger who might have been here before, the stranger whose strong hands have now killed my innocent cat. What does he want, this man who lurks on my roof in the dead of the night?

In an attempt to distract myself, I continue to pick at the pattern. The neckline, I think, is okay; a cowl neck works perfectly on this coat; once more, I try to decide which fabric would marry well with the design. It would be interesting to try it both ways, in a soft fabric and in a tighter weave material that would give it more form. I continue playing with the pattern, forcing myself not to think about Rogue. Buttons, I muse, what sort of buttons would be good?

I start when I hear Lieutenant Burke's voice. 'We've taken casts of the footprints, Mrs Woodruff. Fortunately, like before, there was a base of ice under the snow, and we got some perfect prints. We should be able to be accurate on the size and even the make of the shoe.'

'Oh, that's good,' I say, and rise to face the Lieutenant. 'How on earth would someone get up on the roof?'

'It's not *how* that's important,' the Lieutenant says soberly, 'but *why*. Getting up is no great feat; the roofs here are close together and there are partial fire escapes everywhere.'

I nod, for I have never been out on the roof. I haven't wanted to, especially after I knew that was where Myra died.

'My men are leaving. We need to take the animal for tests.'

I wring my hands helplessly. 'I don't want to think they will just throw him in some trash can, but I have no idea where I can bury him.'

The Lieutenant goes off to arrange things, but returns shortly. 'Please sit down, miss.' I do and he begins telling me the facts. 'As best we can tell, the tracks indicate that the prowler was on the roof between two and three a.m. last night. Did you hear any strange noises – anything?'

'No, I went to bed around twelve. I heard nothing.'

'It's too soon to be certain, but the size of the prints seems to be approximately the same as the ones left out there on the night Mrs Dunhom was killed.' He pauses. 'Of course, it's not the same shoes; we have the others at the station, but we should know pretty quickly the size and make of these.'

He reaches in his pocket, unwraps a peppermint and offers me one, which I refuse. 'Habit,' he finally explains. 'Ever since I stopped smoking.' He leans forward and almost shouts, 'You're in danger, miss! We don't have enough staff to offer you protection.'

'But the windows here are all barred. I should be safe, shouldn't I?'

He looks up. 'That's a skylight. This is a fourteen-foot ceiling . . .' He pauses.

'Can it be opened?' I ask.

'No, but who knows what goes through these crazies' minds.' He sucks thoughtfully on his mint. 'Do you have anyone that could stay with you, or someone you could stay with?'

Quickly I think of Felix. 'I'm not sure.' But I know I will never ask her.

'Well, I'd better be getting back to the station. We'll be working on this.' He rubs his hand over the stubble that is beginning to peek out. 'Those animal shelters have dogs; they bark and let you know when someone's around.'

'I'd feel bad doing that; I'm not sure how long I'm staying in New York. I'm just trying to wind up all my mother's affairs – the shop, the building . . . I've inherited it all.'

'The shop – you're not working down there?'

'Yes, I have been.'

'Alone? Are you working there alone?'

'Yes, on some days I am.'

At that point, the Lieutenant gets very firm with me. 'I don't believe you understand. You're in real danger. It could be that whoever killed Mrs Dunhom is back, and you need to think real hard. Is there anyone here in New York who would wish to harm you?'

'No, I barely know anyone, just a young girl, a fashion student who worked the store with Myra and has been working with me now, and the lady who cleans the shop – she's been in Myra's employ for years. I really don't know anyone else; just clerks in the local stores, waitresses in the restaurants, the homeless guy downstairs.'

'Tonto?'

'You don't think he—' I stop myself.

'Oh no, he's too out of it to be a threat, but we do know he slept in the side passageway at times. We hoped he might have seen something that night, but . . . He seemed real jumpy like he might have, but drunks are unreliable.' The Lieutenant rises to leave. 'By the way, did anything occur to you in the shop or in the house, or did you find anything in her things that you felt was unusual?'

'Yes, I did. I found a Xerox copy of a cashier's check dated a week before she died. I wondered what she might have bought for such a large amount; it was ten thousand dollars. I thought it strange that there wasn't a name on the check.'

'We already followed that up. It turns out she cashed it herself, which is puzzling. We thought she might be being blackmailed, but we couldn't find a connection. Of course, she didn't have any of the components that a blackmailer usually works with. She wasn't married and you say she hadn't been in close contact with her family. No, a blackmailer usually has information that he can pass on to the nearest and dearest. We eventually ruled out that angle.'

'I see.'

'Now you take my advice and get someone to stay with you, or stay somewhere else. And don't, I stress *don't*, hesitate to call if you see or hear anything suspicious. Meanwhile, get a dog!' He winked at me. 'I'm serious. They know a lot quicker than we do when someone's about.'

'Thanks.' And I see him to the door.

'Dropped your cover,' he calls up the stairs. 'Want me to bring it up?'

'No, that's all right,' and I wonder why I didn't mention that I am allowing Tonto to sleep in my hallway.

I'm uncomfortable in the apartment now, and I feel terrible about the cat. Strange that only yesterday we talked about how changing names can mean changing destinies; I should have left him just plain 'Cat'.

I pace the hall. Finally, unable to decide what to do, I put on my coat and go downstairs. Neither Felix nor Clarista is due in today, but I am restless so I open the shop and within minutes a man comes in and lurks around the racks; he seems to be fingering the lingerie and watching me with sideway glances. It suddenly occurs to me that I am alone with him in this cavernous store and the counter is way back here, not visible at all from the street.

Quickly, I walk to the front of the store and begin rearranging the displays in the window. I am extremely relieved when two girls walk in and ask to see the 1940s dresses. I walk them to the right area and they begin sliding dresses along the racks.

'Too boring,' I hear one say. 'I want the Rita Hayworth look – crepe with side drapes.' The girls continue their commentary as they examine the dresses and I, with a great sense of relief, go back to the counter, only to almost fly out of my skin when from nowhere the man sidles up behind me.

'Can I try this on?' he whispers, holding up a black formal with diamanté straps. Wordlessly, I point towards the dressing room and he disappears behind the curtain carrying his treasure.

I drum my fingers on the counter, willing the girls to stay, and am relieved to see that they don't seem to be in any hurry. Now they are deciding if maybe they should look at the racks of the 1950s garments.

It is only a matter of a few minutes before the man reappears furtively at the counter and says, 'I'll take it.' I wrap the dress in tissue as he counts out money from a large wad of crumpled bills. 'Thank you.' Again he only whispers, and I wonder if that is his normal voice or whether it's just that he doesn't want to be seen purchasing a woman's dress.

I hope with all my heart that no one else will enter the shop, and as soon as the girls decide they haven't found anything just right today, I lock the door after them and turn the sign around that reads Closed.

CHAPTER FIFTEEN

Willie walks back and forth, watching the door to the shop. He noticed her when she first went in, but a man entered shortly thereafter, so he had to wait, and it was bad luck that two more people then entered. He's cold as he paces and he pushes his hands further down into the pockets of his shabby tweed coat, where his right hand throbs persistently; that Goddamned cat scratched and bit him in several places. That had forced his final decision. He won't strangle her; killing somebody that way takes too long. He has brought the knife with him – that should be quicker. He has to do it now, today, tonight. Carlos was right; he thinks he's being followed. He doesn't want to think about who really hired him. He has no idea how many hands the woman's picture passed through before he received it. No, he hasn't a clue who put her on the hit list.

His head throbs and he knows the money is dwindling fast. He has to do it; he has to kill her soon.

Suddenly the two girls come out of the shop. He springs into action and dodges and darts among the cars on the narrow street, but when he reaches the pavement in front of the store, she has locked the door and is turning the sign to indicate it is now closed.

He pauses and their eyes meet. She seems younger than the photograph. Too bad, he wanted her to be older. He wishes she had a hard, used-up look about her, but she doesn't; she is fresh-faced and pretty.

He sees his own reflection in the glass – his tousled hair, his face covered by a two-day stubble, his clothes rumpled and ill fitting, and he knows if he knocked she wouldn't open the door to him. So instead, he looks down and pretends to study the red and white Valentine window. Behind the glass he sees the lights going out and before she comes out, he has sauntered down to the corner. He'll play it by ear. He'll watch to see where she goes now. He can follow her.

She comes out onto the street, looks both ways, raises her arm, and in a minute she is in a taxi being whisked away.

He walks back to her building and checks the passageway again. There are only two side windows and both are barred. He knows from being on the roof last night that there is no way in there. He even climbed up to the next level and found the skylight, but it is no good. The ceiling in the place must be fourteen feet high. If he crashed through it, he'd break every Goddamned bone in his body.

Tonight he simply has to find a way in. He can wait now; maybe she'll come back soon. If so, he needs just a small window of opportunity – the right moment to hustle her unseen into the side passage. After all, people are killed on the street in broad daylight all the time.

He walks to her doorway and looks up and down the street before he turns to examine the door to the flat. It is an old one, the original door to the building. It is wood. He rattles the doorknob and can tell by the sound that there is only one lock. There's probably another door inside, up the stairs, but he has to chance it that it's made of wood also. It seems logical that if the bottom door hasn't been replaced by a metal one, then the top one won't have, either.

It's getting colder. His feet are wet from stepping in icy puddles and are almost numb now. Through the pounding in his head, he tries to remember where there is a hardware store, but can't. But he knows that over on Houston there is a junkstore where he can find a chisel or something he can use to force his way in through the door tonight.

CHAPTER SIXTEEN

I find that independence has a down side, for now I really have no one with whom to discuss my concerns, my fears, my half-formed hopes for the future. It's Sunday, so I don't even have the distraction of opening the shop.

I think about the future. What will I do once the property is sold? It's very similar to being a lottery winner, for one day I am an ordinary married woman with ample funds, yet once the sale is complete, I will be independently wealthy. What do they do, these people whose lives change overnight? Travel the world, buy a new flashy car, trade one house in for another? The options will certainly be there, but none of them excite me.

I want change, complete change. I want to find something I can be passionate about, and already I know what it is. I want to be part of this world of design. I deny my interest to Felix and I've never even mentioned it to Jeff or Cindy. Why am I so secretive about it? I examine my motives. Is it because it was Myra's, or is it because I doubt my own ability? I've basked in Felix's compliments, but she is a very young girl, eager and excited with her beliefs that anything is possible, but then I remember Josh Wainwright's compliments and the thing he has arranged – my toile. Am I only a distraction for this jaded, sophisticated man, who wants to prove to this powerful city that he is still a mover and shaker and can make New York sit up and take notice of whoever his eyes have focused upon? If so, then again I have been fortunate, for if I have the courage to choose this thing that I finally realize I do want, I know I can call on his help.

But there are so many other pieces to this puzzle. There are Jeff and Cindy. Jeff certainly wouldn't consider leaving his work in Denver, and Cindy, I'm convinced, would be overwhelmed by this fast-paced metropolis and would probably hate it here. I experience a shiver of fear when I think of the other missing pieces to the puzzle – Myra's murder, the dead cat, Lieutenant Burke's caution that I might be in danger . . . all these concerns I lock away, for there is no one, absolutely no one, that I can talk to.

Sunday is a day I am beginning to dislike. In the distance I hear church bells ringing. I could have gone to church, for there are a number of them nearby, but that is an activity I haven't practiced since Myra left. I do remember the Sunday School I attended when she was still there. I liked it, the stories, the parables, the singing of hymns, the coloring books where we could make Baby Jesus a blond, or a child with black curls. We could fill in the Wise Men in every color offered in the crayon box. I remember all the pleasantness of that Sunday School, but I am not sure it gave me faith. Even though I prayed, it was lists I offered to God in those innocent days. Please, God, let me have the red bike in Sears' window. Please, God, fix Daddy's legs. Please, God, let that terrible man with the black shoes go away. Please, God, take Cindy back . . . He hadn't answered me then. Would He hear me now?

I close my eyes and in the bare kitchen, I say aloud, 'Help me, please help me, for I don't want to hurt them, Jeff and Cindy. I love them both. Please, God, find that man who killed Myra. Please, God, help me with my life. I want to do this thing; I need to try. Let me do it and let me do it without hurting anyone.' I pause. 'Please, God, forgive me for that – you know, what I did to Cindy. I never meant to hurt her. I never thought it would, but now I'm not so sure.' And I stop myself, for I believe in a divine being, but this childish concept of a Santa Claus God, writing down everyone's request list, makes me feel terribly foolish. But I have said them out loud, my concerns, and I feel better, as if there were really someone there in whom I could confide.

I finish my coffee and feel the need to go out and see people, if only strangers gathered here in this big city. I know Houlihans has a Sunday brunch, so I dress and go out into the sun-filled morning, avoiding the puddles where the snow is rapidly melting.

At the restaurant, the waiter finds me a small table in the corner. I am studying the menu when I hear a female voice ask, 'Mind if I join you? It's so awkward when you're alone.'

I glance up; the woman looks familiar, but I can't quite place her. 'No, I don't mind.'

She pulls out the other chair and sits. 'We don't have to talk if you don't want to. It's just . . . most of the time eating alone is okay, but,' she looks around, 'Sunday brunch is different – families, dear friends.'

I nod in agreement and she refuses the offer of a menu. 'I usually do the buffet.' That sounds good, so I follow her to the long table and we fill our plates.

Seated, silently we begin eating, and then something about her jogs my memory. 'The commercial, did you get it?'

'Commercial?' She frowns.

'I'm the lady from the vintage store, "Repeat Performance". Didn't you buy a Fifties dress from us?'

'Oh yes, I did, and I bought the platform shoes that matched. I sure did.' She paused, took a bite of her food, chewed thoughtfully, then said, 'No, I didn't get it, but I've been to at least five more auditions since then. I didn't get those either.'

'I'm sorry,' I offer.

'Yeah, so am I, and I just keep thinking of my little brother and his pithy sayings. Whenever he writes, he never fails to say it.'

'What's that?'

'"Don't worry, Lola, when preparation meets opportunity – *zap!!*" I've been prepared for years, but this guy Opportunity – I haven't run into him yet.'

'If that saying has a grain of truth in it, then I'm really in trouble, for I haven't prepared at all.'

'Oh, you an actress, too?'

'No, I'm an artist, but since coming to New York and working in my mother's shop, I suddenly realize I really want to design clothes.'

'Good luck. I hope you make it,' she says generously. 'By the way, I'm Lola Rivers.'

'That sounds like an actress.'

'It's genuine – that's my real name. I know everybody up here seems to change their names, but I didn't think I needed to.'

Suddenly I think of Rogue. I changed his name and that certainly changed his destiny.

'I'm Trini Woodruff.'

'If you use the name Trini, that sounds like a designer.'

'Do you think so?'

'Yes, I do.'

I thought it odd. Here we were, two complete strangers, discussing things that were really important to us. This would never have happened in Denver, but here in New York, it seemed perfectly natural. I debated with myself and then decided maybe I should mention it. It couldn't hurt. 'The girl who works for me is a firm believer in name changes – something about numerology, names adding up to certain numbers. She's always talking about famous actresses who changed their names. She says it also changed their destiny.'

'Yeah, I've heard of that.'

Boldly I go on, making suggestions to this stranger. 'Well, since you haven't had any luck being Lola, maybe you should think about changing it.'

'Maybe. I went to that psychic on Eleventh Street when I first came to New York, but she's bogus. My roommate warned me about that. I was spending good money to hear compliments, stuff that never does come true. Ever been to one of those psychics?'

'No, I'm afraid not.'

'I don't blame you, it's a waste of money, but I guess there are some genuine ones somewhere. You do hear about the police using them sometimes on difficult cases.' She stops, realizing she might have ventured into sensitive territory.

The waiter clears our plates. 'Dessert cart's out,' he informs us. We both shake our heads no.

'I love that New York cheesecake, but I don't dare,' Lola says, patting her flat stomach.

We linger, both of us reluctant to part with a new acquaintance, for it's hard to find a friend in this large impersonal city. We each pay our check.

'I go your way, my building's right on the corner of Charles Street,' Lola says, 'but I'll probably be moving soon. One of my roommates is getting married and the other one's giving up. She's going back to Dubuque.'

'Are they actresses, too?'

'Yeah, but I wonder, can you call yourself an actress if you can't get any work?'

'I don't know. Can I call myself a designer if I only sketch and never really sew a dress? I can't even sew,' I admit.

'You oughta check out the *Annex*. They offer all kinds of classes.'

'Where is the Annex?'

'Oh, it's not a place, it's a paper that tells all about the different classes that are offered in lots of different venues around New York.'

'I think I will look into it. It can't hurt.'

And as we cross the street, Lola says, 'There's one, in that box over there,' and she jogs over, lifts the lid, and returns handing me a paper. 'I should look into it myself and see if they have any speech classes. When I first came to New York, I spent hours in elocution classes to get rid of my Southern accent and damn, here they are auditioning for a new soap opera, and three of the main characters are supposed to be from the South, and for the life of me, I can't talk that way any more. Those elocution classes really worked.'

We pause in front of the windows of 'Repeat Performance'. 'That Valentine window is really pretty. Your windows are always good; I enjoy looking at them. I do love vintage.'

'Thanks. The girl who works for me does them. She's good.'

'Yeah. Well, bye, it was nice talking to you.'

'Same here. I'm sure we'll run into each other again.'

'Probably will,' Lola agrees.

I search my purse for the keys to the flat and before Lola raches the corner, she turns back, calling, 'Trish, wait!'

I pause and watch her walk toward me. 'Like I said, my roommates are both leaving. You wanna exchange numbers? Maybe we could take in a show, go out to eat. It's no fun eating alone.'

'No, it's not,' and I reach into my purse for a scrap of paper to write down my phone number. 'By the way, it's Trini, not Trish,' I say.

'Oh sorry, I knew it was something unusual. How the heck can I expect to get a job with a memory like mine? I'd only flub my lines.'

I smile and we exchange bits of paper.

'Call me,' Lola urges, 'any time.'

'Me, too, and stop in the shop when you can,' I offer.

'I will. I promise.'

CHAPTER SEVENTEEN

On Monday, Clarista calls early to tell me her youngest child woke up with a high fever and she can't come in to work. It's Felix's day off and I don't relish working alone, so I make up a temporary sign informing the public that the shop will reopen on Tuesday.

I need to distract myself, so I decide to go uptown, travelling by bus. The slow-moving public transport will give me a chance to see more of New York, what's missed in the swift bouncing taxi rides here. Amazing that the city has so many potholes, or the cabs have such bad springs! I find the bus ride as pleasant as I had hoped. Diversity, of shops, buildings and people, is the key word and I'm lulled into a sort of contentment.

When I realize we are approaching 57th Street, I rise, as I do want to see this street of exclusive fashion shops. I've dressed warmly, so the cold is refreshing. The elegant expensive shops are fun to look in. I pause in front of Chanel's window. The mannequins still wear the designer's classic suit in bright colors for spring. How unbelievable, that twenty-five years after her death, her clothes are still so avidly sought after!

I go inside the shop and over to the display to see a classic black collarless suit trimmed in white braid. It's accessorized with a long chain, Chanel's signature look in jewelry. The chic saleslady approaches me. 'May I be of assistance?'

'Not exactly. I am merely wondering about the price range of Chanel suits, this classic style.'

Expertly, the sales clerk flicks the price tag. 'This one is four thousand, four hundred dollars, but they start at three thousand dollars and go up from there depending on the fabric. That's the boutique label, of course.'

'Of course,' I reply, imitating the affected speech of the clerk.

I finger the necklace. The chain is substantial enough and the red and green paste stones combined with faux pearls are of good quality, but to me the price seems outrageous for costume jewelry. I browse through the scarves and handbags, the signature look that is re-created in every color in the fakes on Canal Street.

I leave the shop and move along the busy street, stopping next in front of Jean-Paul Gaultier. One outfit in his window is a stunning ensemble. I can see the influence of Mother Russia in his design. The peaked hat is fur-trimmed, the pants of the gray trouser suit are tucked into high boots, and the graceful flowing cape is edged in darker gray faux fur. The spirit of the Tatars lived in that window. To myself I acknowledge this genius of design.

I peer into the shop and then look in the other display window, where I see another trouser suit designed with an exaggerated silver cone-shaped bra. I grin: designers must have fun, too. Only a high-profile rock star could wear that outfit and get away with it! But it is designed with a sense of humor, I can see that.

I find it odd that I can remember so much of Felix's rambling talk about all the famous designers.

The wind whipping through the canyons of Manhattan is making me feel chilly, so I turn northward and decide to have tea at the Plaza.

Outside again, I look across the busy avenue and see F.O.A. Schwarz, the enormous toy-store. In the pit of my stomach I feel queasy; the thought of babies fills me with guilt. I'm not ready; the time isn't right. I can't explain it to Jeff, or even to myself. I feel like I am waiting for something to happen in my life, but even now I'm not sure what it is.

I know from the guidebooks that Manhattan is an easy city to navigate. The avenues run north and south and the streets east and west. As of now, I have ridden only one bus and I haven't tried to figure out the subway, but I don't have to. I'm rich. There is money, plenty of it!

I raise my hand and the wind tugs at my scarf. Instantly, there is a chorus of honking horns as the yellow taxi cuts across four lanes of traffic to pick me up.

When I enter the flat I hear the phone ringing. I grab it before the tape comes on; it's Jeff.

'Hi, hon, how's the progress?' he asks hopefully.

I bite my lip. 'Is Cindy there?'

'No, as a matter of fact she's not and I really wanted to talk to you when she wasn't here.'

'Is something wrong? How is she? Did something happen at that job you got her? I'm not sure that was a good idea,' I ramble on.

'Whoa, slow down, Trini. Nothing's wrong, she's just fine, she's great. In fact, hold on to your seat, she's out right now with a young man.'

'Who is he? Where'd she meet him?' I ask.

'It's okay, he's a film student, a real nice guy. She's been helping him straighten out his grants.'

I let out a brief sigh. Maybe it'll be all right. Jeff seems able to help her where I couldn't.

'But more about Cindy later. For now, what's going on up there? You sound funny.'

'God, Jeff, I should . . .' and unexpectedly I begin to cry. All the fear that I have held back comes tumbling out.

'What is it, Trini? Should I come up there?'

'No, don't come up here, I'll work it out.' And in that minute I decide to tell him the truth. It's too hard holding all these secrets in. 'I found out Myra didn't die a natural death.' I pause; it's difficult to go on.

'I know you mentioned before that the lawyers said she had died from injuries sustained in a fall.'

I need to share the burden of this frightening knowledge with someone so badly. I take a deep breath. 'She was murdered, Jeff. She was pushed or thrown off her roof terrace.'

'Jesus, that's terrible! Did they catch the person?'

'No, although the police tell me they have clues – casts of the man's footprints on the roof. I've no idea if they have anything else, that's all they've told me.'

'My God, Trini, are you in danger? I could be up there in the morning!'

'No, no, Jeff, I'm fine,' I lie. 'Why would I be in any danger? I hardly know anyone in New York. The police are trying to find a connection, a man, someone she was involved with. They feel he stayed at her apartment. They're looking for someone she must have been in a relationship with.'

'Wow, she was murdered – it's so unbelievable,' he says, still shaken. 'That must really hurt you, to know that.'

'Yes, it does. I told you before we knew absolutely nothing about Myra. She only wrote those brief notes once or twice a year, and what she wrote was a total fabrication, just lies and more lies. Why, when going through her things, I found two sets of divorce papers and one death certificate. Up here, she was married three more times. Thank God my father never knew about this. It would have killed him. Big Jack never stopped loving her.'

'I'm sorry, hon, this must be terribly rough on you. How can I help?'

'By just being patient and by taking care of Cindy,' and in that moment I decide not to mention the second set of footprints on the roof, or the dead cat. Why worry him!

'Trini, please set your mind at ease. Everything's fine here. I know I'm being a bully with your sister, but it's for her own good. She cut her hair, bought some clothes, and with her contact lenses, she looks terrific.'

'She has contacts? It sounds like you've brought about miracles. Cindy with a job and going out on dates. I'm so grateful to you.'

'That's not all. She's agreed to see a psychologist, a woman I know called Lynn Winston, from college. I think you met her once?'

'The name's familiar, but I can't seem to place her.'

'Well, all this progress came about as a result of a nightmare that Cindy had the other night. I heard the sound of her crying and whimpering. It was so sad I went to her room and she was white as a ghost, bathed in sweat, and shaking like a leaf. She was truly terrified.'

'The attic – was she dreaming about the attic . . . ?' My voice trails off. 'She's had those nightmares since she was a child.'

'I figured as much. I know you told me what happened when you were children, but it must still be bothering her a great deal, so I figured it's time to see a professional and get some help.'

'You're right. I did try to get her to see someone in the past, but she wouldn't hear of it. She always said she'd never be able to talk about it. With the stutter, she felt she couldn't say it, wouldn't be able to. You know how she gets when she's upset.'

'That's what's so good about this therapist, Trini. She has expertise in neuro-linguistic programming. I've heard a lot of good things about that field and her.'

'I'm not sure what it involves, but if you think it'll help Cindy, I'm all for it.'

'Good. I didn't want you to think I'd taken over and was bossing around the whole family.'

'No, of course not.'

We fall into a silence until suddenly Jeff says, 'I miss you.'

'I miss you, too,' I answer, but I'm not sure that that's totally true.

They hang up and Jeff looks around the dark house. He couldn't tell Trini what her absence is bringing about. No, he can't face it himself.

There in Cindy's bedroom that night, with the soft magical lamplight shining on her face, he had held her close, patting her back, comforting her, and slowly he became aware of the scent of her fresh skin and the feel of her breast resting against his bare chest. Out of the kindness he meant to offer her, he felt desire and lust rise within him swiftly and unexpectedly. The tendrils of her hair brushed against his cheek and it was electric. He rocked her gently like a child, but he became aware of her totally as a desirable woman. He crazily yearned to touch his lips to the soft place on her neck that was so tantalizingly close. He must have imagined it, but he thought in the sound of her measured breath and the heat of her body that she felt it, too, the animal attraction. Ashamed, he pulled away, untangling her clinging arms from around his neck.

'Better?' he asked.

She nodded wordlessly, but her eyes were downcast, for she could not bear to look at him.

He needed to leave the room, her presence, so he could still his thoughts and calm his body, so he went downstairs to get her a glass of warm milk.

The next morning at the breakfast table, it was he who couldn't look at her, for he felt deeply ashamed. In the five years of his marriage, he had thought of her only as a sad younger sister, but she had changed so much that now these new thoughts about her would stay uppermost in his mind.

It was then that he persuaded her to see the therapist and reluctantly she agreed.

After I hang up from talking to Jeff, I still sit at the telephone bench. Absentmindedly, I rub the phone, a tactile connection to my husband. Home is so far away and Jeff, like my father, always makes me feel safe. He is so capable, so sensible; he is a man who gets things done. Why, it is miraculous what he has managed to accomplish with Cindy in such a short time! The job, and the fact that she is dating – and now he has convinced her to see the therapist, Lynn Winston. That in itself is wonderful.

Then the wayward thought grips me. The treatment can't help Cindy if she holds things back . . . One has to be totally honest with a therapist. My face suddenly burns with shame. What would the woman think if Cindy told her what *really* occurred between us, not only once, when it could be excused as a mistake, but so many times? She would think us perverts, or at least completely deranged, the pair of us; and I am the older sister, I'm the one who led, and Cindy only followed. I know it was my fault completely because I started it, but like an addictive drug, it was Cindy who could not get enough.

CHAPTER EIGHTEEN

Tuesday dawns and Clarista is still absent. She calls to let me know they are all down with the flu, but I have Felix for at least today and Thursday. I need to keep the sale going. A lot of things have gone, but the basement is full of back-up stock and more accessories are packed in the shop's various closets.

Before we open, Felix and I run up and down the basement steps, filling up the half-empty racks. It's fresh stock for the sale and it helps, for the regulars find new things to buy.

Around lunch-time, Lola pops in. 'Hi, how's it going?'

'Just great, but they're running us ragged. I'm short of help, my other lady's home with the flu.'

'I could help,' Lola offers. 'It's not as if I have anything better to do. I haven't even heard from that sluggish agent of mine for weeks.'

'But this kind of work . . . I'm not sure . . .'

Lola interrupts. 'Oh, I'm not too good to do sales. I've been perfume display at Macy's, security guard at Dunn-Reade; I've even done market research on street corners. If it's a question of pay, I could take merchandise instead.'

'No, it's not about pay. I wasn't sure you'd want to do it.'

'Oh, I'd be delighted! I'm going crazy in that apartment. The phone doesn't ring, my roommates are gone, and that ditsy agent hasn't booked an audition for me for ages.'

So I take her over and introduce her to Felix.

'Didn't I see you on the Advil commercial?'

Lola brightens. 'Yes, I did that one.'

'For a commercial, I really liked it. I loved that set, looked like real 1950s, and you, you looked like you could've been a younger version of June Cleaver.'

'Think so? I bought the dress here.'

'I'm not surprised. We've got great stuff,' Felix says with her intense sense of loyalty.

Suddenly Lola looks down at her favorite pair of raggedy jeans. 'Should I put something else on?' she asks.

'Please do. Just choose something you feel comfortable with.'

In ten minutes, Lola emerges from the dressing room in an oriental dress, with her dark hair piled up and held in place with an ivory comb.

'You look stunning. When are you gonna serve the tea?' Felix quips.

Lola laughs and enters the fray, and within minutes she is totally at ease, helping a customer find a Fifties black suit in a size nine.

The day drifts by. Late in the afternoon, Felix takes me aside. 'Clarista's right, there *was* more evidence of mice. Can you bring the cat down?'

I start to tell her what happened when a customer interrupts us. 'I've been looking for ages. Can someone please help me? I need a cloche hat, something dark.'

'I'll show you where we keep them,' and Felix leads her away.

The day is hectic and the three of us can barely keep up with it. When the door is finally closed, we change back to our regular clothes and even Felix is shoeless, rubbing her feet. 'Remind me not to wear those five-inch heels – they're real killers. I don't know how they stood it, walking around in those all day. I'd be crippled.'

'Thanks, everyone,' I say. 'We all worked so hard today. If anyone wants dinner, it's on me.'

'Oh Trini, thanks, but I really can't,' Felix yawns. 'I've got so much reading to do for class I'll be up half the night as it is. It's pizza delivery for me.'

I turn to Lola, but she says, 'I rarely turn down a free dinner, but although I hate to admit it, I must be getting old – or perhaps I've been sitting around on my tush for too long. This honest day's work has knocked me out, but I'll be in tomorrow if you need me.'

'I sure do. Thanks.'

Felix offers, 'I know with Clarista out, you're strapped. If I can, I'll be in late afternoon. If not, I'll see you Thursday.'

We stand outside talking for a few minutes and then Felix asks Lola, 'You live in the neighborhood, right? I thought you might know who the creep is.'

'What creep?'

'That guy on the corner. I meant to tell you, Trini, I noticed him last week. He looks like he's watching the shop.'

When he glances our way, Felix lifts her finger toward him in a rude gesture. He spits in the gutter, pulls his hat further down on his face, and disappears around the corner.

'He sorta looks like that flasher that used to hang around NYU,' Lola says.

'Whatever, you gotta be rude to these creeps to let them know you're not intimidated,' Felix advises.

'If we see him again, maybe I should call the police. That Lieutenant Burke, he's been very helpful.'

'Good idea,' Felix agrees.

I hate to see them go, for suddenly I don't want to be alone. I take my key and go up the stairs to my lonely apartment. It seems cold, so once again I fiddle with the thermostat. This old furnace seems to be very temperamental.

I shiver and go out to the kitchen to find a snack. I'm not very hungry, as we had a big lunch. I can't bear to look at the barred window, so I draw the blinds, shutting out the night. 'Poor cat,' I say aloud, 'you didn't deserve that,' and I find myself missing the companionship of the animal. Who could do such a cruel thing? Suddenly I lose my appetite and I begin prowling though the apartment to convince myself once again that there is no way in. The door is bolted, the couch in place; I re-check all the windows, knowing full well that they are all barred, and last of all I go into the living room and look up at the skylight, where a cold crescent moon slides behind a bank of clouds. I think of the strange man on the corner and feel afraid.

But surely no one wants me dead so fiercely that they would chance leaping through the panes of glass in the skylight and breaking their neck. Surely not!

However, in the bedroom I make certain that the phone by the bed is plugged in and, pushing and straining, I manage to move the dresser in front of the door. I fall into bed fully dressed and pull the covers up to my chin. I must be coming down with something. I think of Clarista and the flu, as I can't stop shivering. That must be it, I'm probably coming down with the flu.

I want not to think about anything – the prowler, the shop, Jeff or, most of all, Cindy. I want my mind to be blank and still as a mountain lake, and I find it, the thing that will chase all bad thoughts away; I begin designing the gown to complement the opera coat. On and on they fly, the pictures in my mind –

separates, tops, jackets . . . and the images float until I finally fall asleep.

The haunting sound comes as only one long, anguished cry. I sit bolt upright in the total darkness and lift the phone to hear the comforting buzz of the dial-tone. With my heart pounding wildly, I turn my head from side to side, searching the night for sound. The hum of the old refrigerator is an undertone and in the distance I hear the whine of car tires in the streets. Maybe I only dreamed it, that eerie sound.

Stealthily, I climb out of bed and tiptoe toward the bedroom door. I stub my toe and my *Ow!* of pain seems as loud as a scream. I place my ear alongside the dresser as best I can. I listen, but all is quiet. After a time, I crawl along the floor in the dark, searching for something that might serve as a weapon. Finally my hand comes upon the umbrella stand and thankfully I reach for what I know is a long black antique umbrella.

Slowly I make my way back to bed and sit upright against the headboard with two pillows behind my back, facing the direction of the bedroom door. With one hand resting on the telephone and the other clutching the handle of the umbrella, I sit terrified, listening out for any misplaced sound. Somewhere a clock ticks and I find this curious, for I'm not aware of any in the apartment that really work. In the awful stillness I can hear only the steady rhythm of my own heartbeat and the sound of my own labored breath.

After a time I calm down, but still on guard I sit motionless with the only two weapons at my disposal in my hands.

I can't tell if it has been an hour, or two, or even three, but when gray light appears under the door and the shadows of things in the room start to be seen, I think it must be morning. Still I wait until the tempo of the city picks up, and when I hear the honking of horns, I know it is truly morning.

On limbs grown stiff, I walk to the door and begin slowly scooting the dresser away. A few inches at a time I move it, then I pause to listen, then pushing and straining, I move it again. When finally the doorway is clear, I open the door just a fraction and listen, but there is no unusual sound. Finally I poke my head out into the hallway, look both ways, then tentatively step out, still brandishing the umbrella.

I tiptoe out into the apartment, where nothing seems disturbed, but a cold draft skitters along the floor, letting me know that something is open – but what? Finally I move the couch from in front of the apartment door, and as I open it, the draft is explained.

Downstairs, the front door is ajar, but Tonto is still there asleep, huddled under his covers. This will not do, I say to myself. He was told to be gone in the morning, and if he is so careless he can't even remember to close the door, then I must take back my offer and not permit him this small kindness of sleeping indoors.

I march downstairs angrily, intending to wake him, but as I draw closer I see dark stains on the duvet, and when I lift back the covers, a terrified scream escapes me, for he seems to be sleeping in a river of blood.

I step out onto the street and hysterically call, 'Help! Help! Help!' and in a matter of minutes someone is wrapping a warm coat around the rumpled clothes that I slept in and I am leaning against a firm shoulder that some stranger has offered, hearing only the sound of people murmuring softly until the wail of an ambulance splits the morning air.

Still I hide against the stranger's shoulder until finally I hear someone say, 'He's still alive.' Only then do I leave the safe cocoon of arms and look, to see Tonto strapped firmly on the stretcher.

'What's happened to him?' I ask as I stagger after the stretcher, which is being placed in the waiting ambulance.

The attendant answers, 'He's been stabbed!' and then out of the throng of people, an officer steps forward as he recognizes me from the incident the other day. He sees the utter terror in my face and kindly places his arm under my elbow for support.

'Was he trying to break in?' he asks gently.

Dumbly, I shake my head no, and with a firm hand he propels me back to my doorway and leads me up the steps one by one. I slump onto the couch and sit numbly until I hear the sound of footsteps in the hall, and when I see Lieutenant Burke standing before me, I let go and begin sobbing, trying to release all the terror I had suffered this night.

I take the clean white handkerchief he offers me and wipe my eyes. 'Is he going to die?'

The Lieutenant shrugs. 'It's too soon to tell, we don't know anything yet,' and he lowers his voice, for he hates himself for having to ask me anything in the state I'm in. 'Can you tell me what happened?'

His question surprises and sobers me. 'I have no idea!'

'Try to think. Was this guy trying to break in? It's within the law to defend oneself, in that case.'

Understanding dawns. 'You think I . . .' I stop and in my hysterical state I begin laughing. 'You think . . .' I can't even continue for mirth.

He reaches over. 'Try to calm down, Mrs Woodruff. We need to understand what happened here. Your door was jimmied and Tonto was found stabbed at the bottom of your stairwell. That's a fact. Now we need to know exactly what happened.'

'I don't know,' I say helplessly. 'I don't have any idea.'

He sits in the corner chair and patiently turns his hat over and over in his hands. He remains quiet, but with a nod of his head he indicates to the officer standing in the doorway that he should leave.

'Tonto didn't jimmy my door; I gave him a key.'

The Lieutenant controls the sudden rush of anger he feels at her stupidity and calmly asks, 'You gave him a key to your apartment?'

I look up. 'No, I gave him a key to the hallway. It seemed inhuman to let him sleep outside in this weather.'

He rubs his chin, and reaches for the ever-present peppermint in his pocket. He runs the scenario through his mind – Tonto asleep in the hallway, someone forces open the door, and finding him inside, struggles with him, and stabs him. 'That it.'

He rises abruptly. 'You're in danger, miss. Someone is evidently stalking you and I don't think you understand how serious this is. You must leave here today. You're not safe here.'

'By why? Why me?'

He shrugs. 'I can leave an officer here for the day until you pack up, but I cannot stress strongly enough that you can't stay here!'

'Where have they taken Tonto?'

'St Andrews. He's lost a lot of blood. The attack must have been some time in the middle of the night. Did you hear anything?'

'Yes, I did, but I thought I was dreaming. I heard only one noise. It seemed to be . . . not a scream . . . I can only describe it as a desperate cry, someone crying out.'

He snaps open a small notebook. 'What time?'

'I don't know. I was so frightened I locked myself in the bedroom, and none of the clocks work.' I look up at the Lieutenant. 'Why would anyone have all these clocks, all these broken clocks?'

He shrugs. 'I can't imagine.'

Lieutenant Burke speaks to the officer and the policeman remains standing at attention in the hallway.

'Please sit down,' I urge the policeman. 'No use standing.' And I go out to the kitchen to make us all a cup of coffee.

I shower and put on fresh clothes, and when I re-enter the living room, I find a well-dressed older woman seated in a chair opposite the officer. She stands and offers a gloved hand. 'I see I've come at a bad time. Pamela Walsh, Manhattan Estates Realtors.'

'Yes, I'm afraid you *have* come at a bad time; we've had a terribly serious incident occur.'

'Yes, I know. The officer told me.'

I desperately feel the need of distraction, so I offer, 'Well, as long as you're here, I guess you could look around.'

'Good.' Pamela Walsh follows me silently through the rooms until we get to the kitchen. 'I'm sure you're in no state to talk about the property right now—'

'No, I really need to, for I have to move today; it seems I'm in some sort of danger.'

'Oh, you poor dear. This city can be crazy.'

She sits down in the kitchen. Out loud Pamela clicks off like a computer the negatives and positives of the flat. 'It's a good size,' and as she speaks she scribbles information into her notebook. 'It has great light, nice high ceilings, the skylight's an attractive feature, the marble mantels in two of the rooms are inlaid, it's possible the fireplaces could be reopened. I noticed that under the rugs, the floors are parquet in good condition. The bathroom is very tasteful; the kitchen's not, but the size is good. What's out there?' she asks, pointing to the kitchen window.

'A roof terrace.'

'May I see?'

'Of course,' and I rise and open the window for her.

'Would you mind if I checked it out?'

'No, of course not.' I fetch the key and unlock the bars, warning her, 'It could be icy out there. Be careful.' And I watch as the woman steps out and gingerly walks around the roof terrace. I don't follow her. I have never gone out on the roof and I don't intend to now – ever.

Re-entering the kitchen, Pamela sits down and scribbles further information in her notebook. 'There was something in my mind about this property – something recent.' She looks toward me for the answer, and when none is forthcoming, she suddenly remembers. 'A woman was murdered here, a month or so ago. Am I right?'

'Yes,' I answer, hoping she won't ask any details.

Being a competent businesswoman, the realtor doesn't pursue it. After all, people forget quickly, and out-of-towners would never know at all. 'What do you intend doing with the shop?' she asks smoothly. 'It's harder to sell a building with an existing tenant unless, of course, it's a prime tenant on a long lease.'

'I'm selling it all out,' I say firmly, and for the first time I know this is what I must do. 'So it will be offered as a vacant shop with an apartment above.'

'Good, it makes it a lot more saleable to offer it that way. Incidentally, my dear, I didn't get to see the room across from the bathroom. I noticed the doorknob was missing.'

'Oh, it's not a room. I think it's a closet, but I never actually got it open,' I say.

'No, my dear, it's a room, I'm sure.' Pamela stands up and goes out to the hallway and looks up and down. 'This apartment is a sought-after E design with rooms jutting out from this main hallway – it's much more desirable than a straight-through railroad flat. Do you have a chisel or a screwdriver – something we could lever it open with?'

I look through the kitchen drawers and finally come up with a rusty screwdriver. 'It's the only thing I could find.'

Pamela takes it from me. 'This should work,' and she begins digging into the door around the lock. 'Damn,' she mutters and stops to suck a broken fingernail.

'I'm sorry,' I offer.

'Not your fault,' and with a final firm dig, the door flies open.

Amazed, I follow her into the large room. 'I've been here for quite a while now, and I never realized . . . I assumed it was a closet.'

'This is good,' Pamela mutters. 'Adds at least twenty thousand to the value.' She goes over to the windows, where the shades are drawn. She tugs and they roll up with a flapping sound.

My heart skips a beat when I see what the room really is. It's a faithful re-creation of our attic in Denver. Under the pair of windows an old treadle sewing machine sits, covered with dust; in two of the corners, dressmaker dummies wait; and on the shelves bolts of material of every description and color are stacked neatly.

Faded with the years, a calendar from twenty-five years ago is the only decoration on the wall. The picture on it is a placid scene of the snow-covered Rockies.

I feel breathless with panic and a sense of sudden loss. Speechless, I follow Pamela back out to the kitchen, where again she sits and scribbles down numbers and, on her calculator, totals them up. 'Let me see,' she muses, and quickly she re-writes more figures, then adds them up. 'I'd say – and I've been in the business a long time – since you're moving anyway, I'd clear out all the furniture, tear up the carpets so the parquet floors show, get a crack cleaning crew in here, paint the entire place off-white . . . You could – you don't have to – open up the fireplaces, but I would.' She stops and looks over at the terrace. 'The trees out there are nice; maybe a few potted evergreens would help, too. Same goes for the shop – clear it out, paint it a light color and you have a real winning property here. I'd say you could expect to get three to four.'

'Three to four hundred thousand?'

'Dear, dear girl,' Pamela laughs, 'you're talking Manhattan commercial, residential, on a prime street in the West Village. Three to four *million*.'

Once more I'm speechless.

'Of course, on the days I'm showing the place, if I were you I'd have an apple pie baking in the oven. Cinnamon and sugar – it gets them every time. Works in the Midwest and does even better here.' Pamela pauses. 'It's a brutal city out there and folks gotta have a safe nest. Do you want to list with my firm? I know we can sell it.'

'Yes, I do.'

'How long do you think it will take you to make the changes I suggested?'

Suddenly I'm in a hurry too, so I say confidently, 'A week, maybe two, for the flat. The store longer, I guess. We need to sell off the merchandise.'

'Good, here's my card. Call me to let me know when we can sit down and sign the listing papers. I do need an exclusive listing.' Pamela wants to have it settled right there and then, but feels it would be too pushy. 'What's your phone number here?'

I give it to her and explain I won't be here after today, but she writes the number down anyway.

I walk her to the door. 'I'm sorry, I've forgotten my manners. I'm Trini Woodruff.'

This time, unexpectedly, the older woman embraces me for just a moment. 'It will be all right, my dear, you'll see.'

This statement from a perfect stranger brings tears to my eyes; it reminds me so much of my father. He, too, was caring and compassionate to strangers.

Feeling motivated now, I walk back to the kitchen, drink a glass of orange juice, sit down and call Sotheby Auction Company. After doing my best to answer their questions on what sort of merchandise I have, they agree to send someone out in the morning.

'Trini! Trini!' I hear someone urgently calling me.

I rush out to the hall to see Felix with Clarista and Lola trailing behind. 'What's happened?' she demands. 'The door's smashed in and there's a policeman in your living room.'

I lead all three of them into the kitchen, where they listen in stunned silence while I tell them of the cat's demise two nights ago and what happened to Tonto sometime during the night.

'Is he dead?' Felix whispers.

'I'm not sure. He was alive when they took him to St Andrews about an hour ago.'

'My God, he saved your life,' she marvels.

'That's right,' I say. 'I didn't realize it before, but of course he did. If he hadn't been there, whoever it was would have gotten in the flat.' I shudder.

'And there was me telling you that you had to be mad to give him a key to your hallway,' Felix sighs. 'Never listen to me again when I give you advice, except about certain stuff.'

Even in this horrible situation we all manage a small nervous laugh, but Clarista looks the picture of gloom as she clutches her large pocketbook. 'I told you, leave names be. The cat, now he's gone, and what are we gonna do about the mice?'

'Get another cat, I suppose,' Lola shrugs.

I know I won't be getting another cat, but I haven't figured out yet how I can tell them that very soon the shop will be closing. They must realize it, for the stock is dwindling rapidly.

'I'd like to call the hospital to see how he is,' I say, and while Felix looks up the number in the phone book, Clarista bustles about putting on the kettle, for today she has brought us a treat – some very special herbal tea.

'This tea,' she promises, 'cures flu in two days, guaranteed.'

The hospital gives out very little information, just that the man listed as Tonto is in a serious condition and is allowed no visitors at this time. As we drink our tea silently, I ask God over and over to please let him live. Strange, I'm calling on God again. Somehow I must help the Indian; I owe him his life, for he saved mine.

I sip my tea and am deep in thought, but I have to keep moving forward. 'Can you carry on without me, ladies, for I really need to make some calls. I have to find a new place to stay today. I'll ring up some of the residential hotels. Lieutenant Burke is right, I'm in danger here, yet I can't understand who would want to harm me, or why.'

Felix shivers. 'It's awful. Why has the world gotten so bad?'

Clarista says one word: 'Drugs.' We nod. 'TV.' Again we agree. 'Violent movies.' Then she gets up and wipes the table. Each of us is caught in our own private thoughts, and none of us has the answer to why the world has become such a scary place.

When they leave, I get out the Yellow Pages and with pen and paper in hand, begin looking through the lists of hotels. But before I can make the first call, the telephone rings.

'Mrs Woodruff? It's Pamela Walsh here.'

'Yes?'

'I heard you mention that you needed somewhere to stay. I don't know why I didn't think of it at the time, but I have the ideal place for you. It seems like a perfect match!'

'Really, where is it?'

'It's a loft – a fabulous place, so roomy you could land a plane in it – and it's as safe as a bank vault.'

'It sounds good. When's it available?'

'Right now. The owners are currently in Europe. It's one of my listings and it's really up for sale, but I do have the option to rent it out for short periods while it's on the market. It's in Soho – a great area. I must admit the streets do get a bit deserted at night, but the place itself is totally secure – there are alarms fitted to all the windows and no access, even without them.'

'It sounds perfect. How do we proceed?'

'I could meet you there – shall we say in an hour?'

I agree and quickly scribble down the address. Downstairs, detectives are dusting the door for prints and a gloved technician with a small pair of tweezers is picking up bits of paper, cigarette butts, and debris that has blown against my doorway.

I duck under the yellow police tape and go into the shop, where Felix is already serving a couple of customers. Lola's helping a lady who's trying on hats and Clarista is busily dusting the shelves. When the customers have left, I ask if the three women can stay until closing, as I have to go look at an apartment.

'Gee, I wasn't thinking. You could have stayed at my place,' Lola says.

'Thanks, but I do need something for at least a couple of weeks.'

'No problem. If you decide you want to, the offer stands. I told you my roommates are gone, at least one of them, and the other one will be totally moved out by the weekend.'

'Thanks again, but I'm meeting a realtor about a place in Soho.'

Lola nods. 'Look – you have the full crew today. If you don't need me to work, I understand.'

'No, please stay, Lola. There's so much to do I can use all three of you, honest!'

'Good, I really enjoyed it yesterday and you never can tell – I might run into somebody in the business who could give me a lead part or something.'

'That's possible,' Felix says. 'We do get actors, and agents. Why, the other day we had Josh Wainwright in.'

'Shame I'm not taller, I might try modeling,' Lola muses.

I go outside, intending to hail a cab, but Lieutenant Burke waves to me and comes over. 'Where are you going, Mrs Woodruff? You really must take precautions. As I told you, I feel you're being stalked.'

'I know, but I'm just going over to see about an apartment. You made it clear that I shouldn't stay here another night.'

'Good, I'll have one of my men drive you over. That way you can be certain you're not being followed.'

'Thank you. That's very kind. I do appreciate it.'

He nods. 'And if you're working in the shop, I suggest you hire one of my off-duty policemen.' He reaches into his pocket for the ever-present notebook and writes down the number of the off-duty police available for work.

I get into the unmarked police car, and the driver carefully zigzags up and down the streets of the Village for a full fifteen minutes, to throw off any tail, only to finally arrive at a street some seven or eight blocks away. Here exclusive art galleries sit next door to large expensive boutiques, and on every corner there seems to be a fashionable restaurant which even at this early hour is filled with people lunching.

At Prince Street, the driver finally stops. His caution has been successful; it isn't possible that anyone could have followed us.

Near the corner, I notice Pamela Walsh standing in front of a massive building that at one time had been a warehouse. Its façade resembles a fortress; all of the display windows have been cemented in, but with sheets of concrete that sport attractive sea-life designs, and the huge steel double doors that are covered with copper have an abstract pattern hammered into the soft metal. It's an impressive building.

Smiling, Pamela says, 'I told you it's a bit like a bank vault. But a pretty one.'

'You're right, it's everything you said.'

She uses both keys and when the double doors open, I see a two-story airy entrance hall; inside the staircase a spiral of shining steel going up to the living space above. The owners must love the sea, for even in the stairs I see the design copied from nature, the gracious curve of steps dwindling smaller and smaller as they reach the top, a giant chambered nautilus in steel.

We find ourselves in a massive room. In the very center is a huge boulder of crystal balanced atop a copper stand. The eight terminals of the fantastic rock catch the light and send rainbows into the cracks and crevices of the elegant room. The couches and chairs seem dwarfed by comparison.

'How big is this apartment?' I ask.

'Oh, let's see. This, the main room, is four thousand square feet, the bedroom is thirty by twenty-four feet, the kitchen is galley style and it's twenty by twenty, and the apartment has two full baths. Both have Jacuzzis.'

'It's stunning,' I manage.

'And safe,' Pamela finishes. 'And also, it has very good light, for the owner replaced all the skylights with these,' and she points up to the ceiling, which seems very far away. I see eight narrow panels of glass in strips slanting across the ceiling. 'They don't open,' Pamela continues. 'It's solar heat in industrial-strength glass; they don't break either. The owner's an architect and he used only the finest of materials.'

'It must cost a fortune.'

'The selling price is. The rental . . . well, I have your listing on your building and you seem to be in immediate need of accommodation, so I'll shave the price a bit.'

We come to an agreement that I can lease the place month to month with the proviso that Pamela can show the property to prospective buyers with ample notice.

I sigh wearily. 'Cheer up,' Pamela urges. 'You have a fabulous apartment at an unheard-of price . . .' She pauses. 'And most of all, you'll be safe here.'

I nod in agreement.

'Come on, I'll drive you home to get your things.'

The move was accomplished in less than an hour, for I took only two suitcases full of clothes and one box full of important papers.

Now, with three people to work the shop, I was free to call and meet with workmen. Sotheby's auction evaluator arrived and he committed to take the bed – it *was* rosewood – several art glass lamps, and a piece of bronze statuary for their spring auction. The estimates on the pieces were truly impressive.

In his free time, the local kid from the pizza parlor moved everything else down to the shop and with the flat empty, the company I hired to renovate it moved at a swift pace.

Pamela Walsh was delighted and began showing the property, while I settled into my new surroundings, feeling as satisfied as if I had designed this place myself. I am a person who is influenced by beauty and from my childhood in Denver, I always feel the need of raw empty space. It calms me.

Everything suddenly feels right. I have Steve, the patrolman, drive me to the shop each day and return me to the loft each night. I am taking care, I feel in control again, and the fear I felt at the apartment has dimmed.

I have tried on several occasions to explain to Jeff exactly what has been happening here. I list the progress that I am making, for now the flat has been cleared out and the auction company has taken the bed, which turned out to be a very valuable piece. And I've moved the 1950s furniture down to the shop and a few pieces have already sold, and the other things I donated to a local charity.

I explain to Jeff that the flat is now freshly painted, the floors sanded, and both fireplaces reopened. The realtor has shown the place twice to prospective buyers and one of them seems very keen on it. But I get the impression he's not really listening to me as I talk about the shop's fifty-per-cent-off sale, and when I tell him that I should be done with everything very, very soon.

The only thing I cannot bring myself to mention to Jeff is that I have been working frantically on designs. A fuzzy, incomplete idea has taken root in my mind. I now know what she meant when I read Myra's notes of *I must find it*. Even Clarista has said it: 'Those damn designers are always looking for it.'

It is the genius in the cloth they are looking for, the design, that elusive thing that makes the garment a work of art. I understand that now – how in cloth, with the right talent, you can create a sculpture in the unorthodox medium of fabric. As an artist, this fact interests me – no, it grips me! It is such a challenge, for one has to design within the constraints of a three-dimensional female form that does not change.

Now Jeff no longer asks me when I will be returning to Denver and I am grateful, for I know I cannot give him an answer.

[illegible]

[illegible]

[illegible]

[illegible]

[illegible]

CHAPTER NINETEEN

While emptying the closets in the shop, I suddenly remember Cindy's request for a few things that had belonged to Myra. She had asked me this when I first came to New York and I had completely forgotten. Now I have the time, so I begin my search, trying to guess what she would like. The old Cindy I could have predicted, but the one Jeff now describes, I can't be sure of.

First I select a necklace, a double strand of genuine pearls with a ruby clasp. I pick through the jewelry until I find a perfect set of button pearl earrings of the same pink cast. These would be perfect for day wear. Again I search the cases: the pair of pearl drop earrings are not as perfect in color as the others, but they are stunning and meant for evening, so they will do.

I also take a cameo set in a delicate gold frame, and an amethyst cross on an intricate Victorian chain. I pick more earrings, blues and greens, for I know if she ever wears them, they will be perfect with her eyes. I select plain sets of gold tone in Trifari, necklace, earrings, and bracelet. I choose the same idea in silver by Monet. I go on selecting, choosing a whimsical brooch of a Scotty dog, a bracelet of Bakelite dice . . . until I have gathered up a mound of diverse jewelry before me.

Like a giant grab bag, Cindy will love it, unwrapping all the secret gifts. I can almost see her face, so eager, full of surprise. She'll love it, this treasure hunt. I begin looking for a box or something to put it all in. I pass on the jeweled music box with the ballerina on the top; it is so like the one Myra had in Denver that I almost believe it *is* the same one. I search until I find the perfect box. It is purple velvet with hand-painted violets on the lid.

'Where's the tissue paper? Are we out of it?' I ask.

'No, I'll get some. We have more in the storeroom,' Felix answers.

'I'll wrap them for you,' Lola offers.

'Thanks. They're for my sister. She wanted some of Myra's things.'

Lola looks through my untidy piles. 'She should love this stuff. It's great.'

'I hope so. And now I've got to find a few other things.'

I dart in and out of the cubbyholes of the shop until my arms are full. I have retrieved the Schiaparelli bust perfume bottle that is still half-full. I also take a Bakelite bag that has a poodle and the Eiffel Tower on its lid. I find a red velvet dressing gown and a black crepe formal with slip straps, and then I see it lying atop an unsorted box from upstairs, the oriental gown with the chrysanthemum design. I'm not sure why, but I put it in the stack to be sent to Cindy. It has a connection to her, even though she will never know it. It is the same robe that attended at her conception.

Once I have started, I know I should look for what *I* wish to keep from my mother's past.

I know for sure that I want Myra's books. She had collected volume upon volume – some of them rare – on the famous designers, those who changed social history. There were books on Poiret, who liberated women from their Victorian corsets, Vionnet, whose bias technique gave the female form a gracefulness that in the past it had never possessed, and Chanel, who taught women they could be elegant and comfortable at the same time. In those volumes, Myra had searched for a common denominator, the clue to their genius. It eluded her. It would probably elude me, too.

Apart from the books, I take a few more couture pieces and examine them closely, staring at the tiny perfect stitches, the interfaces; such detail, such perfection in places no one could really see. The cloth of these garments that were fitted for only one woman in the entire world was certainly special! A couture garment was cut, fitted, ironed and stretched, and refitted again several times until, molded with perfection and total precision, it must have been worn by the lucky woman with the confidence of a second skin.

In principle, I wish that my interest were not there, for it was Myra's calling and I do not yearn to follow in my mother's footsteps. But try as I will to dampen it, it will not die, this interest . . . and that's when I receive a phone call from Josh Wainwright.

When I overcome my surprise, I remember to thank him for the delightful present of the toile. I had sent him a thank you note earlier.

'I had hoped you'd like it. I also hoped it would fuel the fire.'

It feels odd that this stranger knows me better than I know myself, and I find myself answering him truthfully. 'It did, Mr Wainwright. I find the fire blazing. I've been working on designs.'

'Good, good, bring them along, and your little girl's invited, too – my partner in crime. That's for Wednesday dinner, about eight-thirty. It's 243 Park Avenue – the penthouse.'

I scribble down the address. I couldn't refuse the invitation – I wouldn't have known how.

His phone call is followed by one from Pamela. 'I know you've got your hands full, but when do you suppose you can clear out the sewing room? The paint looks good, the floor's nice, but it ruins the whole effect, that one room still being so cluttered.'

'Oh Pamela, you're right. I've been meaning to do it and I'll get on it today.'

'I don't want to be premature, but I do think that couple from Miami will be making an offer soon,' Pamela says.

'Good, I hope so.'

I leave Felix, Clarista, and Lola in the shop and go upstairs to the transformed flat. It is spacious and light now, the parquet floors gleam with wax, the windows sparkle, and in the kitchen the painted cupboards have been stripped down to their oak finish and look wonderful. All in all, it is a desirable living space. I almost feel nostalgia about it, for in my mind's eye I can see it freshly furnished and know it could be done so tastefully.

The extra room has lost some of its eeriness, for all of the things have been shoved together on one side.

I begin folding bolt upon bolt of cloth when in the corner I come across a large wrapped package. When I tear it open, I find a note addressed to my mother.

Dear Myra,

Don't ask me how, but I found forty yards of it. It hasn't been around for twenty years, but this warehouse in Tribeca had just one bolt of it. Once you touch it, you'll be able to see why they call it 'the fiber of the gods'. It makes silk feel like burlap. This vicuna is the most precious fabric in the world.

Be careful – make something spectacular out of it.

Barney.

I run my hand over the tan cloth. The author of the note was right – I have never felt a fabric so soft, so luxurious to the touch. It would be such a great pleasure to design a suit or a dress in this 'gift from the gods'.

I phone downstairs. 'Felix, can you locate Bruce, you know, Bruce from the deli. I've got some stuff upstairs that I need taken down to the shop. He likes odd jobs. Maybe he could do this on his lunch-hour.'

'Oh, I thought you had it all cleared out,' she says.

'It is . . . I did . . . except the one room where Myra had some cloth and a sewing machine.' I pause. 'I found a whole bolt of vicuna; it's simply gorgeous.'

'Vicuna? What's that?'

'Shame on you, a fashion student and you don't know vicuna. It's that incredibly expensive fabric they used a while back. It's made out of goat or llama hair. You know, those animals from the Andes.'

'Oh, is that the stuff they said Al Capone had all of his overcoats made from?' she asks.

'Yeah, I think so, and I also seem to remember some government scandal – I think it was in Eisenhower's time. Some of his aides got in trouble over gifts of vicuna coats.'

'Historic stuff, huh,' Felix muses. 'Okay, I'll give Bruce a call.'

I begin piling the bolts of fabric up in an orderly fashion. Then I find it – the sketchbook – my drawings from when I was a small child. She had saved it all this time, and I am touched. I see my drawing of a Christmas tree surrounded with presents, and I had drawn only three people – Daddy, Myra, and myself. That was before Cindy.

I leaf through the yellowed pages, remembering that I always wanted to be an artist and both my parents had been very complimentary and encouraging. Often the refrigerator door was decorated with one of my drawings. The pages of the pad are a vivid trip through my distant past, but on the last page of the art pad I find her note.

Trini,

I know someday you will find this. I can't say Dear Trini, for if I do, planes could fall out of the sky, drunk drivers careen out of control, and who or whatever picks the names for the lottery for terrible accidents might call your number. Even those tiny, invisible intruders, the germs who carry all manner of horrible disease, could suddenly find the address and zip code of Downing Street.

I think of those women in remote parts of the world like Asia who live with my same fears and name their children Teaspoon or Broken Cup. They know, as I do now, that an endearing name might attract the jealous gods.

Do you remember sitting on my lap in the window seat, always asking me to read? I even read those adult stories to you, for you begged me to. I'm sure you didn't understand about peoples in remote uncivilized places. I cried then for those ladies who named their children Teaspoon, but I understand their wisdom now.

I read you stories about women who shared their most precious things. I know you didn't understand, but you claimed you liked the sound of my voice reading on and on in those quiet afternoons, and you asked me to read over and over the story of the blind man who knocked at the door of the poor and ugly. You never understood my stories – I think you just liked sitting in my lap in that comfortable window seat, and my voice weaving strange tales caught your imagination.

I cannot help but wonder if, on 11 November, he had been named Henry or Perceval or Mark instead of Jack, if the strap would have held; if suddenly someone had called up to him and named him Edward, would the strap on that rig magically have held fast? I can only wonder.

In my imagination I give you and your sister many lives. I create happiness and health and talent and I enjoy you both in many ways.

But you must understand that that day, 11 November, transformed me like a whiteout in Colorado and I am snowblind. I see only the face of fear and feel the pain of my frozen heart. For I love him so much, I cannot watch. I love you and your sister so much, I cannot stay.

I need to become someone for your sakes – so that my desertion has meaning. For now, I reach out only to that which is inanimate; I chase that unknown quality called fame, but it eludes me, for I am not good enough. No coward ever is.

Forgive me,
Myra.

I stare down at the note and my tears drop and smear the ink until it is a smudged message, as smudged and confused as the words written there.

She asked for my forgiveness. A month ago – two weeks ago – I could never have given it. But now I have found pieces of my forgotten mother. I have dreamed of the Denver mall and root beer so sweet it brought tears to my eyes; I have relived the parachute game, and I remember only the good things. I can almost hear her melodic voice reciting stories – yes, stories I did not fully understand then, but loved. I only need the thread of her voice weaving, weaving me into a cocoon of safety in that time when the world was new . . .

'I do not completely understand, but I forgive you,' I say to the empty room. As I rise to answer the bell, I shift the bolts of cloth, they spill over against the old machine, ancient parts are jarred into action, and I hear the whir of the treadle as it goes back and forth only once.

CHAPTER TWENTY

It's on Friday that I accept Lola's invitation to have dinner; she has tickets for us to go on to an off-Broadway production of *The Glass Menagerie*.

'I almost got the part of Laura, but the director gave it to his girlfriend instead,' she tells me.

'That's too bad. Connections are always helpful,' and it makes me think of Josh Wainwright and the forthcoming dinner. I know I can have his help if I decide to pursue this newly hatched dream of mine.

We eat at the Gotham and I can feel the adrenaline of the clientèle.

'I like it here,' Lola says, 'it's always full of writers and actors. This room just buzzes with creativity.' And on the way to our table, she stops to greet acquaintances, and once or twice stoops down to exchange casual cheek kisses. 'I need to be seen out more often,' she murmurs. 'If you hide at home, everyone knows you're doing bad.'

'It could look like you're just too busy.'

'No, in this town, if you're out of circulation, it just means you're on the way down.'

I order lobster tail and it is cooked to perfection, but the salad, with its assortment of unknown greens, is a bit alarming.

We're both feeling mellow after the wine and when we reach the theater, Lola manages to persuade the usher to give us front-row seats.

'I just love Tennessee's stuff, don't you?'

'Yes, I do. It's uplifting somehow. I always end up feeling lucky, for I'm not as damaged as most of his characters,' I say, but as I watch the actress playing Laura limp across the stage, I begin to feel uneasy, for it makes me think of Cindy, and I watch with interest as the mother pushes and prods this daughter, trying to make her into something that she isn't.

Maybe I should have been more forceful with Cindy, more demanding, but at least in the play it doesn't work.

'Geez, her accent is terrible,' Lola hisses. 'They don't talk southern in St Louis.' And I can see her agony at watching something she could have done so much better.

Afterwards, we walk along the now-quiet streets. 'Wanna stop for coffee, or is it too late?'

'I don't mind,' I say. 'Or we could always do tea.'

We find a small intimate grill and when we're seated in the booth, Lola wails, 'I don't know why I do this to myself! I go see other actresses in parts that I could have had, and honest, Trini, I know I could have been so much better.' She stops talking, for she has noticed. 'You seem upset, too. What's wrong?'

'It's my sister. When I see or read stuff about afflictions, it upsets me.'

'Oh, I'm sorry. Is she crippled?'

'No, nothing like that. She has, or I should say *had*, a bad stutter. She's better now, but it makes me think about how unhappy she was when she was growing up. It made her extremely shy.'

And we sip our tea and nibble on raisin cookies and discuss other Tennessee Williams plays.

Outside, we look up and down the streets, which are pretty deserted now; no cabs are in sight. As a man walks by mumbling something under his breath, Lola says, 'I forgot, you didn't use the policeman tonight. Was this safe, your going out like this?'

'According to Lieutenant Burke, probably not,' and we continue walking towards 5th Avenue to find a taxi.

Lola gives the driver my address. 'It's best you are dropped off first. I'll wait until you get in.'

The cab waits until I open the double doors and I am inside. I am home. I am safe.

CHAPTER TWENTY-ONE

The day of Josh's dinner arrives. Felix and I decide to wear vintage and I pick a 1940s waist-hugging suit by Adrian. He seems to be one of my favorites. It is a soft beige with wonderful Bakelite buttons. I find a pair of dark brown suede ankle-strap platform shoes with a matching clutch purse, and Felix talks me into a turban that hides my hair completely.

The ensemble is totally dramatic and I feel it would be outrageous to dress like this for anyone but Josh Wainwright.

'Now that you've picked a suit, I've got to wear one, too,' Felix wails, and she runs about the shop frantically.

'Wear whatever you like,' I offer. 'Pick anything.'

'No, I mean we have to have the same style or we'll look terribly silly, and suits don't look that good on me and my feet are too big – none of the platforms fit.'

'Hurry up, Felix, Steve is supposed to be off work at five. I hate to make him wait, he's been such a comfort.'

I look towards the young policeman who has been working for me for the last couple of weeks. 'Sorry, we'll hurry, Steve, I promise, or we could take a cab.'

'No, no. Lieutenant Burke said I should drive you as always.'

'All right,' and I look towards Felix annoyed, for she should have picked out her outfit earlier.

'The Dior, it'll do.' She hastily grabs a stylish 1950s suit and a plain pair of black leather court shoes.

'We're ready,' and we dim the lights, lock the door, and begin our ride, which takes us up and down the maze of Village streets. As usual, Steve makes lefts and then quick rights to be certain we aren't followed, and then he walks us up to the door of the building when we arrive.

Inside my new apartment, Felix is beside herself. 'This place is wonderful!' and she walks up and lays her palms against the crystal.

'The vibes are fantastic in here!' She whirls around the large room. 'Oh Trini, buy it! I've never seen an apartment this large or this special.'

'Yes, yes, I love it, too. But all planes going west go to Denver.'

I show her the bathroom that she can bathe in and go to my bedroom, lay my clothes out, and begin running my own bath.

We dress and I feel somewhat like an actress. Is this what Lola's work feels like, I wonder. I suggest we could go out on Spring Street, where we'd be sure to find a taxi.

'No, you don't,' Felix warns. 'If Lieutenant Burke feels you need protection, you need protection. We'll call for a car,' and she proceeds to dial Courtesy Cars.

As we drive up 6th Avenue towards uptown, I feel compelled to ask Felix, 'Why do you suppose he asked me, or I should say *us*, to dinner? I find his interest in me a little unsettling.'

'Oh, it's nothing like that – he's gay.'

'I didn't mean romantic interest. I just meant I'm not that interesting, or at least no one in my past has found me so.'

Felix sits back in the bouncing car and in a minute replies: 'I know he loves finding protégés. Last winter his magazine did several pieces on a young and upcoming actress. He likes beating people to it – finding the next artist whom he thinks will somehow make a mark. I wish he'd take an interest in me.'

'But how do I fit in?'

'The design thing. He seems to see you as an up and coming young designer.'

'Oh that,' I say, knowing it is hopeless repeating that I have obligations elsewhere and it is unthinkable that Jeff and Cindy would move to New York.

At the penthouse, the door is answered by a Filipino houseboy who ushers us into the large living room, where the entire wall is made up of panes of glass. From the eighteenth floor, the city looks like a glittering puzzle laid before us.

Josh rises from the luxurious leather couch, strides forward and grips my hands. 'My dear, you look simply stunning! Joan Crawford couldn't have given it as much style.'

He leads us to the couches. 'Martinis,' he orders from the boy. 'They're back in fashion, you know.'

We sip our drinks and I can tell that for once Felix is so intimidated she is strangely silent.

Under the shaggy brows, Josh's dark eyes pierce mine. 'Have you found the fabric for your coat?'

'Not yet, but I have thought about it.'

'Good, good. Now about the sketches – have you brought them?'

'I have,' Felix speaks up, and I am surprised, for I hadn't realized she had carried in the portfolio. I had totally forgotten that he'd asked for them.

He picks up the folder, goes over to a table, switches on a bright light, and begins laying the sketches out side by side. He seems to have forgotten us and after ten minutes or so of silence, he turns to us. 'My collection – it's in there,' and he waves towards a room through a fantastic archway. 'Go on, you both could learn something.'

Holding on to her drink, Felix accompanies me into the room. The houseboy follows discreetly and works a row of light switches. Before us, in Plexiglas drawers of sorts, the garments are laid out.

'My God, it's a genuine Fortuny,' Felix whispers.

Silently, the servant walks up and pulls out the drawers so we can examine the garments closer. The pleated gown which Fortuny was so famous for is lying there. 'The color is so soft,' Felix marvels. 'I've never seen purple that is so beautiful.'

'That's because he only used natural dyes,' Josh says as he comes up to join us. 'He used South American insects for red, Brittany straw for yellow, Indian indigo for blue. This is one of the very first Delphos gowns – it's dated about 1907. He created this finely pleated garment with a pure Greek influence. His clothes were designed flat and were meant to be slipped over the head and fastened only with a drawstring or a tie. He made many variations of this dress over the years.'

Josh pushes in the drawer and opens the next one, containing a sumptuous brocade tunic over trousers – by Poiret. 'He was influenced by his visit to Russia in 1911 when he fell in love with Turkish and Persian costumes. He was one of the first. He loved designing trousers, soft billowing trousers, which were very new then, *très avant garde*.'

Josh pulls out drawer after drawer. Many names are new to me, but Felix, as the fashion student, is literally trembling with excitement. The names reel past – Worth, Vionnet, Mainboucher,

Hardy Amies, Charles James, Jacques Fath, Madame Grès, Givenchy, Dior . . .

'Last, but not least,' Josh pulls out the final drawer, '*Coco!* I met her once after the war,' and he touches the suit. 'This is one of the first – 1939. What an artist that woman was! You know she demanded comfort with elegance? She would make her mannequins stand for hours wiggling their arms and swinging their legs, to be certain that her clothes could be worn in utter comfort.'

'My God, the Metropolitan doesn't have a collection as important as this,' Felix marvels.

'But someday they shall. I intend to leave it to them. Now, which did you like the best, my child?'

Walking past the cases, Felix studies them, trying to make a choice. 'The Fortuny. I like the freedom of it and its classic lines and the color. It's fabulous.'

'And you, my dear, which did *you* like the best?' he asks, directing his attention at me.

'I couldn't decide that,' I answer truthfully. 'I can see the uniqueness in all of them.'

'Yes, genius is obvious – it shouts,' and he claps his hands. 'I'm hungry. Being the tour guide almost always makes me ravenous.' He rings a bell, and magically dinner is served.

'In honor of the lady from the west, I thought filet mignon,' he announces.

We sit at the long glass table while Josh makes small talk and then with a sense of regret says, 'Haute couture is a dying art. The Paris houses exist on licenses for the prêt-à-porter, the scents and the scarves . . . which is all that most people can afford, for the cost of one haute-couture piece can be more than the price of a new car. But design artists will always have the urge to create.'

We both nod and he looks at me and bluntly states, '*You* feel it. I can tell by the stroke of your drawing pencil.'

'In the face of such genius, it seems pretentious to even think about it,' I say.

'Never mind. That was yesterday – that sort of artistry is gone – but there is always the female form and the artist who must decorate it.'

'That was Myra's dream,' I say.

'And mine,' Felix speaks up boldly.

'Patience, child, your time will come.' He looks up. 'Coffee and Cointreau,' he orders the servant, 'in the living room.'

When we are seated on the couches once more, he tugs at his gray ponytail and seems deep in thought. 'Would you like to see your designs come to life?' Again his eyes bore into mine, questioning.

I sip the Cointreau, stalling for time so I can formulate a truthful answer. 'Yes, I would be curious and anxious to know if they worked.'

'Then it's settled. You must do it.'

Felix enthusiastically nods yes.

'I've explained this to Felix. Myra knew the components of sewing, but I haven't a clue. I don't know the first thing about it. I can't even sew on a button.'

He reaches over and gently takes my hands into his. He examines them closely. 'These are the first hands, my dear. Under that stylish turban you gave birth to the design, you've sent the message to these, the first hands. There are others who can turn your dreams into reality. Some designers cannot draw, some designers cannot sew – it's the original idea that has importance.'

Politely, I draw my hands away. 'I don't understand. It's very kind of you to have given me and my sketches so much thought and time, but they are not remarkable, I know that.'

He sinks back into the softness of the sofa. 'Oh, my dear, I'm an old man. I've traveled the world, seen many things, succeeded at many things, failed at some. I've led a decadent life and with this comes boredom. So now I play the game of power; I find the stars and talent in those who don't even know they have it. I enjoy it, finding that gem inside an ugly rock. I love it, astounding the other bored New Yorkers by *finding it first*. I'm the little boy who at the Easter-egg hunt always found the golden egg, for I will settle for nothing less.'

I finish my liqueur quickly and my head begins to swim.

'The lady at Parsons . . . Madame . . . what's her name?' he asks.

'Madame Opensky,' Felix says, and they begin talking over me, around me.

'I'll call her in the morning. She has that entourage of Europeans who are from the old school. She'd like to be featured in the magazine, I'm sure, and I'll promise her that.'

'Yes, of course,' and Felix understands the carrot he will hold out to Madame.

Finally, as if remembering that I am still there, he says, 'Pick nine pieces. I can arrange for the models – but the venue . . .' Again in thought he pulls at his ponytail. 'They are doing some offbeat venues these days, old warehouses, boat docks . . .'

Felix comes alive. 'Trini's loft is wonderful. It's huge! I think it was the old Haase warehouse.'

'The Haase warehouse . . . I know the owner, Foster. I believe he's in France. I've been there – it's ideal. A perfect venue.'

And in a heartbeat, it is settled. I am to pick nine designs and they are to arrange for the seamstress, and in only a few weeks we are having a fashion show where Josh Wainwright will introduce me to the Big Apple as his latest find.

Lieutenant Burke sits at his desk studying the papers. It doesn't make sense. Both shoe casts from the Dunhom roof are the same size – 10½ – yet the shoes are very different. The first set of prints was made by an expensive shoe which has been identified as a man's Gucci loafer; the label is worn out, but the cut of the heel convinced the technicians of this, and one or two other characteristics made it a given. They have these shoes in the lab.

The second set of prints from the roof, made on the night that the cat was killed, is from a cheap pair of trainers; the pattern on the sole identifies them as a label called *Runners* – an inexpensive import sold mostly at street fairs or in the row of shops on Canal Street.

The imprint depth of the trainers indicates a man weighing approximately 140 to 150 pounds, while the loafers indicated someone a great deal lighter. In fact, the imprint depth did not register anywhere on their scale, which means that it could have been a very small woman or even a child, wearing them. It makes no sense! Something important has been overlooked.

He drums his fingers on the desk as he flicks through the statements obtained from the two paid informants. Both mentioned that the rumors on the street were that there was a hit out on a woman named Myra Dunhom; someone a while back was looking for a shooter. The men named a couple of bars in the East Village where the rumors had started, but each one named a different place. Questioning the bartenders turned up nothing.

Lieutenant Burke goes over and over the facts. A professional assassin doesn't push a woman off a roof and then *place his shoes in her closet,* nor does a professional climb up on a roof looking for an unprotected window and leave the dead body of a cat.

The whole thing reeks of an amateur or a psycho! Myra Dunhom was not killed by a professional; he is convinced of that. And the incidents with the daughter point strongly towards a psychotic. They are by far the most dangerous criminals of all and a lot harder to catch, for no sane man can really imagine what motivates a man to stalk and kill a perfect stranger.

He gives some thought to the Indian. Tonto is improving; he is doing well in detox, but questioning him threw no light on the matter. He remembered nothing, only struggling in the dark with a stranger.

The Lieutenant sits back in his chair. He feels responsible for the daughter. It alarmed him in the beginning that she didn't seem to take it seriously, but now he can breathe a sigh of relief. He talked to her last week at the new place and it is a strongbox, all right. What's more, she took his advice and hired the off-duty policeman for the days she opens the shop.

He closes the file. Motive, he can find no motive, and without one he can't even get an accurate profile on the killer.

CHAPTER TWENTY-TWO

I justify my desire to do the collection. What can it matter now if I stay in New York a few more weeks, and I convince myself that I really do owe it to me to make this dream a reality. Later I will see if I can decide what to do next, but I will not think beyond that time and I see no purpose in explaining it to Jeff. I'm certain he wouldn't understand, for this is a completely new interest, one I never knew I had until coming here.

I no longer work in the shop, as stock has run down to the point where Lola and Clarista can handle it. So Felix and I begin haunting the garment district, looking for fabrics. She does not give an opinion, she only helps by telling me what she knows about certain materials. I choose bolts of different colors and weights and fabrics, for I'm planning on doing the nine different designs that Josh selected from my sketches. I am learning, and again I think of the vicuna. One suit Josh has selected would be perfect in this fantastic material.

I feel like a whirlwind caught between the shop, the garment district, and the loft, where I often work late into the night perfecting these nine important designs. Like me, Josh is in a frenzy of excitement, for this is really his event, too. If it fails, he will have orchestrated a tremendous flop, and others will suspect he has lost his golden touch, his ability to see into a crystal ball.

Josh sends endless faxes to Madame Opensky. She responds, and he checks and re-checks all the details: how many women to work, how many cutters, how many seamstresses, and one who can iron and stretch. He demands to see examples of their work and messengers are kept busy ferrying between the college and his office. He feels that I am lucky, for I have a perfectionist at the helm, and eventually he can teach me, should I decide to carry on.

It's late on Friday when Tonto comes to the shop. After drying out he is still feeling shaky, and he has trouble passing the many liquor stores in Manhattan. His mannerism of licking his lips every few minutes has become so ingrained that he cannot control it and it looks peculiar, like an annoying tic.

While he was recovering, Felix and I visited him several times in the hospital and after repeatedly thanking him, I found myself falling into an awkward silence. Both Felix and I wonder what his plans are, now that he is sober. We sense he has no plans, for it was over five years since he walked the steel beams in the sky like a talented circus performer, and how many wine bottles have there been since then and now? Now his hands visibly shake and he walks slowly, even though he has not yet turned fifty.

He stands before me clean and trim in a blue work shirt; at the shelter they also gave him a pressed pair of khaki pants and a leather jacket. 'I came to say goodbye and give you this.' He holds out to me three dirty crumpled envelopes; he is glad that they were still there in his grocery cart among the rags and papers.

'She paid me to mail them and I didn't. I think you should have them,' he says solemnly.

Felix draws a little closer, but I look so nervous that reluctantly she moves away out of earshot. At the counter, I seat myself on the high stool and frown as I look at the strange addresses on the envelopes. I open the first letter. My forehead creases into a furrow of concentration, as I cannot figure it out. My head begins to pound – *what does it mean?*

I open the next letter and the next. Quickly I put them in my purse. 'When did she give you the letters?' I ask.

'That night, the night she fell. I didn't keep my word. I meant to, but . . . but . . .' He stops and looks down at his hands.

'It's okay. Thank you, Tonto. No, your name's not Tonto. We never officially met. I'm Trini Woodruff and I don't know if you ever introduced yourself to my mother. Her name was Myra Dunhom. And now that we've met, it would be so nice to know the name of the man who saved my life.'

He straightens up and for a moment he seems proud. He hesitates, for it has been years since anybody asked or cared. 'John . . . John Sandaval.'

'That's a lovely name, John Sandaval, and I'm glad that you seem well.'

'Well, you know then, what they explain in the hospital. This was a sickness I had, such a strange sickness where people hate you, spit on you, blame you . . . If I had a cancer, would I be so despised?'

'I'm sorry. It's true. So many people don't understand this sort of illness. I don't know a great deal about alcoholism myself.'

He still stands awkwardly before me like a disobedient child, and I almost say, 'What are your plans?' But after five years of sleeping in doorways, what sort of plans could he possibly have?

As if reading my thoughts, he says, 'I'm going home.'

'Where is home?' I ask.

'Gallup, New Mexico.'

'You must give me your address.'

He nods and slowly writes down a rural route number. 'This is my cousin. He brings honor to the name Sandaval, for he designs beautiful Indian jewelry.'

I reach into the drawer. If only I had known he was coming today, I would have had more cash to give him. I don't feel I am insulting him, for I know he has no money and suddenly I have so much. I glance at my watch, but it is too late – the bank is already closed. But now that I have his address, I can send him more.

I press the wad of bills into his hand. 'That's all there is in the shop, but if you'll come back in the morning, I will have a lot more.'

'No.' He shakes his head.

'You must take this,' I stumble over the word, 'John.'

I look intently into his thin dark face. His eyes now are clear, but there is a sadness in them and I wonder if it will ever leave him.

He looks down at his awkward hands that are now holding the crumpled bills. He is no longer a man who can refuse charity. He looks off to a spot somewhere behind my face. 'I thought I'd go back someday, but not like this. No, I thought I'd go back with my pockets stuffed with money. I would have been generous to my sister, my cousins. It was big money they paid me, big money. I thought I'd drive cross country in a big red Cadillac. I thought I'd go back in style,' he says sadly.

'You couldn't help it,' I say. 'No one can help getting ill. But John, please come back in the morning. I can't think of any other way to repay you. You saved my life and it almost cost you yours; we both know that.'

He nods but I know he won't be back. He has enough money for the bus; Greyhound is good enough for the likes of him now. When he came to New York, his eye was accurate, his arms powerful, and his steps confident. The company paid for a first-class plane ticket for a man like that.

I walk him to the door. We shake hands, while Felix and Clarista only nod a silent farewell. I watch his tall figure disappear down the street until he grows smaller and smaller in the twilight.

He makes his way down to Wall Street and for a few minutes he stands looking up at his building. It makes him feel good to know the eagle feather is safe in the cornerstone where he placed it. He says his goodbye and heads for the subway that will take him to the bus depot.

The letters in my purse trouble me. I have to give them to Lieutenant Burke, for I don't understand what they mean. Suddenly I feel tired. It is exhausting opening the shop every day, going home each night accompanied by the policeman who was hired to be in the shop. We always take a circuitous route so we won't be followed and it makes me feel safe. And when I can, I stay up late redoing the designs until I know they are perfection.

I have to put these strange letters out of my mind for tonight, for there is nothing I can do with them now, and in the morning I will call Lieutenant Burke.

CHAPTER TWENTY-THREE

It was an ordinary bust, two junkies picked up on a street corner in the East Village scoring some crack.

It was the sort of thing the police on the beat would have chosen not to see – they'd have looked the other way, except this time it was on the corner of A Avenue across from a grade school.

There are so many cases like this that the police know an appointed lawyer will be down and the junkie will be back on the streets before dark. But today they get a break. One of the men arrested is Willie Butts, and he's crashing bad. 'I need a doctor!' he screams. 'I need a doctor! I'm sick, man, real sick.'

'All right, we'll see to it,' and the Sergeant puts in a call for him, but the public sector doctors, as usual, are running behind schedule and in a couple of hours Willie is sweating and hallucinating. At the station, they are familiar with Willie – he has been in several times. Same problem – drugs – only this time he was arrested before he had a chance to score. His joints ache and his head pounds unbearably.

He wails and beats the walls of the cell until his knuckles bleed. 'You're doing this 'cos you think I killed that woman. Goddammit, I need a doctor. I didn't kill that woman, I only killed the cat!'

Bells ring and the Sergeant, hearing this, puts in a call for Lieutenant Burke, who comes down within a hour. In the interview room, Willie squirms with discomfort and Burke feels the adrenaline rush; he is going in for the kill.

'Listen, Willie, the doctor's on his way. Things are looking up; you'll feel better soon. He'll give you something to smooth you out.'

'Look, man, I need it now,' Willie pleads as he scratches his arms savagely.

The officers stare at Willie as he squirms and scratches. 'Let's run through it quick,' the Lieutenant urges. 'How'd you get in, Willie?'

'Get in where?'

'Over on Charles Street.'

'I didn't get in,' Willie blurts out. 'There were bars on the window and that Goddamned cat, he scratched the shit outa me. That's the only reason I strangled him . . . biting and scratching. Oh man, when's that doctor coming?'

'He's here now, Willie, he's in the building, but we haven't finished talking,' the Lieutenant says, knowing how cruel this is.

'He's here? Get him, please! Please! Oh man, *please!*'

'Just a few more answers, Willie. You can get him in here faster if you answer real quick.'

'I'll tell you anything you want to know; just bring the doc in. I'm sick, I'm telling you, I'm real sick.'

'Yeah, Willie, yeah. Just tell me about the other night, the night you pushed that lady off the roof.'

'No, man, no!' And Willie backs up to the corner and begins crying. 'I didn't do that; I sure as shit didn't do that. I was there . . .' He stops, realizing he has said too much, and begins sobbing uncontrollably until the Lieutenant allows the doctor in. The latter gives him a couple of capsules that calm him down.

The Lieutenant reaches for a mint, offers Willie one, and then patiently begins to question him again.

Slowly Willie begins. 'I was there one night, but I was tripping.' He pauses. 'I thought I saw a woman up on the roof and she was talking soft to someone, but it was a still night, real still. There was a halo around the moon and all the streetlights, they blurred, and I thought I saw her float down – just float down soft as a snowflake, but I could be mistaken.'

'You saw her fall?'

'No, man, I thought I saw that, but I didn't. Carlos told me that woman is still alive and I've still got her picture from the man who hired me. Carlos was right; she *is* alive. I saw her myself.'

'Where is this picture?'

'Um . . .' Willie looks up at the lights. They are good, now; they have halos, too. He tries to think. 'Under the mattress in my room, or maybe in the Bible on the bedstand, or maybe . . .'

'Never mind, Willie, you can go back to your cell now.'

Lieutenant Burke dispatches a team of men to the sleazy hotel and they find the small snapshot of Myra Dunhom hidden in the light fixtures. Its edges are burned, but it's still clear.

Sleaze-bag junkie, the Lieutenant thinks. He is so out of it that he thinks Myra Dunhom and Trini Woodruff are one and the same!

It will be difficult, if not impossible, to find out now exactly who hired Willie to be the hit man. Generally it would pass through a bunch of hands until given out to the designated killer. In this case, they hadn't looked for a professional, just a cheap guy who might or might not do it right.

In his cell, Willie dozes. They've said they'll send him to the hospital – a drug rehab. He's happy about that; he doesn't want to be out on the street. The money is gone and he didn't do it, what they paid him to do. For now, he'll mellow out. That's all he can do.

The Lieutenant goes home disgusted. He is no closer to finding out who killed Myra Dunhom. Willie stabbed the Indian all right, but he insisted he was never inside Myra Dunhom's house, nor did he ever own a pair of Gucci loafers. He admitted he was given Myra's picture, her address, and one thousand dollars to kill her.

Now in jail under the doctor's care, Willie alternates between pain and relief according to the time and frequency of the pills. He only knows one thing – he doesn't want to be out there on the streets. In the haze of his mind, he is convinced he screwed it up. He searches his mind for what he could give the Lieutenant to plea bargain; he *needs* the hospital, the rehab. He sure as shit can't cut it in jail.

He doesn't know what charges will be brought against him, but he is certain of attempted murder. They know he took the woman's picture and the money and that he lurked around her porch, killed her cat, and struggled with somebody in the dark where he used the knife. But he has to make them understand he really wouldn't have killed her, 'cos deep down he isn't sure he could have. She's okay; he saw her, but there is something funny going on. He noticed it when he told the cops about the picture. They rolled their eyes and looked at him like he was crazy. So he goes over and over it in his mind. Is there something he could tell them about the picture? Something that would help him plea bargain?

He tries to remember exactly how this job came about, and in the middle of the night he suddenly remembers something. It might be important; it might help with the plea bargain. He gets up from his bunk and bangs on the bars until his fist hurts. The turnkey tells him to shut up, but he keeps yelling that he needs to see the Lieutenant – he has something important to tell him.

'Yeah, shut up. It's three o'clock in the morning. Whatever it is, it's gonna have to wait until tomorrow.'

Finally, Willie's throat gets hoarse and his hand hurts where the damn cat scratched him, so he lies back down, and when Lieutenant Burke comes in the morning, he has trouble remembering what it was he wanted to tell him. After an agonizing half hour, he finally remembers.

'It's about the picture. Will the judge know I'm being cooperative? Will you let him know?'

'Yeah, but so far you haven't told us anything that's helpful.'

'Well, I got something now. I wasn't holding back, I just now remembered it – no, I did last night, but the damn guard wouldn't get you.'

'Well, I'm here now, Willie, so spill it. I ain't got all day.'

'It was a woman who ordered the hit.'

'How do you know that?' the Lieutenant asks, as he feels the heat of excitement rising in his gut.

'The guy who gave me the money and the picture said so.'

'Exactly what did he say?'

'He said . . .' and Willie looks up, rubs his chin with a shaky hand. 'He said, "So much for the weaker sex." He handed me the picture and said, "This dame is your mark and guess what, Willie, it's a lady who wants her gone. Sun glasses, blonde hair, mink coat, looking enough like the picture to be her sister or maybe a cousin."'

'Let me get this straight, Willie. The person paying for the hit was a woman who resembled the picture of Myra Dunhom?'

'Yeah, that's it.'

'Are you making this up? I told you there's a mother and a daughter and the mother's dead. You still don't have your story straight about the woman on the roof; you saw her, but it wasn't you that pushed her.'

Willie begins to shake. 'No, man, I think I saw her, but I was tripping. I thought I saw her and I heard somebody talking, but it was like whispers. I couldn't make it out.'

'No good, Willie. If it wasn't you, then who was up there on the roof with her?'

'Nobody. As God is my witness, I didn't see nobody up there but her.'

'You got nothing to sell, Willie, it's all bullshit!' Lieutenant Burke leaves the cell. As much as he wants not to, he believes him, for the Gucci loafers were tried on Willie and they were far too narrow, and if he *had* worn them, why hadn't they made a measurable impression? And this junkie would never have had Myra's key or have been invited into her apartment.

It's his day off. He leaves for his apartment, planning on just lying around taking it easy and maybe watching the sports channel.

But when he gets home, he listens to his messages and there is one from Trini Woodruff asking to see him.

CHAPTER TWENTY-FOUR

I awake late, to hear the phone and doorbell ringing simultaneously. I peek through the eyehole in the door and see the comforting sight of the police uniform. 'I'm late, Steve, it'll be just a few minutes.'

'Okay,' and he goes to the car to wait.

It's Cindy on the phone and I feel rushed. I'll have to cut the call short, but she seems so happy and fairly bursting with news I haven't the heart to cut her off too quickly. We finally hang up with me promising to call later tonight.

I check my watch. I am really late and I know Felix and Lola will be waiting on the sidewalk. I always meant to get Felix a set of keys, but I haven't gotten around to it yet. I throw on my clothes and Steve has me in front of the shop in less than five minutes.

'Hi,' I greet Felix and Lola. 'Someone remind me to send Clarista down to get another set of keys; we don't want you out in the cold catching pneumonia, now do we?'

Felix removes her hat, fluffs out her mane of red waves, saying, 'I take Vitamin C; I don't get colds.'

'I do, and I take Vitamin C,' Lola says.

Felix follows me around as I hit the various light switches and go from lamp to lamp. 'That theater group is coming in today,' she says. 'Can you work with me so I know which pieces you want to give a better discount on?'

'Certainly.'

'God, we've got so much to talk about. It's so exciting, and there's still a lot to work out. Uh oh, here they come – that theater group.'

'I hope they're gone before the Lieutenant comes in; I need to talk to him.'

'Have they charged him yet, the man who . . .' Felix stops, for we both know what she means.

'Willie the druggie? I don't know. Lieutenant Burke said they're sure he's the one who stabbed Tonto, I mean John, but according to the Lieutenant he is a down and out who would never have owned a pair of Gucci loafers.'

Felix stops midway on her journey to the office to make the coffee. 'Lola, can you get the coffee? I need to talk to Trini.' Felix pulls me aside. 'Did you say *Gucci loafers*? What does that have to do with it?'

'It seems the man on the roof with Myra that night wore a pair of Gucci loafers, size ten and a half; they found the shoes in question in Myra's closet afterwards . . .'

'Afterwards?' Felix echoes, puzzled until it dawns on her what I am saying.

'Yes. That's why they asked so many questions about a man in her life – did she have a boyfriend, a live-in, someone in a relationship with her, someone who had access to her closet. They couldn't find anyone who knew anything about such a mystery man. They still haven't.'

'That's because there wasn't one,' Felix says firmly. 'I knew her better than anyone; I would have known. No, it wasn't a man who owned those shoes: they came from right here in the shop. They were brown, hand-made Guccis from Italy, size ten and a half. They had a loose heel and Myra took them home that night. I assumed she was gonna take them to the shoemaker.'

'Are you sure about this?'

'Of course I am. I almost sold the damn things twice, but both times the man who was interested noticed the heel was loose. The cheapos, they should have bought 'em; a shoemaker could have fixed it for a few bucks.'

When Lola emerges from the office with our steaming mugs of cappuccino, we stop talking, but Felix is still muttering to herself. 'There was no man in her life. No, she was worse than I am about being a designer. All she talked about was when she'd do her collection and become famous. She was totally obsessed with it. That's why I knew where to find Madame Opensky and Gemma. I believed her for a long time about doing a collection, but then I came to realize that all she had was that sketchbook full of designs that didn't really work.' Felix is quiet while she sips her coffee, but in a minute she turns back to me. 'God, I hope that doesn't happen to me, to want something so badly and not have the talent to really do it.'

'I'm sure you'll be fine,' I assure her.

'Maybe, maybe not, you've never seen my sketches. I haven't tried making a toile on any of them yet; I guess I'm afraid to.'

Our talk is interrupted by the theater group needing assistance. Felix walks off to join Lola and help the group, meaning to call me only when they make their final selections. It depends on what they choose. I'm willing to go up to seventy per cent off on some of the garments. I hope they buy a lot, for I am anxious to be done with the shop so the workmen can get it renovated. The property would show so much better empty, and Pamela so far has had no offers, as she expected, from the couple from Florida.

Lieutenant Burke walks in shortly afterwards and apologizes for being early. I lead him back to the office where we can talk privately. After making him a cup of coffee and having him sit comfortably in the one armchair, I hand him the three letters. He reads them, his forehead wrinkling with puzzlement.

'Where did you get these?' he asks.

'Tonto, I mean John Sandaval, gave them to me a day or so ago before he left for Gallup. He claims Myra gave them to him the night she died and paid him some money so he would mail them the next day. Naturally, he got drunk and forgot to do so.'

Puzzled, he reads them over. 'They're outrageous – obituaries written by a lady before she knew she was gonna die – or did she? Is any of this true – "famous designer on the brink of world recognition"? I thought she only sold vintage clothes?'

'That's right, none of it is true. She wasn't a designer; she only wanted to be.'

He scratches his head. 'Could she have imagined that the *Times*, *Women's Wear Daily*, or even the *Village Voice* would print any of this information without checking it out?'

'I don't know, Lieutenant. I didn't know my mother very well; in fact, I didn't know her at all. I did have the impression from my father that she was a willful, spoiled child of a woman who craved attention and always needed to be at the center of it.' I pause. 'And my employee said she obsessed about being a famous designer.'

He is clicking the thoughts around in his head when I come out with another bit of information.

'Felix,' and I point towards her, 'that's the girl who did an internship with Myra and I've kept her on – she told me that Myra took a pair of men's Gucci loafers, size ten and a half, home the night she died.'

He sits up, all attention. 'I'll need to speak to this Felix when she's free.'

'Of course. She also mentioned that one shoe had a loose heel and she assumed Myra was going to take it to the shoemaker.'

He jumps up and paces the room. Suddenly it has all fallen into place. The dead woman got what she wanted after all – attention. He stops, reaches over and pats my hand gently. 'I think you can relax now; you're no longer in danger. The man we have in custody will be going away for a long time.'

I wonder about him, this murderer who killed my mother. I need explanations, I need to understand. 'Why did he kill her? Was it robbery, was it someone she was involved with? Lieutenant, I need to know why!'

He pauses in his pacing, his mind tumbling over words. How can he say it so it might prove a comfort to her? 'She – she . . . Mrs Dunhom wasn't murdered.'

'You mean it was an accident?'

'No, not an accident, but a very clever suicide staged to look like a murder.'

'Suicide.' The word bounces around in my mind like a crazy ball, and I feel nausea rise up in my throat. Tears spring to my eyes, for I realize she must have been so unhappy, so desperate; only someone without a ray of hope would do such a thing.

For some reason, I fight against this explanation which, deep down, I know is true. 'But the shoes, the check, the man's footprints on the terrace! The man in jail – he killed the cat and you're telling me he stabbed Ton— John Sandaval – and yet you're certain he did not kill Myra.'

'He didn't kill Mrs Dunhom,' he says firmly, and sits back down.

The inertia of sitting still is too much for me. I feel my nerves jumping like restless fish, so I do the unthinkable – I reach over to the desk and light one of Felix's long brown cigarettes. I cough and sputter until the Lieutenant holds out one of his mints. 'I gave that up and traded it for these.' I stub out the cigarette and gratefully suck on the mint.

'I'll go through it so you can understand. It's all very clear and explainable now, the whole affair. The shoes, our crucial clue, never did make sense; they didn't test out right. It seems no one was wearing those shoes that made the imprints. She must have made the impressions earlier and, not thinking clearly, put the shoes back in her closet. Your mother, Mrs Woodruff, was an unhappy woman making her passing much more newsworthy. She wrote the anonymous letters for her obituary, which weren't lies but I guess they were just wishful daydreams; and the cashier's check for ten thousand dollars, she cashed it herself and paid the killer. But someone with her sort of ego wouldn't allow a killer to decide where and how she died. No, she would have wanted to orchestrate that herself, but still she wanted a police force out there looking for her killer, one who had been hired but not allowed to do his job.'

My head reels with what he is telling me, but finally it all makes some kind of weird sense and I find a kernel of comfort in it. It was painful to think of Myra terrified and being chased across the frozen roof by a vicious killer. Far easier to accept her choosing her own destiny, but as ever in Myra's selfish way, a helpless creature, the cat, died, John Sandaval was almost killed, and I've been in grave danger from a drugged man. I hadn't known my mother before I came here and I don't know her much better now, but I'm aware of some facts and I'm beginning to understand a little about what made her tick.

'People do bizarre things when they're unhappy,' the Lieutenant says as he is rising to go.

His words strike me like a sharp knife. I did something just as strange and inexplicable, but I always justified it by saying I didn't hurt anyone in the process. Then I think of Cindy and know that isn't true, for someone will be hurt in the end. This thing hidden inside us is like a snowball gathering momentum and racing downhill growing bigger and more important to Cindy, and I fear Cindy has turned it into some sort of twisted reality.

I am safer here, for Jeff has led Cindy out into the world and out of that sad house filled with shameful secrets. Maybe in time my absence will help her. I know a part of my reluctance to return is based on that. If we never mention it again, will it disappear from our thoughts as if it never happened? But if Jeff ever finds out, I feel he will despise us both.

CHAPTER TWENTY-FIVE

One last time I let myself into the flat. I walk the empty rooms and I no longer feel Myra's presence here. I go into the kitchen, which looks like a completely different room, transplanted here from a different house.

I take the small key, open the bars, and hesitate, but I force myself to step over the sill and go out onto the porch. My footsteps crunch into the layers of snow and I know this is the same sound that accompanied her on her last journey.

The trees rustle in the wind and as I look up, I see a curious sight. In the west, the sun is setting, but between buildings in the east, I see the sliver of a crescent moon. Day and night missing each other by just a few miles.

I walk to the edge and know it is that spot, for the potted tree is crookedly shoved aside and I see the storm gutter is bent outward as if a foot were caught there for only a second.

I kneel down, unaware of the cold on my knees and look over the edge. It is not so far down. At least it could have been only seconds until she arrived at the destiny she had chosen for herself.

I look down at the courtyard, which is a pristine carpet of white, and there in the center, where I imagine she must have fallen, I see a group of dandelions pushing their way up through the snow. Curious how most things desperately want to live. They know, these weeds or flowers, something I did not know. It will be an early spring.

It is not so terrible, this way she chose for herself, and whatever devils drove her, at last she is free; and my journey here has given me a taste for freedom, when all the while I didn't know I was caged, trapped, by what I perceived were others' needs far more important than my own.

Finally, I am honest with myself. I release Cindy to live her own life. I release Jeff, too.

Soon I must go to Denver to make them understand!

CHAPTER TWENTY-SIX

The riddle of Myra's death has been solved; it is certain that she killed herself and it gives me a sense of closure. Particular details may never be fully explained, but it is over.

I'm told Willie Butts has been sent to a hospital – a drug rehab unit – and it isn't clear whether he will be doing time at Rikers Island or not, but Lieutenant Burke maintains he always knew that Butts didn't have the stamina or attention span to be a killer.

The trail is cold now, and the Lieutenant may never be able to find the hands that this supposed hit went through, but it is clear that Myra had hired what was supposed to be her own killer. Yet, from all the facts about Myra, it was a ploy, a smokescreen; she would never have trusted anyone with such an important job. In her eyes, her passing needed the drama of a perceived murder.

Lieutenant Burke was delighted to close the case. He wished me well and told me that if I wanted to move back to my own property, he could guarantee it was safe.

But no, I don't want to occupy the newly renovated apartment, for at this stage even the shop is emptied and the remaining stock boxed and stored safely in the basement.

No, I feel the vibes in the building are not right; I am afraid that a tiny essence of Myra would always haunt me – her elaborate cry for attention gone wrong, with no media hype, no more frantic detectives searching for a phantom murderer. I wonder whether the dead feel failure, for Myra failed in some of the most important things in her life. Suddenly I feel a deep sorrow for that pathetic woman who was my mother. I even feel that at some point, without being totally aware of it, I have truly forgiven her, and by doing so, I have freed myself.

No, I don't wish to go back to that apartment. I find in my new environment something magical that I respond to – the space clears my mind, it brings me dreams of a different life, a different occupation. I yearn to create.

With the shop now closed and being renovated, I have the free time to devote myself to the design project with a vengeance.

True to his word, Josh sent this marvelous woman, Madame Opensky, to me. From her I learned that there is an army of women out there who are skilled in the art of sewing, and my dream of a business that needs no factory was born. A cottage industry seems like a simple idea that will be possible to start. I feel alive and energetic and I tell myself that after all, many people change their occupations in midstream.

I pooh-pooh Felix's idea of an exclusive design shop with only haute couture. 'This isn't Paris, Felix – I have no interest in designing for the very rich. That was Myra's dream, not mine. Nor do I want to design for women so slim they need to throw up before getting dressed. No, I want to make clothes for average women, classic clothes you don't have to get rid of every season.'

And again I roam the streets of the garment district teaching myself the properties and the secrets of cloth. The idea of a casual fashion show, to which buyers from the major department stores will be invited, is born and with Josh and Felix's help, it is going to be a reality. I am excited by change. I can offer the designs off the original pattern in high fashion ready-to-wear.

And in a dark sleepless night, when my overactive mind makes resting difficult if not impossible, it comes to me. In the twilight between sleep and wakefulness, I leap out of bed. 'How wonderful!' I shout aloud. 'It will work, I know it.'

It seems to me a brilliant idea; no one in fashion has ever done this that I know of. I take a sheet of paper and began scribbling out the plan. I will make only fifty copies of each dress in the three most popular sizes, exclusive limited editions of my designs with a canvas label issuing the number from one to fifty, no different from numbered prints. Why not? This could work in clothing as well, for I now think of clothing as art. I can't wait for morning to tell Felix and Madame Opensky my plan. It might put me on the fashion map and I find myself consumed with ambition.

The work stretches out to where my life seems to have a purpose now. I know all human beings, male and female, strive to succeed at something. I never felt this ravenous hunger before, for I had drifted along, doing Rockwell copies, not knowing how much I yearned to do originals.

It's settled, I will have to stay in New York. The cloth, the accessories, the models, this won't work in any other city. I need a showroom on 7th Avenue.

I know one other reality – I need a divorce. I have never been fair to Jeff. I never loved him in the right way. I try to think back. He was simply there, I guess, at the right time, for most of my friends were already married and the truth was we both settled for something less than we had dreamed of!

There was so much distance between us before, and now he probably wouldn't know me at all, for I feel I have changed profoundly. I will call him in the morning and commit to a firm date that I will be back in Denver. I shall walk into the travel agent as soon as they open in the morning and buy the ticket for one week after the fashion show.

Josh has already pressed me to settle on a date for the show, and it is good. I always work well with tight deadlines.

CHAPTER TWENTY-SEVEN

I interview Madame Opensky and she assures me she has a crew of women who are expert seamstresses, many from Europe, and a much older woman who has actually worked in a Paris *atelier*. She admits her own sewing days are over, for arthritis has fused her fingers, but she can instruct – she knows how to press and shape the cloth.

So overnight the living room becomes my factory. Tables, chairs, high-density lamps, ironing boards, and irons of every size and shape are installed.

Five seamstresses are hired and Josh very kindly sends down one young girl anxious to model, so with Gemma, and I've enlisted Lola, we have the three needed for the show. Each will wear three different outfits, so for the first couple of days, Gemma comes in to be measured and fitted.

I have my crew of loyal workers. Felix, Clarista, and Lola do any job that needs doing, and they go about the work without being told.

The bolts of fabric have been delivered and we only need nine prototypes, one completed garment for each style. The models come for fittings and my flat is a beehive of activity.

I am not even fazed when Pamela Walsh calls in to say she has a firm offer on the property, and when she arrives, she says, 'My goodness, what is all this? Noise, women ironing and sewing, girls running around in their underwear . . . it looks just like a fashion show.'

'That's exactly what it is, or will be in two weeks.'

'Who . . . why . . . what?' she laughs.

'Me. I've designed some things and I'm presenting a fashion show to the industry.'

'I didn't know you were a designer. I guess I misunderstood. I thought you were selling out the shop and going back west.'

'I was, but I changed my mind. I'm interested in working in the design field.'

'I've heard it's a hard one to crack.'

'Yeah, I heard that, too. Funny you should mention it. A friend of mine, who's in acting, keeps quoting this pithy saying: "Things happen when preparation meets opportunity". Well, I met opportunity and I wasn't even prepared, but I will be now.'

'That's great, you're a lucky lady, but since you're staying and need living quarters and workspace, have you changed your mind about selling the building?'

'Oh no, I still want to sell. Too many bad things happened there. I definitely want to sell.'

Pamela exhaled. She had been holding her breath, for it was such a large commission she would have missed. She opened her briefcase. 'Their first offer was two million one hundred thousand. I didn't bring it to you, for I thought they could be pushed a little higher. I was right – they came up with two million five hundred thousand.'

My heart raced. Were these numbers *real*? 'I'll take it.'

Smiling, Pamela pushed the papers over to me to sign. 'I thought you would. It'll take about six weeks until we close.'

'Great,' and as I walk her to the door, we pause and watch the activity at the east end of the mammoth living room.

'Looks official,' she comments. 'Where's your venue?'

'Here, right here, all centered around the crystal boulder. I'm told they like offbeat places for shows.'

'It's perfect,' Pamela agrees. 'My God, Trini, you should buy this place.'

My heart hammers with excitement. I can only whisper, 'How much are they asking?'

'Two million. It's residential, not commercial like your place.'

Quickly I calculate. Five hundred thousand left, but after the commission, I'm not sure. 'How much would they take?' I ask, my voice squeaky with nerves.

'They turned down one point five.'

'Oh Pamela, what do you think? You must know.'

'I think one point eight would get it.'

'I need to think about it. There's my sister to consider,' I say.

'How so? She wasn't on the deed to the property.'

'No, she wasn't, it was mine to sell, but . . . It's too hard to explain, but Pamela – stall them, please! It's perfect here, almost *too* perfect. It scares me when something fits too well.'

'All right, honey, but remember I told you it'll all work out in the end.'

I walk her to the door and go back into the hubbub. 'Felix, can you manage? I've got a splitting headache. I thought I'd lie down.'

'Sure, everything's under control. By the way, I'm glad you insisted on Lola. She's good. Shame she's not a little taller, but maybe the trend to beanpole models might be over.'

'I wanted someone like Lola to show the clothes on, someone of average build, average height. After all, I'm designing for ordinary women. I always thought it was a shame to show beautiful clothes on such tall slender women, then the lady who buys it has a real letdown, for it doesn't look at all the same on her.'

'You're right,' Felix agrees, and when she notices my hand shaking, asks, 'Are you okay? You look terrible. Your face is white as a sheet.'

I reach up and smooth my forehead. 'It's just a headache, a bad one.'

I go to my bedroom and lie down. I love it here, this house, this place. Already I feel like I belong here. I will have the money to buy it and enough left over to fund my design project. Myra left it to me and legally it's mine, all mine, but morally I know it isn't, and just half of the proceeds isn't enough. Who would give me a mortgage for so much money, me, with only a dream and no set income.

I must stop thinking about it, but again and again I go over it. I could have it, it is mine, legally it is all mine to do with what I want.

I take two aspirins, for truly this has given me a very painful headache.

When the first toile has been turned into the actual material to be used, Madame Opensky urges, 'Go on, touch the cloth, smooth it on the body. You must be satisfied that it is your idea, your dream, faithfully re-created,' and timidly I reach up to smooth the cloth. Then, with more confidence, I either compliment or criticize what I do not like on the garment.

Again and again the dress is pulled off Gemma, taken to the iron, and stretched until it hugs her body correctly. Next it is given to the most experienced seamstress, who works the body or framework of the dress and is responsible for the interface as well. The others work on the sleeves or press seams flat, and I am hypnotized by the tiny expert hand-stitching of their capable fingers.

'That's what makes a couture piece so special. With hand-stitching there is only one thread, so the garment can always, if needed, be successfully altered. Machine stitching leaves a line, tiny holes,' Madame Opensky tells me, and I learn, I work with the cloth, and watch how they, like magicians, turn my ideas, my dream of a garment, into reality.

When I am finally satisfied with the piece, I watch the women run their fine needles through beeswax and begin on the finished garment, which has been ripped apart several times.

Josh comes by several times a week, and during the final week, when we have two of the models working, he watches with a satisfied smile as I drape the fabric over the still-as-a-statue model, only to take it off again – the iron, the pressing, stitches ripped out . . . and the cloth put back together again.

'It is truly sculpture in cloth,' Josh says to no one in particular. Madame Opensky nods in agreement, for she too knows the talent it takes to create in two-dimensional fabric something that fits like an easy skin on a three-dimensional form.

It is a frantic time, the house full of dedicated women who take pride in fitting in their piece of the puzzle.

CHAPTER TWENTY-EIGHT

On my calls to Denver, I have been silent about the fashion show. I feel I can't explain the project to either Jeff or Cindy – even to me, it seems far-fetched!

As of late, my conversations with Jeff have become so stilted we both seem to be waiting for the other to say something. I know I am holding back. I need to be free, but after all this time, it isn't fair to be so impersonal as to ask for a divorce over the telephone.

Jeff, too, has drawn away from Cindy, for now he is afraid of himself. He is too aware of her as a woman, and without Trini there to shelter her and keep her in the shadows, she is someone totally different. Her lonely years have made her an avid reader, so she is able to converse on so many different subjects and is a very interesting person. He had never realized this before. He had always thought of her as a sad, unhappy child.

When he persuaded her to attend another function at the University, some casual acquaintances mistook her for his wife. He was proud to be with her, and it was more than the simple pride of coaxing her out of her shell. She is an attractive, warm, caring woman, and it startles him to realize they have more areas of common interest than he ever had with Trini.

Slowly, unexpectedly, he is falling in love with her.

Now he, like Cindy, subconsciously does not want Trini to come back, not yet, not until he can understand exactly what it is that he is feeling.

Like a concerned father or a jealous lover, he finds himself peeking out of the blinds whenever Cindy returns home from a date. He can hear the soft murmur of voices and it pains him to think she is out there kissing someone under the protection of the large stone porch.

He is torn with indecision about going on a week-long trip to the oil fields in Wyoming. It is crucial to study the new bits where it really counts – in the field – and the time is right, for it is now almost the end of February and an unexpected spring thaw is in place. He makes his plans to be away, and that will leave Cindy alone in the house for a week, but she doesn't seem alarmed at the prospect. With a shock, he becomes aware that Trini has been gone almost two months.

In the beginning, he thought he missed her, but now he isn't sure, for life seems easier, more comfortable, yet exciting without her. It's nice to have nights free from squabbling, for they had taken to quarreling over nothing, when he knew deep down it was only one thing that they really fought about. He wanted a child, a boy or girl, it didn't matter. He wanted to leave this link of eternity behind him. He wanted a child to love, to teach, to watch him or her grow, and he couldn't understand his wife, for she felt no need of this, nor did she seem to understand that he did. This one deep division made their relationship flawed and he wondered about it. Why had they never discussed it before getting married? But he hadn't realized there would be any reason to.

CHAPTER TWENTY-NINE

I work feverishly with Felix, for we have committed to produce the show by 10 March. 'It's the Fall line, that's good; we can get the orders in plenty of time,' Felix muses.

'Are you sure?'

'Yes, this is an offbeat time for a show and because of it, it will get more attention.'

'I need a theme, something to tie this style show together,' I muse. 'They all seem to have a theme.'

'Trini, "style show" is outdated. It's called a fashion show.'

'I know, but we don't have catwalks or bands . . .'

'Never mind, this loft is perfect. It's a unique setting. Josh was delighted with it.'

'What kind of setting you call it?' Clarista asks.

'Unique, it's very unique,' Felix says importantly.

'I don't care about this house, seems too big, you could be lonesome here. You still got your medal?' Clarista asks.

'Of course,' I answer as I pull it out from under my shirt, and I can see that Clarista is extremely pleased.

'What is it?' Felix asks as she leans closer to examine the pendant.

'It's the Sacred Medal of the Virgin of Fatima. You living in New York without one, you a foolish girl, Miss Mary Jane,' Clarista scolds.

'Well, I just better get one,' Felix quips. 'I'll just hurry along to Canal Street right away.'

'No use making fun of it. It kept Miss Trini safe when all that danger was underfoot.'

'Yes, it did,' I say, 'and I thank you for it.'

Clarista moves off to watch the ladies sewing and make herself available for anything they need her to do. But she is still muttering under her breath that the Pope didn't think it was funny – it saved his life as well.

'What was all that about?'

'Felix, you don't make fun of other people's beliefs,' I scold. 'Now let's get down to work. I've been thinking about the invitation. I've been wracking my brain for something different – something they won't just throw away.' I purse my lips. 'I've been thinking of something in cloth tied around a real flower.'

'With Josh sponsoring it, they won't throw it away, but what is it? Go on, Trini, tell me what your idea is.'

'Well . . .' I take a sketchpad and begin drawing. 'A calla lily, with a red or purple ribbon, the invitation in gold script on the ribbon.'

'No.' Felix shakes her head. 'Too Easter – and Deco stuff always used lilies.'

'I know, but roses are boring.'

'How about sunflowers?' Felix chirps.

'No, they're everywhere, even on babies' hats; that seems too home-grown.'

We put our heads in our hands thinking, and after a time Felix breaks the silence. 'The flower-ribbon connection is a great idea. I like it – you'll just have to decide which flower.'

'Yeah, I'll come back to that. We have the models, two size five, five foot nine, and Lola, size nine, five foot six. Do you think Gemma can do it? What if she's not up to it on the night of the show?'

'Trini, she'll be okay. That's her bag really. She can pull herself together when she needs to. She's desperate to succeed at modeling again. That's why she's bulimic, but it's ruining her looks. She used to be real good – she had a lot of work before and she almost made it to the top rung.'

'So, we have three models, each with three changes,' and I continue writing all the particulars in the book. 'I saw the guy from NYU, the film student. He showed me the slides he'll use – seascapes, skyscrapers et cetera – and his friend had the taped music, everything from *La Mer* to Pink Floyd. I think it worked, but maybe I should have him back to run through the program for you?'

'No, Trini, trust your own judgment. You're a natural. Josh and I believe in you.'

'Have the programs been delivered?'

'Yes,' and Felix goes over and unpacks the printing.

Rapidly, I read the program. Each design is described in detail – the material, the buttons, belts, even the threads used in the garment are given weights and quality control – and each item contains information on the number of garments to be offered and describes the canvas label that will be in each garment, with the pertinent information that the garments will be numbered and offered in only limited editions.

Josh is pleased with it. He feels it is a very original idea that will catch on, and in the sincerest form of flattery, he is certain it will be quickly copied by others.

The only thing left for me to decide is what flower to use for the invitation. No particular bloom comes to mind, so I choose apricot-colored roses, as the invitation is printed in gold lettering on a chocolate-brown velvet ribbon.

The couriers are dispatched and within days we receive forty-five yes's from people who will attend out of the sixty invitations that were sent.

Felix squeals with excitement. '*Women's Wear Daily* and all the fashion magazines! Wow! I knew Josh's name would get us noticed.'

'But the stores . . .' I sputter. 'How many stores? After all, they place the orders.'

'Ten, all the majors.'

We both sigh with relief.

It's all in place. Huge four-foot candles are delivered and placed in strategic places in the room and the rented folding chairs are scattered in groups in three different sections of the large room. We had a rehearsal yesterday and there was only one hitch; the maids hired had to be instructed to blow out the candles exactly on time, for certain dresses needed to be seen under strobe-lights and accompanied by the right music, and then the maids needed to relight the candles for the softer designs with the background of seascapes and *La Mer*.

The food arrives on time – a selection of exotic cheeses – and the champagne is to be served with new strawberries flown in fresh from Florida.

In the excitement, I overlook what I am to wear. I am so jumpy that nothing in my closet seems right, and at the last minute Felix goes back to the basement of the shop and roots through all the boxes until she finds something suitable for both of us to wear. She comes back to the loft with a Schiaparelli gown, a bold print design of circus acrobats, one of her signature pieces, and a hooded bias gown of forest green by Valentina.

She holds up the dress and begs me to try it on. 'You'll look stunning in this.'

I slip on the Valentina – it is rather a tight fit.

'It's so dramatic, it's perfect on you. Oh, wear it, Trini!'

'Are you sure? I feel like Meryl Streep in *The French Lieutenant's Woman* with this hood.'

'Gee, Trini, just don't eat much before the show and hold your tummy in a little. It's so good on you; you've got to wear it.'

I turn again and again and look at myself in the mirror. Felix is right – it is total drama, it makes a bold statement. 'I didn't know I owned a vintage Valentino,' I say.

'No, no,' she corrects. 'It's a Valentina.'

'Who's that?' I've never heard of her.

'Oh, you've simply got to learn,' Felix scolds. 'Valentina was great – she was a Russian from Kiev. She was an actress, dancer, and a model in the Twenties. She worked in Paris dress-shops and somehow she ended up in New York. She loved clothes, and I think it shows. In the Thirties or Forties she opened her own shop – with a very exclusive clientèle.'

'Wow, and I'm wearing one of her originals tonight. I feel special.'

'You should. She even designed the clothes Grace Kelly wore in the movie *The Philadelphia Story*.'

'That settles it, I'm wearing it,' I say as I tuck my tummy in a little further.

Clarista comes in with a late RSVP. 'Who is it?' Felix asks.

'He sounds important – a Mr Trevor St Paul, Esq. What does Esq mean? I never heard a name Esq,' Clarista states.

'I'll say he's important. He's that yummy British designer – a household name in street fashion.' And Felix continues to hold the card.

'I'll learn,' I promise, and we begin putting on our make-up, as excited as two young girls going out on a first date.

It has all been arranged and rehearsed. Clarista will answer the door and Madame Opensky will greet the guests, take them over to the hospitality area, and introduce them to one another on the rare occasions when they aren't already acquainted. We know Josh will arrive fashionably late and flit through the crowd like a butterfly.

* * *

I fidget in front of the bedroom mirror. The dress is wonderful, the viscose, or whatever this old clinging cloth was called, hugs my body and it sways seductively as I move. The hood lays softly on my shoulders and I have adorned the dark green bodice with one large brooch, a stylized diamanté figure of a praying mantis, a rare design by Eisenberg. With my blonde hair pulled back in a severe chignon, the large round diamanté earrings are the only things that compete with my face. On my left arm I wear one slender tennis bracelet that sparkles, and at the last minute I take off my wedding band and replace it with a well-made large square ring of crystal.

I study my reflection. I am confident I feel and look like a designer, or what I imagine a designer looks like.

After twenty or so of the guests have arrived and I have gulped down two glasses of champagne, I decide I can't hide in my bedroom any longer. Peeking through the door, I can see Felix is already confidently circulating among the crowd. I open the door and enter the room.

Within minutes of my arrival, Felix brings over a young man with a crisp manner who is from a magazine and wants a very quick bio.

'You're new in New York?'

'Yes, but my mother had been here for many years. We worked on the designs together.'

'So that's why your label is "Myra Dunhom and daughter"?'

'That's right.'

'What part was Myra Dunhom and what part – I'm sorry, I didn't get your name?'

'Trini Woodruff, and I'd say design credit was fifty-fifty.'

'How refreshing – a designer who doesn't want to hog all the limelight.' In that moment, the reporter decides he likes this Trini Woodruff.

'I should have said the late Myra Dunhom,' I add. 'My mother passed away before she could see the collection.'

'That's a shame. Do you plan on changing the label at some future date?'

'No, I have no plans to do so,' and before the reporter can ask me any more questions, Clarista whispers to me, 'It's a phone call, your husband. I'm sorry, I wouldn't have bothered you, but he said it's urgent.'

'Please excuse me,' I apologize. 'I'm afraid it's an urgent phone call.'

My heart is hammering with fear; something must be wrong, terribly wrong. Breathless, I pick up the phone in the bedroom. 'Jeff, what is it? What's happened?'

I am greeted with an eerie silence. He must have hung up. 'Jeff, are you there?' I am practically screaming now.

Finally his voice comes over the phone, ominous in its simplicity. 'It's Cindy.' He pauses.

'My God, what is it, what's happened to Cindy?'

Again I am greeted with silence until finally he says, 'She's pregnant,' and I can hear the anger in his voice. He has other secret reasons to be angry, for he now realizes he has fallen in love with her. 'Did you ever talk to her, tell her about things?' His voice stridently accuses me.

'Of course I did, Jeff. Calm down, it's not the worst thing in the world. She's not a child, she's twenty-four years old.'

'That's what I always told you – that she isn't a child but you always treated her like one.'

'Please, Jeff, I have guests. I can't talk about it now.' As ever, he makes me feel dishonest, for I hadn't mentioned what was really going on. 'Please, I'll call you later, after they've gone.'

Without another word, he bangs the phone down, a harsh sound in my ear.

I have to put it aside for now, but I feel trembly with the news. Maybe it's Jeff's fault, not mine. He took her out into the world. She hadn't known any boys or men; she hadn't dated before. She probably fell for the first guy who said, 'I love you.'

When I return to the room, Felix sees the look on my face, takes the mike, and invites everyone to sit down.

On cue, the maids light the tall candles and the strains of *La Mer* fill the room as people scatter and take their seats.

Gemma is first. She comes forward, looking professional, the exaggerated gait of the catwalk firmly in place. She pauses before the crystal, twirls in front of the large precious stone, then gracefully flips off the opera coat to expose the matching sheath. Rainbow colors bounce off the rock, and the off-white gown is a masterpiece.

I scan the faces of the audience and I notice the buyers, writers, and assembled fashion people quickly look down at the program to read the description of this particular design. Around the room, with appropriate pauses, Gemma deftly replaces the coat over her shoulder and retraces her steps. Her exit meets with the soft sound of polite clapping.

Next comes the evening gown in chiffon, the color an acid green, a curious marriage of color and fabric that merges tastefully. On one shoulder is the designer's helpmate, a huge soft exaggerated black chiffon rose. The blonde model wears it magnificently and this design is greeted with a louder applause of approval.

The tempo changes and against the wall the silhouettes of skyscrapers become the background and the next design, a suit in red jersey with a fitted jacket and row upon row of blackeyed susan buttons, is an instant hit. Lola swirls, then stops and deftly unzips a side panel. Stepping out of the ankle-length flared skirt, she exposes a shorter mini skirt with a straight line.

This ensemble is like a chameleon; it has changed in style and appearance and the suit, usually seen as something done in wool, works incredibly well in this unlikely fabric. Lola is on stage and her shorter stature is somehow a plus – you can see the women in the audience thinking it would look great on practically anybody. This design meets with a roar of approval as well, and the clapping of hands continues long after the model leaves the area. Between each outfit, there is soft music, heightening expectations.

In a fog, I watch the parade. The little black dress is done in brown only to surprise them, for after exiting, the model reappears and the reversible garment is now that classic black cocktail dress. This is the design that gave me the most problems. It is so difficult to do reversibles and still maintain pure lines. By the sound of their approval, I know I succeeded in this innovation.

I can't tell how long it takes; it was scheduled to be a mere half-hour.

At its finish, Felix and Josh bring me forward and Josh says simply, in his impressive voice, 'The designer, Trini Woodruff.' I am greeted with the sound of applause and approval, and as each model reappears, she in turn takes her applause with a small nod of acknowledgment.

I find myself surrounded by pushing women and my ears ring with their questions. 'How long have you been in New York?' 'I understand your name's not on the label?' 'This limited edition; do you intend to stick with this posture?' 'Will you decide to only let out one design to one buyer of all fifty limited editions?' Over their heads, I can see Josh's satisfied smile. Once again he has won the game he plays so well.

Later, when he comes to kiss me, that caress tells me everything I need to know. I have made him proud and when I see Lola, I whisper to her, 'That man, his name is opportunity,' and I pull her forward and say, 'Lola, I'd like you to meet Josh Wainwright.'

Thankfully, Felix and Madame Opensky begin answering some of the questions and I feel a firm hand on my elbow leading me away from the crowd. A male voice is saying, 'Don't look so pained; they liked what they saw.'

When he has steered me behind the eight-foot seguro cactus, I turn to see my captor. He is a tall man with a thatch of dark unruly hair. His brown eyes look amused. 'Where on earth did you come from, luv?'

His London accent makes me smile. This must be that 'yummy British designer' Felix talked about. 'Denver,' I answer simply.

'Where on earth have you been hiding in the Big Apple? I've never seen or heard of you.'

'I've never heard of you either,' I say, the remark meant to be teasing.

'I see, you're one of those newcomers who don't know the designers, don't know the business . . .' and he touches my chin, forcing me to look up into his handsome, suntanned face '. . . but all you do know is you've got talent, real talent.'

I smile, extremely pleased.

'Hey, they know it, too. You wait here while I get us some champagne. You deserve a toast; you've earned one.'

I watch him move away; he walks with the confidence of one who has already arrived. He is dressed casually in a pair of gray slacks and a tweed jacket that is a departure from the norm – it is without lapels. I wonder if he designed it. It is different and I like it.

He returns in a minute with two overfull glasses. 'To you, Myra Dunhom!'

'No,' I correct him. 'I'm Trini Woodruff – weren't you listening? But let's toast Myra anyway.'

'To Myra,' he says, and raises his glass.

'To Myra.' I raise my glass as well.

He drinks quickly and I feel he is already a bit tipsy. When I excuse myself, I am surprised, for he allows me to leave without protest. I mingle with the crowd and answer their questions as best I can.

And when the crowd has thinned, I find myself searching the room for a tall man with dark unruly hair but, disappointed, I don't see him.

Felix comes over. Earlier she had noticed Trevor St Paul whisking me away. 'He's gone,' she whispers.

'Who?' I question.

'The guy you're looking for – the Brit.'

'Oh.'

Then Felix smiles wickedly. 'But he asked, so I gave him your phone number.'

'Felix,' I say tiredly, 'you know I'm married. By the way, can we just leave this mess and pay the help to clear up tomorrow? I have to call Jeff. Something came up in Denver and it's bad.'

'I'm sorry. Anything I can do?'

'Yes, what I asked you to. Just take care of the guests – see them out, and leave the mess. We can talk and gloat in the morning and have the maids clear up then.'

'Okay, Trini.' And Felix is surprised, for I reach over and give her a warm hug and whisper, 'I don't know what I would have done without you. This was your idea – the whole thing. It's more your success than mine.'

'Nonsense,' Felix says. 'It was Josh's idea and you're the talent. Those who can, do, and those who can't, teach, or it goes something like that.'

'Thanks.' And I go to the bedroom, take off the Valentina dress, and hang it up carefully on a satin hanger.

I put on my old flannel robe; it makes me feel safe. My head is a little fuzzy, but I sit down to call Jeff even though it's very late.

CHAPTER THIRTY

[illegible]

"Felix," [illegible] "you know [illegible]"

[illegible]

[illegible] hope you'll [illegible] your buyers want you to be creative, but not too drastic. They want change, but not too much."

[illegible] but I feel exhilarated by the challenge.

[illegible] Felix, with a [illegible] wink, hands [illegible] the phone.

CHAPTER THIRTY

The morning dawns, and it is a hectic one.

By eleven, several stores have already called, asking for the fax number.

'You have to get one, Trini. Nobody, absolutely nobody, can exist without one,' Felix nags. The apartment has been cleared, and my little team are sitting around, enjoying a morning-after coffee and gossip.

I phone and make my reservations for the flight to Denver. 'Some of this is gonna have to wait. I'm leaving in the morning and I'll be gone at least several days.'

'You leave now?' Madame Opensky asks, incredulous that after the very positive reception I would even consider disappearing off the scene.

'Family problems,' I explain. 'They can't wait.'

'Hard to get never hurts a lady,' she says kindly, and smiles.

The phone rings constantly, some retailers asking if they took an entire run, could they split it, and have a few different colors?

'I told them no,' Madame Opensky says with a haughty air. 'Young lady, remember the tail doesn't wag the dog.'

I smile, but know I mustn't get carried away. It was a success, sure, but I have read enough to know what designers really go through. Next season, there is always a next season . . . when your critics hope you'll fail and your buyers want you to be creative, but not *too* drastic. They want change, but not too much.

It is a tightrope-walk, but I feel exhilarated by the challenge.

Then finally he calls. Felix, with a conspiratorial wink, hands me the phone.

'Morning, luv, it's a beautiful day, sun's shining just for you. Shall we have lunch?'

His voice thrills me. 'No, I can't. The phone is ringing off the hook and I have a million things to do.' I pause. 'I'd like to, but I really can't.'

'Then at least you can't refuse me dinner. I thought we could do Windows of the World.' The timbre of his voice sounds familiar, yet unfamiliar, like someone who will be important to my life in some way.

I hesitate, then: 'All right, if we can make it an early one. I'm off to the wilderness, Denver, in the morning.'

'You wicked girl, you can't stand everyone on their heads and then run away – it's not fair. How about seven-thirty then – is that early enough?'

'All right, seven-thirty, but I am like Cinderella, you know. I must be home by midnight.'

He laughs. 'You have my word. I wouldn't want you losing any glass slippers.'

When I see him tall and handsome standing at my door, he is every bit as exciting as I remember. He is even able to maintain a dignified air in the bouncing taxi that seems to hit every pothole in the city. When we arrive at the World Trade Center, the elevator whisks us up to the 107th floor. He is recognized and his presence causes a stir. Women glance admiringly in his direction and couples lean towards each other and I hear his name whispered. I am pleased to be with him.

Expertly, he orders for us both – prime rib, potatoes Lyonnaise, and a simple salad.

I look out the window at the city; it is a wonderland of lights. They wink, in this Christmas-tree city, and I feel a jolt of excitement.

He notices my rapt look. 'Enjoy it, it's yours, or it will be.'

I blush, for that's exactly what I was thinking. I want it to belong to me, this marvelous city. Thinking of Myra, I say, 'How many of us have stared at those lights and had dreams, big dreams!'

'A lot of us. Mine came true, and yours will too.'

'Promises, promises,' I laugh, 'but it's a brutal city out there, too.'

'Only for those who have nothing going for them.'

'You sound so cold about it, Mr St Paul.'

'I won't have it – Mr indeed! It's Trev. Funny name it is, too, but one thing I need to tell you, young lady, these New Yorkers are a snobby bunch; don't ever try to pretend you're one of them. No, they'll cut you down like a weed. They take pride in being the genuine article, but I found they like their imports, too. If I were you, I'd cultivate a Southern accent.'

I laugh. 'No . . . I couldn't do one of those if my life depended on it.'

'Then do a little western; a bit of a twang never hurt. Why, some of the most sought-after dinner guests are those with a fat wallet and a Texas accent. They make great clients when they decide you're trendy.'

'You're making it all sound so phony,' I observe.

'Not phony exactly, but everyone plays a game, wears a mask, wants to be part of the inset.'

I find his observations unpleasant. 'I can't ever be like that. I'm dreadful at games. I just want to design, and I hope enough people like my designs, that's all.'

He smiles and reaches over to take my hand. Erotically, his fingertips trace mine. 'I didn't mean to scare you,' he whispers. 'You're on the right track, darling. Do your thing and the hell with them.'

Slowly I extricate my hand from his and try to recover from the effect his touch seems to have on me. 'That's better, you're telling me I can just be me,' I say.

'Yup – but I must admit I've got plans. We would make an unbeatable combination, with my wild zany stuff and your designs – pure classic, pure elegance.' I smile and sip the after-dinner drink.

Again he reaches for my hand. I do not draw away and across the table his eyes catch mine. The heat in them frightens me. Is it desire, ambition, or a range of emotions I can't quite identify? His fingers touch it, the white space where my wedding ring had been. 'How quaint, I'm guessing this is where a wedding band used to be,' and his eyes hold mine, telling me to deny it.

'I don't wear it any more. My husband and I are separated; we're getting divorced.'

I hate myself for being so predictable, but there is something about him that makes me remember what it was like to tease, to flirt. Really all I want to do is reach out and touch his lips to see how they feel.

The evening goes by in a blur. Because of my confusion over what I am feeling, I drink the wine more quickly than I have ever done.

His talk, his plans, whirl about us like a dizzying wind. 'This spring we'll do London, the King's Road. You'll love it. I want to show you where my inspiration comes from. I want to bring it back – the excitement of London street fashion that burned so brightly in the Sixties. You know that was where the mini-skirt started, and hot pants, and these wild, wild platform shoes . . .' He stops. 'Have you thought about doing shoes, accessories?'

'Not really.'

'You should. That guarantees that your outfits are worn correctly.' He stops. 'I'm homesick for London now, and I can't wait to show you Vivienne Westwood. The woman's a genius, an Alice in Wonderland.'

'You're going too fast,' I say. I need to learn so much. I need to read, I need to study . . .

'In London we can go to the V and A,' he interrupts, 'but my God, you know they have a fabulous collection of haute couture right here in New York – at the Met. We should go soon.' He stops and looks at me, and his admiration and desire are clearly visible in his dark eyes. 'I promise you, we'll see the catwalks in Paris and Milan . . .' Finally realizing that he *is* going too fast he glances at his watch and calls for the bill. 'I always keep a promise,' are his final words before we leave.

Back home, the combined effect of the wine and his presence makes me feel a bit shaky, and I dig through my purse unsuccessfully searching for the key. 'Here, let me,' he offers and takes the bag, holding it nearer to the streetlamp until he finds the key.

'It's late, you might have trouble finding another cab,' I warn. 'Should you keep this one?'

'No,' and he dismisses the cab. 'It's not that late and I can always walk up to Houston.'

He follows me inside and I click on the lights, wondering how we will proceed. Casually, I drop my coat upon the couch. And when I turn, he reaches for me and gently takes me in his arms. He looks down into my face, studying it carefully, until finally his eyes rest on mine and he leans down, finding my lips. The kiss at first is tender, then it deepens in intensity. He releases me and again looks deeply into my eyes, searching.

I feel hot and faint, as if I can't breathe. I want to look away, but I feel it too strongly, the emotion that has been missing from my life for so long. It is as though his desire has ignited mine. He senses it and his lips meet mine again, harder and more insistent, and I respond to this demand, for I want the kiss to go on and on. I don't stop him when I feel his hand cup my breast. I am acutely aware of his body running the length of mine, and I know he can feel my trembling. Again his hand smoothes my back, then reaches up to touch, with expert fingers, the nape of my neck.

When this kiss finally ends, he pulls away reluctantly and whispers, 'Call me when you get back, luv.' Then he turns and I hear his footsteps running down the stairs.

I stand in the middle of the room feeling totally foolish for wanting so much more. My face burns, for I know he knew it!

'Arrogant bastard!' I say, but deep down I know I will call him when I get back!

CHAPTER THIRTY-ONE

I've brought a stack of books to read on the plane. I'll be better prepared for Mr St Paul the next time we meet. I skim the books and read about all the famous greats in the design field. It makes fascinating reading, for little-known facts jump out at me from the pages: Chicago-born Mainbocher was the first to design the strapless evening gown; Elsa Schiaparelli was said to be the first designer to use a zipper; English-born Charles James was considered a 'sculptor in cloth'.

The greats came from the ranks of philosophers, artists, architects, and even poets, but somehow found their way into the exclusive world of design in haute couture. The books mention that the heyday of couture was the 1930s and 1940s; even at that time, one fitted costume was the same price as an automobile.

Couture is a dying art. Most of the Paris houses couldn't survive in the 1990s with only couture; no, now they sell license for everything from lipsticks to golf clubs, and of course, the original designs are made into high-fashion ready-to-wear.

What a curious field, I think, and most of all I find it odd that a man had really been at the forefront of it all. Charles Frederick Worth, a British designer who moved to Paris in 1858. He was the first to offer four fittings and every garment hand-stitched. He was the father of haute couture.

I feel elated that I may have contributed something new to the fickle world, of fashion with my limited sets of numbered designs. It seems almost providence that I didn't start out to be a designer; most of the names I read about didn't either.

I'm not fooling myself. I know why I keep my nose in the books; I don't want to think about the hurt that I will be causing Jeff and Cindy until the very last minute. Will Cindy feel abandoned by me? Would it be possible to suggest New York? But does my new life have room for a pregnant woman and later, a baby? I think not.

When the plane lands and I see the snow-covered peaks of the Rockies, I feel a swift tug of nostalgia. I can understand how those who love the mountains need to stay close, but to me the peaks only speak of broken promises and tears. Looking at them will always bring back painful memories of that long-ago winter when Cindy's accident occurred; the accident that welded my sister and myself into our unhealthy partnership.

Maybe, by chance, my absence has dissolved it – or at least weakened it. I give myself no credit, for I know that my absence has actually helped Cindy. Now I have to face the hurt I will be causing. But a part of me knows that Jeff doesn't love me either, not in the right way.

I didn't tell him my arrival time for I felt I needed a couple of hours alone in the house to frame what I want to say to both of them in the kindest possible way. I pray for their understanding and forgiveness.

When the taxi pulls up in front of the house on Downing Street, I blink and for a moment think the driver has brought me to the wrong corner; the house seems so changed.

I stand on the pavement for a few minutes gazing up at it. The pussy willows are in full bloom and I inhale the perfume of the abundant forsythia. Cheerful jonquils line the path, and a wind-chime tinkles happily on the front porch above a swing that's swaying slowly in the wind.

I walk up to the front door and reach for my familiar set of keys. When the wide oak door opens, I catch the fragrant smell of cinnamon and apples; it makes Pamela Walsh's words come alive – for it truly is the homiest and most welcoming smell in the whole world. For a moment I wonder if some clever person has made the scent into a room freshener, but later I find the source of the glorious smell, for two recently home-baked apple pies stand on the kitchen counter.

The house has been given a second chance to be a truly welcoming place, a real home. Gone are the drab green drapes that had shrouded the rooms in shadow; they have been replaced by light mini-blinds that invite in the sun.

The living room now is a delight. A Navaho rug in red, white and gray is at the heart of the room and a soft gray corduroy couch is flanked by two comfortable-looking chairs in the same fabric. Above the fireplace, a Georgia O'Keefe numbered print in the same colors seems to reach down and tie the room into a pleasing whole. One or two large turquoise Van Briggle vases hold cut branches of pussy willow. Cindy and I always loved that special pottery – the Van Briggles from the studio in Colorado Springs. The room is open and free; it breathes.

Timidly, like a thief who doesn't belong here, I walk through the rooms and find subtle small touches of Cindy's that have transformed the entire house.

When I get upstairs, I look toward the attic door and realize I have to face it sometime. So slowly I climb the stairs, to find this is the only space Cindy has not touched. In the corner under the eaves, the old Singer sewing machine sits covered with a layer of dust, and dressmaker dummies still hold court as they group together in the far corner.

Reluctantly, I walk toward the infamous window. It seems harmless enough now – a picture-frame holding a scene of mountain and sky in its center. I reach forward and touch the pane of glass, which is warm from the rays of the sun.

If only I had, my thought begins. If only what? If only I had grabbed my sister's small sturdy body and in one brief second of pain had pulled her swiftly away, that would have saved a lifetime of pain. I'm certain I wouldn't have had the wisdom or knowledge to have dashed a pan of warm water over the glass as my mother did.

Unexpected tears spill over, and I find myself sobbing, 'I'm sorry, Cindy, I'm so sorry.'

My journey through the house is really a journey through my past, and I feel so nervous, for the worst is yet to come. I have to tell them both that I won't be coming back. After drinking a cup of tea, I decide to lie down, for it's hours until either of them will be home.

Briefly I glance into the bedroom I had shared with Jeff. It is unthinkable to lie down on that bed, so I go into Cindy's room – but it, too, is changed. Before, it had seemed like the room of a child or a teenager – full of stuffed animals. These are gone now, and the old furniture has been replaced by a lovely bedroom suite. The room is a soft combination of white and sunny yellow, and on the wall above the bed is another O'Keefe, smaller, less lonely than the one in the living room.

It comes as a shock that Cindy has wonderful taste. I hadn't known that, for in the past she hadn't been allowed an opinion; she hadn't chosen anything.

I open the door to one of the guest rooms. It, too, has been repainted. It is now a soft green and the room has been cleared of clutter. In its simplicity, it is too inviting.

I lie down on top of the spread and hear the sounds of my childhood – the chatter of birds in the new spring and the wind that always whistles around the corners of the house and at times reminded me of a favorite song. The house creaks intermittently and even upstairs I can hear the hum of the furnace as it switches off and on. Hypnotically, I watch the pattern of leaves dancing with sunbeams on the wall. I watch and my eyes grow heavy.

Later, like a sleeper aware of subtle changing sounds, the familiar monotone roar of the Jeep pulling into the driveway awakens me. Quickly I smooth down my hair and give a quick glance in the mirror; I am rumpled but still presentable.

I walk to the staircase and catch sight of Jeff as he enters the entrance hall. He discards the windbreaker jacket to reveal a blue plaid flannel shirt. I notice he has boots on, so he must have been doing fieldwork today – work which he enjoys so much.

My heart quickens at the sight of him, for he is so dear to me, it is heartbreaking. It isn't fair that the one essential component of physical love is missing. I watch the familiar gestures that I've seen him make over the five years of our marriage. Like a blind woman, I could trace his movement in Braille. First he takes the mail from the hall table, then he dives into the dining room to find a succulent apple. He nibbles on the ripe fruit as he leafs through the mail, deciding which to open first. I can only see his long legs stretched out, as he is sitting in the first chair in the living room. I watch as he discards junk mail into the waste basket without opening it. I hear his playful, *'Yes!'* when he pitches the envelope successfully into the basket instead of having it land on the floor. I know so well the look of intense concentration that he wears on his face when reading the other mail.

Suddenly I feel uneasy about spying on him, so I call out, 'Jeff, is that you?' and I begin walking down the stairs.

He rises to meet me and an almost happy look comes over his face, but it changes rapidly to one of annoyance. 'If you had let me know the time, I would have met you at the airport.'

'It wasn't necessary,' I say, realizing my voice is reaching for sharpness as well. I walk over and sit in the chair opposite his, a stiffness in my posture that mirrors his.

He looks down and studies his hands. 'You had a responsibility to her, Trini, and you let her down,' he says softly.

I swallow and pause, for I feel tears already welling behind my eyelids, and wanting to choose my words carefully, I begin. 'I've had a responsibility to her all my life, even when I wasn't old enough to handle it. I don't understand how you can blame me; she's twenty-four years old, she's not stupid, and you make it sound so awful. She hasn't done anything that a lot of girls in love, or not in love, have done.'

He continues looking down at his hands and I see the hurt and disappointment in the slump of his shoulders. 'She's not that kind of girl, or I didn't think she was,' he says.

I feel my anger rise. 'What kind of girl is that, Jeff, a normal healthy woman who has feelings and desires like every human being?'

He looks up and almost wants to confront me on some level. I know what he's thinking: how can I know about normal human beings, I who can't bear to make love in the light as if it were a shameful dirty thing. He holds it back, his insult.

He picks up a small framed photo from the end table that was not there before and holds it, examining it carefully as if he could find the flaw. 'I'm disappointed, that's all.'

'That's a lovely picture of Cindy. Who took it?'

'I did, when I took her up to the oil-fields one afternoon. She mentioned how she always wanted her father to take her, but of course he couldn't.'

I still feel tears threatening to fall, so I change the subject, saying brightly, 'The house looks wonderful.' I am allowing myself breathing space to think, for Jeff sounds so disappointed, like a man who has more than a brotherly interest in Cindy. Is it possible that somehow in my absence he has seen Cindy in a different light – no longer the little sister whose hair he would casually ruffle? If only this hadn't happened to Cindy, this baby, there might have been a chance for them, for I know that Cindy has loved him ever since the first night he entered this house. Missed connections can be so sad and irretrievable.

Finally I blurt out, 'I'd like to talk about a divorce, Jeff. I'm sorry, but you know we haven't been good together for a very long time.'

He nods. 'I expected as much. We haven't really been good together *ever*,' he says, and his honesty surprises me, for I never knew he felt the lack as deeply as I did. 'That's fine, file whenever you like. I guess you'll be going back to New York?' I nod yes and abruptly he gets up. 'I need to shower. I'll be eating out; I'm having dinner with some guys from staff.'

I can't tell if he is angry, or if it is just that we have grown so far apart that we really have nothing to talk about. We are so distant, and the gulf is so wide, we cannot even hurt each other.

I hear the sounds of his moving about the house and I go through to the kitchen and stare out of the window. The yard looks lovely, and I watch as a squirrel darts among the few remaining autumn leaves retrieving forgotten hazelnuts. It is refreshing to see the blue sky and the incredible green of spring after months of the concrete jungle, but with a sadness, I realize it doesn't call to me to remain, only to sip its beauty and store it away for another time.

Later I hear the door slam and the sound of his Jeep pulling away, and I feel the loss of his friendship deeply. I wonder if sometime in the future we can retrieve it and begin again on a different plane, the one etched out for dear friends. I wander aimlessly about the house. It is truly transformed; it has the thing Felix talks about, good vibes, and the warmth of a real home now is apparent. Not my home, but Cindy's and Jeff's.

In the den that was Big Jack's, Cindy has altered very little. She has only touched it lightly with a sensitive hand. The pictures of happy men working the oil rigs still grace the walls; the worn chairs replaced with comfortable ones of leather. I see the notes on the desk and know Jeff still works there at the desk that was my father's – and suddenly I realize why I married him. He, with his good humor and caring ways, filled the vacuum that had been left by Big Jack's passing.

I look at my favorite picture of my father, his face streaked with oil. 'I've screwed it up, Daddy, I've screwed it up bad – Cindy . . . Jeff . . . I feel exactly like Myra must have felt. I feel selfish, but I do understand her at last. How can one live a lie? Must one be expected to live only for others? I know it sounds shallow, but I've found something I desperately want to do . . .' and a few tears that I have been holding back escape me. I go to the drawer where he kept the album and find a bit of happiness in some of the captured moments of my life.

Feeling like a stranger in the house that I spent most of my life in, I decide to change clothes and *do* something – for this trip through the past serves no purpose. I need activity! Once changed, I dust the furniture, vacuum the rugs. It's harder than I had imagined, this waiting, and I still have to face my sister.

CHAPTER THIRTY-TWO

It is almost eight o'clock when a strange car pulls up in the driveway and I am quite surprised to see it is Cindy climbing out of the driver's side. She had flunked her driving test twice when she was eighteen and never tried again. Her arms are full of packages and I rush to the hall and open the door and Cindy drops her bundles to embrace me, saying over and over, 'Trini, oh Trini, I'm so happy to see you,' her voice warm and tender, without a trace of a stutter.

'Me, too,' I say, returning her bear hug.

As we pull apart, I am amazed to see how transformed my sister is. The dark hair that had been worn straight and lank is now shaped into a fashionable wind-blown style, and Cindy's face is alive with color, her large blue eyes enhanced with eye-shadow and mascara, and the contacts make her eyes a deeper blue.

'You look beautiful,' I say.

'If I do, it's because I'm so happy,' and with an unconscious gesture, Cindy reaches down and touches her small mound of tummy.

We leave the packages on the floor and go out to the pleasant kitchen, where our roles are now reversed. I am merely a guest and I am urged to sit while Cindy bustles about making us both a cup of herbal tea. When we are seated comfortably at the small intimate table, I say, 'I can't believe it, the house and you, everything so beautiful.'

Shyly, Cindy looks down and picks at a nail. 'It was the money. You sent so much, maybe I was carried away . . .' She pauses. 'But Jeff liked it – all the changes, I mean.'

'I'm sure he did; it's wonderful,' I say. 'The cash-flow has stopped, for the shop is shut now, but as soon as the property is sold there will be a lot more. We'll both be wealthy.' I bite my lip, for I am thinking about the money and what it could buy me – the loft, the chance to design.

'That's great, for I need to take care of him, or her,' and again Cindy reaches down and gently touches her stomach.

'When are you due?'

'October. I can't wait,' and Cindy looks away, her eyes misty. Abruptly, she changes the subject. 'I'm starved, but I have to watch my weight now. I have some pasta salad in the fridge, is that okay?'

'Sounds great,' and with that Cindy bustles about the kitchen preparing our supper. She has stopped talking about the forthcoming baby, so I respect this and don't ask the questions that are flooding through my mind.

'Tell me about New York,' Cindy urges.

I sip my tea. She is an adult now, as capable as any of us. Should I stop shielding her, should I tell her what really happened – the detective, the shoes hidden in the closet, and about my brush with danger? She would like to hear about John Sandaval and how he saved my life, but I think of the baby growing in her womb and I see her bubbling happiness and I know I will keep it from her, all these anxieties and mysteries that have been solved. It serves no purpose now to worry her.

So I begin. There is so much to tell. I describe the city, the flat, I talk about Felix and Clarista and Josh, and in detail I try to explain about my design work and the fashion show and its success. I keep my secret. I do not mention Trevor St Paul.

'God, Trini, it sounds great, but then you always could do anything you set your mind to.'

Reaching for a way to explain it, I say, 'I always hated Myra, at least I thought I did, and I guess I never wanted to be interested in anything connected with her. But around the clothing in the shop, I began to remember how magical the attic, her studio, was to me when I was little. I loved the feel of the cloth, the smell of the thread, and the mystery of it all; it was like a great big puzzle that you could put together and find you had created something beautiful.'

'I don't remember her studio,' Cindy says. 'She never allowed me in it. I only remember . . .'

'I know, after a while she never gave me permission to go there either, but I used to sneak up there. I got in trouble lots of times, for she'd find my dirty fingerprints on the fabric.'

'You never told me about that.'

'It was way before you were born,' and with a flash I remember when and why I stopped going up there.

I need to tell her about the loft. I don't exactly know what I expect her to say, but I begin. 'You know the loft I've rented? It's perfect for living and working in, and having the fashion show.'

'Will you keep renting it? It sounds ideal.'

'No, I can't. It's really up for sale. The realtor, Pamela Walsh, a real nice helpful lady, arranged for me to rent it while our place was being fixed up.'

'Well, maybe you could buy it, Trini. It sounds just right for you.'

'It is – but it costs a great deal of money.'

'How much?'

'It's one million, eight hundred thousand.'

'Whew,' Cindy breathes, and sits down heavily in the chair. 'I can see why you can't buy it, Trini. I guess I don't understand places like New York.'

'We have an offer on Myra's place for two million, five hundred thousand.'

'What? What did you say?'

'That's right, Cindy, you heard OK – two million five hundred thousand.'

'Oh, my God,' and I can see Cindy looking at me, searching my face to check whether it's some sort of joke.

'It's true, Cindy, all true. The final papers will go through in about six weeks.' '

'Gee, she was really something, our mother. Such talent, such intelligence, such business sense. She did all this for us! I wish I could have told her money's not all that important. I wish we didn't have it and we just had her.'

'She left a note and tried to explain it to us. I'll read it to you if you like.'

'Yes, where is it?'

'Upstairs in my luggage. Shall we go up?'

We put the dishes in the dishwasher. I go up to the guest room, retrieve the torn sheet from the sketchbook, and join Cindy in her room. I smooth the crumpled page and begin. *'"Trini, I know someday . . ."'*

'She didn't say Trini and Cindy?'

'No, I guess she wrote this when you were too young.'

'Oh.'

But I can see Cindy's hurt at the omission. I begin again. *'"Trini, I know someday you will find this. I can't say Dear Trini, for if I do, planes could fall out of the sky, drunk drivers careen out of control, and who or whatever picks the names for the lottery for terrible accidents might call your number. Even those tiny invisible intruders, the germs who carry all manner of horrible disease, could suddenly find the address and zip code of Downing Street . . ."'*

Cindy interrupts. 'God, she was so worried about us and she seemed so superstitious. I never knew that about her.'

I go on reading. *'"I think of those women in remote parts of the world like Asia who live with my same fears and name their children Teaspoon or Broken Cup. They know, as I do now, that an endearing name might attract the jealous gods . . ."'*

'Gosh, her letters are like poetry. Teaspoon or Broken cup. Do you suppose anyone was really named that?' Cindy wonders.

I suppose, as I frown at the next part, that I'd better explain. 'This is before you were born, Cindy, before Daddy was sick. She had a lot more time then.' Again I begin reading. *'"Do you remember sitting in my lap in the window seat, always asking me to read? I even read those adult stories to you, for you begged me to."'* I pause and squint down. 'It's kinda smudged here,' for I want to skip over the part about the blind man who knocked on the door of the poor and the ugly.

'I wish she had read to me,' Cindy says wistfully.

'This next part's about Daddy,' and in a low voice I begin reading. *'"I cannot help but wonder if, on 11 November, he had been named Henry or Perceval or Mark instead of Jack, if the strap would have held; if suddenly someone had called up to him and named him Edward, would the strap on that rig magically have held fast? I can only wonder."'*

I stop to catch my breath. 'Daddy's accident happened on 11 November,' I explain.

'That's before I was born,' Cindy says.

'This next part is nice. It's about us,' I say. *'"In my imagination I give you and your sister many lives. I create happiness and health and talent and I enjoy you both in many ways."'*

Cindy smiles. 'That was nice. She said both of us. She'd be proud of you, Trini, you have talent, but the other part about health and happiness, I have that. I'm ordinary, I know that, but I don't care, for I never wanted to be anything else. Most of us are ordinary. I just want what I have now – my home, my health, my work for now, and soon I will have my baby to love, and someday maybe I'll have a man, a husband who will love me back.'

'I'm sure you will, Cindy, you must believe that.'

'Oh, I do. What else does she say in the letter?'

My voice starts to break, but I control it and keep reading. '*"But you must understand that that day, 11 November, transformed me like a whiteout in Colorado and I am snowblind. I see only the face of fear and feel the pain of my frozen heart. For I love him so much, I cannot watch. I love you and your sister so much, I cannot stay."*' I pause, for I am out of breath.

'She really did love us, and she must have loved Daddy, too, but I guess artistic people are so different from ordinary ones. If it were me and I loved us, I would have never left.'

'Maybe we don't understand her note completely,' I say, 'but she is trying to let us know that she loved us very, very much.'

Cindy nods and my voice goes on. '*"I need to become someone for your sakes, so that my desertion has meaning. For now, I reach out to that which is inanimate; I chase that unknown quality called fame, but it eludes me, for I am not good enough. No coward ever is. Forgive me. Myra."*'

'I wish we could have told her that being famous or earning all that money for us wasn't really important,' Cindy says softly, then she searches my face. 'Do you think she was a coward?'

'I don't know,' I answer truthfully.

'I don't either. Did you forgive her, Trini?'

'Yes, I do. I did.'

'I'm not sure,' Cindy says as she touches her stomach lightly. 'Now that I will have someone to love, I know I could never leave him or her, certainly not for those kinds of reasons, so I'm not sure if I do forgive her, and I guess it's not important anyway.'

I'm surprised, for it was always Cindy who treasured her brief notes and handled the fake label as if it were something precious, but I can accept her reasons, for she is a person now in her own right, entitled to her own opinions.

'But, Trini, I'm glad for you,' she goes on. 'You found what you want. What about Jeff?'

'I've told him I'm filing for a divorce. You know, Cindy, better than anyone, how unfair I've been. He's too nice, too good, to be treated like that. He doesn't care about the divorce; he's relieved.'

Cindy reaches over and we hug. 'Oh Trini, I'm so happy for both of us. We both got what we wanted.' She pushes me gently back as the thought occurs to her. 'You can have all or any part of my money so you can buy that place.'

'I couldn't ask you for that.'

'No, I want you to, Trini. All my life you gave me your stuff, your best toy, your best dress, your best box of candy. No, for once *I* can give. Don't rob me of that.'

'I don't know how much of your money I'd need,' I say truthfully.

'It's okay, for now I have a nice house to raise my child in, I have a pretty good bank account started, I can keep my job for months and months yet. Course, someday, you'd pay it back.'

'Of course I would,' and I wonder what she would have thought if she knew that I had no obligation to give her any of it.

'It's settled then,' Cindy states, and her generosity gives her stature and new self-esteem. She rustles the bags that are piled on the bed with us. 'Baby clothes and more baby clothes,' she announces happily, and we begin poking around in the bags, holding up the tiny pajamas and gowns, admiring the embroidery.

'I mainly bought white, yellow, and green,' Cindy says.

'With ultrasound you'd be able to tell.'

'I don't want to know. Women in the past never knew and I don't want to. I'll love it no matter whether it's a boy or a girl.'

I smile, for that is so like Cindy.

It is still early when we hear the front door slam and the uneven tread of Jeff's footsteps in the hall. We both know it means he has been out with the guys and has been drinking. He pops his head in the doorway. His hair is disheveled and his face is red, letting us know for sure that he has had a few drinks.

'Are you okay?' he asks, looking directly at Cindy.

'I'm fine,' she answers, 'just fine.'

'Did you go to the doctor today?'

'That's not till Monday, Jeff,' she explains patiently, but she's pleased at his concern.

'I see,' and he weaves unsteadily in her doorway, seemingly totally unaware of me sitting on the bed alongside Cindy.

'Night,' and we hear him stumble down the hall.

'He's real disappointed in me.'

'I'm sure that's not true,' I say. 'He seemed very concerned about you and the baby.'

'Oh, he is, but I notice he can't even look me in the eye.'

'He's old fashioned,' I say gently. 'It's what I always loved about him.'

'I know, I love that about him, too, but I need this baby. Finally I'll have somebody that's really mine, mine to love.'

That statement makes me bold. 'Is there any chance you'll marry the baby's father?'

'No, he's already married, and anyway, I couldn't marry him. He doesn't love me.'

This makes me squirm with guilt. It's my fault, for I didn't prepare Cindy for the real world. We should have discussed things like this – married men who lie to innocent girls. It's so unfortunate that she has become involved with such a one. 'People do get divorced,' I say. 'Even Jeff and I.'

'You're really getting divorced? You mean it?'

'Yes. I know I can't explain it in a way you'd understand, but New York and the work I want to do . . . it's not possible here – and Jeff and I have grown so far apart we have nothing in common any more. I'm not sure we ever did.'

Cindy smiles and the vision comes back swiftly of how it had been then – was it only six months ago that we had sat on this very bed?

The talk then had been about love, and Cindy's eyes were full of tears as she asked, 'What's it like, Trini? What's it like to be in love?'

Then I had felt the sadness of my sister's empty life. 'You know, you want to be with the person, you want to share things, do things for the person, your whole life is a partnership.'

'No, Trini, I don't mean things like that, I mean the physical part. What's it like, what's it *feel* like, the lovemaking between a man and a woman?'

I remember how embarrassed I had been at her question. 'I can't explain it, Cindy, not really. I just can't explain it.'

'Please, Trini, please try. I want to know, I need to know. The movies, the love stories, it's all so mysterious. Please tell me what it's like when Jeff makes love to you.'

'Jeff . . .' I couldn't explain lovemaking with Jeff, for it was pure fantasy. No, in the dark it was never Jeff I responded to, it was the other, Cal, my first love.

'Please try,' Cindy urged. 'I really need to know.'

I closed my eyes to try to remember. 'His hands touching me feel like soft velvet; nerve-endings I didn't know existed come alive; the feel of his tongue, warm and moist, sends currents through my body, an electricity of sorts, and when he's inside me, it touches unknown places I didn't know existed either. The rhythm of lovemaking is a dance you know, without knowing how; the feel of skin upon skin is like a warm fire, and your whole body is alive in places that lie dormant at other times; and the release when it comes is like letting go of all tension. You feel drained, satisfied, and at the same time renewed. And after, I always want to touch his body, the one that gave me so much pleasure. It's pleasure, an ecstasy like no other.'

Tears had fallen from Cindy's eyes at my words. 'Jeff makes you feel like that?' she whispered. 'It sounds wonderful.'

'No.' I hesitated and finally I said, 'Do you remember that blond-haired boy named Cal when I was in University? I felt that way with him.' I lowered my voice. 'It was never that way with Jeff.' I hesitated again and then went on: 'No, with Jeff I turn out the light and pretend it's Cal.'

Cindy lunged at me and scratched my face. 'That's terrible! That's so unfair – how can you!' She began to cry hysterically. 'You bitch, you horrible bitch!'

I grabbed my sister, holding her to still the anger. 'I've never told anyone that; I'm so ashamed,' I admitted.

'I hate you,' Cindy whispered, 'and he should hate you, too. You don't deserve him; he deserves somebody who loves him, who really loves him.'

We had drawn apart and I searched my sister's face. 'You're right. He deserves somebody who really loves him – like you do.'

Cindy started to protest, then stopped.

It was then I had The Idea – so bizarre, so crazy, that I was never sure where it came from. I slipped off my wedding band and eased it onto my sister's finger. I pinned up her hair, pulled off her flannel gown and replaced it with a silk one of my own. I sprayed with perfume the pulse that beat wildly in her throat.

'It's always in the dark; he expects it to be,' I whispered, and gently I eased my sister into the hall and watched her hesitant steps. I saw her stand quietly in front of the bedroom door and pause, but only for a moment.

'Go in, Cindy, go in. You deserve his love, I don't,' I said silently to myself, and presently I saw the door open and Cindy go in.

How many times had it happened in those five or six months?

Now I look at Cindy with newfound knowledge. 'It's Jeff's, isn't it?'

Cindy nods yes. 'But I could never tell him.'

'You can. You must,' I urge. 'A child is what he wants most in the world.'

'He'll think we were crazy; he'll hate us both. You said so.'

'Everything's changed now, Cindy. He's not in love with me, I don't think he ever really was. You see his concern for you and his disappointment.' I look in my purse and find the gold wedding band and, as I did in the past, slide it on my sister's finger. She studies the ring, opens the dresser drawer, and when her clothes drop in a heap at her feet, she draws a black silk gown over her head. She looks at me. I nod yes and say softly, 'If you love him, fight for him. Make him understand that you always loved him. Only this time, turn the light on afterwards.'

As before, I watch my sister's hesitant steps walking down the long hall and her predictable pause before the forbidden door. In a second she enters.

Suddenly I remember. It is here someplace, that book my mother read to me so long ago. She said she didn't know why I even enjoyed listening to stories that I didn't really understand, and it comes to me that she read from it the story in which mothers named their children Teaspoon or Broken Cup so the jealous gods wouldn't seize them.

And then I remember the other story – the one of the blind man who called at the poor widow's house, a widow with three daughters and no money for a dowry. The mother persuaded the blind man to marry her eldest daughter, which left her with two who had no husbands and no chance of ever finding one, for she knew only a blind man would knock on the door of the poor and ugly. And as the years went by and no other suitors called, the sisters, who loved each other, called upon the lucky eldest, who would then slip off her golden ring and, for a night, lend her sisters the wedding band.

In remembering this strange tale, I feel a torrent of guilt somewhere in my unconscious. I had deemed Cindy so hopeless, so unworthy, that I had to give her what was mine, and I know now it wasn't generosity which prompted that insanity. No – a gift is not a gift if you are only giving something you do not want yourself.

I know now why I never wanted children, for I had already been a mother. I had been given a child to raise and I had done a very bad job, for it is not love that protects too much, it is guilt. I have faced the past and come to terms with my mistakes. Now I can forgive myself and go on.

I leave the gaily wrapped package on Cindy's bed among the tiny baby garments. It is a suit I had designed for her, a perfect size nine, in the precious vicuna. I wonder if she will treasure this label as much as she did the other. After the baby, I'm sure she will wear it proudly, as I will, for I have its twin in my closet.

The world tilts. She is no longer less and me, more. Her generosity in giving me my dream of owning the loft has told me that, and my secret of giving her half, if only on paper, somehow makes us equal.

I must hurry down to Daddy's study, as I know on one shelf are Myra's forgotten books and among them, I will find the slim volume of strange tales from around the world, and when I do, I put it in the trash compactor. It would not do to have Cindy find this book with the tale of the blind man. I put lettuce leaves on top and the remains of the pasta salad.

The whir of the compactor has buried this secret for all time.

I go out into the back yard. I shiver, but the night air feels good. In the distance, the Rockies gleam with snow, the Colorado sky is alive with twinkling stars, the air is heavy with perfumed flowers . . . and I am saying a silent goodbye to this place of happiness and pain.

For I know that Cindy and I hear the beat of a different drummer.

I'm not ready to settle down and create new life, for I am my mother's daughter after all; prizes and future triumphs call out to me. Strange cities, distant places lure me with a siren's song.

And in time, upstairs, I see the lights go on and against the shade I witness their tender embrace. I feel a sense of closure: one door closes and it is good, but another door opens and I sense the future awaiting me, bright and full of promise.